SEASON OF ROT

ERIC S. BROWN

Permuted Press
The formula has been changed...
Shifted... Altered... *Twisted.*
www.permutedpress.com

A PERMUTED PRESS book
published by arrangement with the authors

ISBN-10: 1-934861-22-7
ISBN-13: 978-1-934861-22-6

This book is a work of fiction. People, places, events, and situations are the product of the author's imagination. Any resemblance to actual persons, living or dead, or historical events, is purely coincidental.

Cover art by Joshua Ross
Title page art by Flickr users pdgibson and Pam Rosengren
Interior by Ryan C. Thomas

10 9 8 7 6 5 4 3 2 1

INTRODUCTION

YOU hear their moans and the sound of them pawing over each other to get to you. Swarms of them now flood the room as you load the last of your rounds into your gun. They've devoured your family, your friends, and you are the only one left, alone, isolated, empty, your soul shattered. They will kill you now in unimaginable ways, but you are determined to take some of them to hell with you. You aim and pull the trigger . . .

Sounds like a nightmare, doesn't it? Welcome to Eric S. Brown's *Season of Rot.* Here you will find a sense of paranoia, dread, isolation, shock and horror, and all of it adeptly woven into one tasty, flesh-eating morsel.

I have worked with Eric firsthand on some projects in the past, and his stories have always captivated me. His bleak, intense world vision gets under your skin and makes you face the biggest, scariest "what if" you could ask . . . What if the undead took over the world and the last hope of humanity was an inch away from oblivion? Well, the zombie man, as I like to call him, delivers again with *Season of Rot.*

Eric has become known for turning out the most original end of days, apocalyptic, zombie-mashing tales around. From the get-go, his stories assault you with relentless action, twists and turns and enough human drama to give you nightmares for weeks. They'll make you stay far away from cemeteries for as long as you can until the end finally comes.

Season of Rot does all this and much more. This isn't just a zombie fest. It's not just an end of the world scenario. It's a glimpse into a universe, one created and orchestrated by Eric himself. If you think you know where this story is going, think again. It's not your mom's zombie story. Forget that old black-and-white *Night of the Living Dead*—this is full-blown color in your face. *Season of Rot* takes the zombie convention and turns it on its head.

I guarantee that you won't know where the story is going until Eric wants you to know. He successfully reinvents zombie fiction and makes us think. His mix of characterization, plot and action is well done and makes us care. You will be with these characters all the way; they are alive, they breathe and you will beg to know what happens to them next. You will pick a favorite and follow them all the way through. You will feel their horror, their fear, their sense of isolation, their hopelessness and helplessness. But you will also feel their courage, their sense of community, their determination to live and their hope. Yes, hope. Hope in a world gone to hell. There are glimmers of it here and there, but you never truly know how it will play out, and just as you think you know, it sucker punches you.

In recent years Eric S. Brown has spawned more zombie fiction than you can shake a corpse at. From *The Queen* to *Zombies: The War Stories*, to his most recent *Zombies II: Inhuman*. In these tales you will find no ordinary zombies. They think, act in groups, plan, communicate, run, and kill with intelligence. Through these tales you discover how much like us they are. They really are us. The enemy is within. They are our sisters, our brothers, our neighbors, our fathers and mothers. Everyone you could trust and love is now out to kill you and ravage your flesh, and it happens in the blink of an eye.

If anything Eric's tales have made us analyze ourselves and the human condition, our interaction with each other and the world around us. For the battlefield, when it comes down to it, is the entire world. Eric has turned the formula of the living dead into a world-ending apocalypse. As if nuclear war, the greenhouse effect, disease and starvation weren't enough, now we have the undead rising from their graves to end the world. And this is his universe, spanning volumes of stories, chapbooks, collections and novellas, all woven together to tell the ultimate tale of humanity's survival.

Add to this *The Season of Rot*—a fine collection that only enhances this universe. From beginning to end, the book sucks you in with its seemingly simple premise, but then snags you deeply, forcing you to ride alongside these people as the unreal unfolds and the real story takes hold.

You might think that after all the zombie fiction there would be no new way of telling this tale. Eric shows you that is painfully untrue with his new offering of undead delight, a feast for his fans, an homage to all those who love the living dead.

It's clear that Eric has much more to say on this subject, many more poor souls to thrust into a world overrun and overthrown by legions of the undead. It's clear that Eric isn't done twisting and turning this new icon and reinventing it. This tale, like his others, is no ordinary zombie tale . . . it has bite.

Prepare for the *Season of Rot*; it's going to be a rough season, one you won't soon forget. Grab your shotgun, your hunting knife and food rations, and turn the page, brave fan. The *Season of Rot* has just begun.

9/6/07

—John Grover

Author of *Terror in Small Doses*, *Shadow Tales*, and *Space Stations and Graveyards*. Visit his site www.shadowtales.com.

THE SEASON OF ROT

ONE

DANIEL dangled his feet over the edge of the demolished stairwell. Two floors below, the creatures waited, stretching their decaying arms toward him. Frustrated, unable to reach their prey, they pushed each other and occasionally knocked one or two of their brethren off the jagged end of the stairs. Daniel imagined the bottom of the stairwell, dark and littered with broken bodies, masses of them crawling and dragging themselves about, unable to work their way back up the stairs or find their way out of the hospital.

When Daniel and his group took refuge here, they destroyed the stairs and cut the cable to the elevators, leaving the dead no way up to reach them. The effort had proved well worth it; now the refugees could sleep in peace.

Daniel shifted the rifle across his lap and checked its chamber, then lifted the gun to his shoulder and aimed at the horde below. Only a headshot, or general destruction of the brain, would send the things back to Hell. Daniel found a target and squeezed the trigger. The rifle kicked as the high-velocity bullet tore through the dead thing's skull in an explosion of wet pulp. It was a futile gesture, really: millions of people, nearly everyone in the city, had turned into walking mounds of rotting flesh whose sole purpose was to tear off your face and eat it; Daniel and his group could never kill all of them. But he enjoyed it from time to time. He joked that it was his tiny piece of vengeance.

No one from the floors above came running to investigate the shot. They knew Daniel was on watch today and were accustomed to his habits.

Aside from Daniel, more than four dozen living souls called the hospital home. They collected rainwater on the roof, tried to grow crops in or on the building wherever they could, and rationed out the dwindling supplies from the hospital's cafeteria and emergency stores. They'd moved the generators and the fuel supply to the upper floors and had limited the use of electricity as much as possible. Even so, their time here was running out. One day soon, if help didn't come, they'd all be forced to pack up and move . . . assuming they could find a way through or past the thousands of creatures occupying the bottom three floors of the building and surrounding its walls outside.

Daniel sighed and lit up a cigarette. He was down to three packs and getting nervous about the supplies running out. Luckily only two other people in the group smoked, or the cigarettes would have been gone already. He took a deep drag and held it in, savoring the taste before exhaling. Glancing at his watch, he noticed his shift was almost over, and hoped it wasn't an omen of some sort. He stood up, thanking God he could return to his real job in the communications room, and headed out of the stairwell to meet his replacement.

LAURA sat up in bed as the coughing fit hit her. She threw back her blankets and slammed her bare feet onto the cold tile in a frantic dash for the bathroom sink. She stumbled into the room, wearing only a t-shirt, and she grabbed the sink's edge to support herself as the coughing grew more intense. What she hacked up was more solid than mucus and drenched in blood. She stared at it in horror as the coughing died down.

Letting go of the sink's edge, she slid to the floor and tried to catch her breath. *I'm a doctor, damn it.* This kind of thing wasn't supposed to happen to her. She had never touched a cigarette in her life. She worked out and ate right, yet here she sat dying of cancer in a time where people needed her skills and knowledge more than ever.

No one else knew how sick she was. She hid it well and put up a good front. The hospital was stocked with the medicine she needed, enough medicine to curb her symptoms and keep her comfortable most of the time. At least it *had* been enough until things began to get worse.

With her t-shirt, she wiped the blood from around her mouth and got to her feet. Today was going to be a busy day. Not only was she the doctor of the group, she was also a member of its leading tribunal, a responsibility she shared with Jack and Vince.

She was also *supposed* to be finding a cure for the plague, but that was a joke. She wasn't a research scientist, just a doctor, and even after months of studying the plague she knew little more than when she started.

Today, her focus was on her administration duties and helping Jack and Vince agree on an evacuation plan for when the time came to find a new home. According to Jack's last inventory check, even with their rationing system they had a month, tops, before people started starving and their tiny piece of the civilization collapsed into mutiny.

Laura changed into her day clothes and put on her happy face. Then she headed out to meet up with the boys.

JACK stood on the roof of the hospital, looking out into the city, parts of which were still ablaze. Dark smoke joined the usual clouds of lingering smog, making the day seem pale like the rotting flesh of the creatures on the streets below.

It was hard for Jack to remember what the world had been like before the creatures came. Less than a year ago things had been normal, but the plague had spread so fast that no one, not the government, the military, nor the C.D.C., had been able to stop it. The city around him had changed from his home to a sick version of Hell on Earth where only the strong and the determined stayed alive.

Jack was a tall man and well built. Standing there on the roof he looked every inch a king, and in a sense he was. This new world had forced the burden of leadership upon him.

He lifted his binoculars to his eyes, trying to figure out a path through the dead. The only vehicles he had at his disposal were locked away in the hospital's garage. They were mostly simple cars built for civilian use, not for fighting through a horde of hungry, flesh-eating monsters. The only larger vehicles were a few dump trucks left behind from his work crew. None of them were what he needed, and even if they were, reaching them would be a problem.

The safest way to the garage was a long and difficult climb down an elevator shaft. At the end of the shaft dozens—maybe hundreds—of the creatures waited; like the first three floors of the hospital, the garage was infested with the dead. There simply hadn't been time to close it off when Jack and the group had taken refuge here.

Some of the other refugees still believed help was coming, but Jack suffered no such delusions. Any survivors out there were certainly in the same sort of mess his group was in, or at least incapable of breaching the armies of the dead to rescue them. There would be no help coming. It was up to him, to *them*, to find their way out of the city—if there was one. Any attempt to escape would cost them lives, but Jack was willing to accept some losses for the greater good as long as some of them survived to carry on. And as long as his ass wasn't one that got chewed off along the way.

CLUTCHING a beat-up Daffy Duck doll in his sweaty palms, Chris made his way down the winding hospital corridors to the nursery. In a few moments he would see his daughter for the first time. The doctor, Laura, hadn't let him stay during the delivery last night. There had been complications with the birth beyond his understanding. He'd been forced to wait outside as Natalie entered the world and his wife Rebecca left it.

He had watched as Jack and Mitchell carried her to the roof, her body wrapped in bloodstained sheets bound with thick ropes. Chris had cried and screamed, had even tried to attack Mitchell, but Jack calmed him down. "Think of your daughter," he had said, as if giving an order. "She *does* need you." Chris knew he was right and did his best to hold in the sobs.

He tore the hospital apart after that, looking for a gift he could take to his new daughter. At last he found Daffy inside a desk drawer in one of the offices. He sat and stared at the doll for hours, weeping for Rebecca, himself, and Natalie. He managed to pull himself together just as Laura found him and told him he could visit his child whenever he was ready.

Before he went in, Chris walked around and gave himself time to prepare, letting his excitement drive away the horrors of the world. Finally, he was ready. He ran the last few steps to the nursery proper, and as he rounded the corner he saw his daughter and stopped dead in his tracks. His breath left his body as if someone had punched him in the gut.

Beyond the nursery window, a nurse cradled the newborn, trying to soothe her as she cried and waved her tiny arms. Chris took a deep breath and stepped into the room. The nurse smiled and held Natalie out to him just as he held out the doll. He reddened, embarrassed by the mix up. And then he took his daughter into his arms, and his heart nearly burst with pride.

JACK and Laura waited in the conference room for Vince to arrive. As usual he was late. Jack gritted his teeth and, scowling, checked his watch again. Laura hoped Vince would show up soon; it looked like Jack was on the verge exploding.

She picked up the stack of inventory reports Jack had brought her, then thumped them down on the table, straightening the pile of papers.

"Jack," she started as the door swung open. Vince came in and plopped into a chair at the table. He hadn't shaved in a day or two, and he wore a battered t-shirt, jeans, mismatched socks, and sneakers that had seen better times. Vince's appearance was another sore point with Jack, who believed those in power should set an example for those they led.

"Good morning, guys," Vince said cheerfully, ignoring Jack's glares. "Sorry I'm late. I had a busy night."

"So did we," Jack pointed out. "Rebecca died in childbirth last night."

Vince's cheerful expression crumbled. "God, I'm sorry. Why didn't you call me?"

"We did," Laura said. "You didn't answer your radio."

Vince shifted in his seat. "Oh yeah, I had to leave it behind. I was doing some work up on the roof."

"I was on the roof this morning, Vince," Jack said. "You weren't there."

"No. I turned in around three or so."

"What were you doing up there, Vince?" Laura asked, heading off an outburst from Jack.

"Brainstorming." Vince smiled.

For a second, Laura thought he meant brainstorming for one of his novels. Although he had worked as everything from a dishwasher and taxi driver to a bookstore owner and photojournalist, Vince was primarily a horror writer, with the mindset and attitude of an artist. If he started talking about his writing, that would set Jack off like nothing else.

"I think I've come up with a way to solve our supply and escape woes," Vince added.

Laura relaxed a bit. She really hadn't felt up to playing her usual role as levelheaded mediator between Jack and Vince. Without her intervention she often thought the hospital would either become a pseudo-military dictatorship or fall apart completely from neglect.

Jack still seemed dead set on making her job difficult this morning. "Do tell," he said sarcastically.

Jack was a hardheaded son of a bitch any way you looked at him. Before the dead rose and claimed the world he'd been the foreman of a construction crew contracted to remodel the hospital. He wasn't a fool—the man held degrees in engineering and architecture. He was just too accustomed to being in charge. He'd grown up in a military family, so structure and discipline were almost holy to him. It was as if he saw himself as the group's commander in chief. And at times he felt his way was the only way.

"Well, my plan's pretty simple really," Vince said. "The hospital has a helipad right?"

Laura sighed. "Vince, there's no way we can get our hands on a helicopter, much less one large enough to move all of us and the supplies we'd need."

"That's it?" Jack asked Vince. "You were up there most of the night without your damn radio and all you came up with is the fact that we have a helipad?"

"Whoa, settle down, big guy," Vince said, laughing. "We all agreed that we couldn't reach the airport to get a helicopter, that's true, but I was going over the maps of the city again and did you know the WKT station is only a couple of miles from here? You can't see it with the binoculars, but I borrowed Chris's telescope. The station's got a copter sitting on its roof."

Laura shook her head. "It's too small for what you're thinking, Vince. At best, it'd hold four people with minimal gear."

"Yes, we couldn't use it to escape as group, but we . . . " Vince saw that he had lost their attention. "Just hear me out, okay?"

Laura motioned for Jack to stay quiet for a moment.

"We send a small strike team to fetch the bird, but we don't use it to escape. Once we have it, we'll have a viable means of traveling around the city. Do you know how many other hospitals and buildings have helipads? A damn lot of them do. So we use it to reach those buildings, loot their supplies, or even fly out and land in less populated areas of the city to make ground raids. Sure, some of us will have to risk our asses to do it, but it's a damn sight better than risking the whole group trying to make it out of here on the ground.

"And here's the beautiful part: not only would food no longer be an immediate problem, but some of the buildings I'm talking about have fuel depots for birds like the one we'd be using. We'd also have a way to reach the airport and steal us a larger bird if we really needed to get out of here."

"It's risky, Vince," Laura said. "There are so many things that could go wrong every time our raiding parties took the helicopter out, and dozens of ways we could lose the helicopter after we've got it . . . if we can even get it. One failed raid and we could be right back where we started with nothing to show for it except some of us being dead."

"A *strike* team?" Jack laughed. "Just who the hell out of our little group fits that description? None of us have any military training. Hell, half of the folks here have barely even used a gun more than once or twice in their lives, and those times were in desperation after the plague hit."

"Actually, Jack, I thought we'd go. Me, you, Mitchell, and Chris. And Daniel, of course. He's the only one who knows how to fly a bird."

"You'd take three of our strongest people *and* our only engineer on this fool's errand? You'd actually leave Laura here with no one left to head things up if the hospital had to be defended?"

"In case you haven't noticed, Jack, we all have 'basic experience' or we wouldn't be alive, would we?"

"Vince," Laura said, "what you're suggesting might work if the creatures outside were like the ones in the movies, but they're not. Those things out there move like us. They're fast and there are thousands of them. There's no way a team could fight its way through them to the station."

"You're right, but they could leapfrog to it," Vince said with a grin.

"Leapfrog?" Jack muttered under his breath.

"All we'd have to do is jury-rig some grappling gear. We could hop from one rooftop to another all the way to the station. How many creatures have you seen on the roofs? Not many. Only a handful of the things ever wander that high, and most of them either fall off or leave when they find that the roofs are empty. Chris used to be a professional mountain climber. With his help, it'll be easy."

"Chris's wife just died last night," Laura reminded Vince coldly. "He has a daughter to think of now. Even if he wasn't an emotional wreck, I'm not sure he'd agree to be a part of your plan."

"Leapfrog?" Jack repeated, laughing aloud this time. "Holy shit, you are crazy. This isn't the fucking Matrix or something. We're not superheroes. Going from roof to roof would be nearly as suicidal as facing the creatures head on."

"Do you have a better idea?" Vince asked.

"Making a break for it with the damn cars locked up in the garage seems like a better idea than that," Jack said. "And we all know there's way too many of those things out there to make it, even if we armored the vehicles and wasted all our firepower trying."

"I'm sorry Vince," Laura said, hoping to cut Jack short. "Everything you're suggesting is just too risky. Let's drop it and move on okay?"

Vince shrugged and gave up. He knew if Laura sided with Jack it was pointless to continue, even if he was right. That's one of the things Laura liked about Vince. Though occasionally temperamental, he was generally laid back and didn't care how things got done as long as they did get done.

She turned to Jack. "According to these reports, we have nearly four weeks of food and water left, right?"

Jack nodded.

"Then that gives us some time. Maybe we can come up with some other options . . . One other thing from your lists that concerns me is the lack of weapons and ammo. If it *does* come down to a plan like Vince's, Jack, can we realistically equip a team to send out and still have enough firepower here, should something happen?"

"Honestly, no. Even without splitting the weapons, if the dead found a way up to us right now we wouldn't have enough here to make a real stand . . . but I don't think that's going to happen, or it would have already."

"Point taken," Laura said and leaned back in her chair.

"So then what the hell do we do?" Vince asked.

They all sat in silence.

TWO floors above the informal tribunal meeting, Daniel had returned to his obsessive work in what he considered his own field. Though he had actually been a pilot before the plague, he'd also been a HAM radio fanatic and was the closest thing the group had to a communications expert. Since his first days in the hospital he'd been trying to reach other survivors using the radio equipment he'd found in the building. His efforts weren't entirely futile. More than once he'd made contact with another group or person still alive in the world outside, even a few in the city itself. But they were always cut off from the hospital by either the dead or a lack of transport. The other survivors might as well have been on the moon.

The part that really depressed Daniel was that he never managed to stay in contact with any of them. They simply disappeared from the airwaves as if they had never been there at all. He told himself those poor souls had just ran out of power to broadcast or that they'd been rescued.

Daniel had boosted his signal as much as he could. His range was huge for the equipment he had available, but he still wished for more. He told himself that if he just kept trying, one day he would reach a group capable of coming to the hospital's aid. He'd spent the last few days scanning the civilian bands, so today he switched back to the military channels. His only radio contact with a military unit had been scary as hell. The soldiers demanded his location as if they intended to raid the hospital rather than come to their rescue.

They hadn't said that outright, but Daniel could read voices. They were his passion. Hell, for all he knew they'd already tried to reach the hospital and had been consumed in the attempt by the dead. He'd certainly never heard from them again. He never even told the others about them, and they were the one party he never tried very hard to reestablish contact with after they went missing.

Still, he was desperate. He hadn't reached anyone in a long time, and he wanted, maybe even needed, to hear the voice of someone outside of the group. He needed to know they weren't the only ones left.

Daniel made some additional adjustments on his gear, then sent out his usual message. "This is Saint Joseph Hospital calling anyone who can hear us. Please respond?" Daniel leaned back in his chair, running a hand through his unkempt blond hair. He nearly toppled over when the radio crackled with a reply.

"This is Installation Phoenix. I copy you, Saint Joseph. It's good to hear another voice."

Daniel rocked forward, grabbing the control console to answer his new friend.

"You have no idea how good," he said, and then he laughed over the airwaves.

ALYSON raised her head and looked down at Mitchell. A smile stretched across her lips as the bed sheets shifted over her naked, sweat-drenched body. "Was it good for you?" she said with a chuckle.

Mitchell ran his hand through her short, wet red hair. "You know it was. But I've got to get back to work. I'm on sentry duty, honey. Jack would tear me a new one if he knew I was here."

Alyson rolled off him, her sweetness suddenly gone. "Just don't forget to pay up on your way out," she told him, stretching out on her back and closing her eyes.

Mitchell got out of bed and got dressed. He placed the packet of drugs on her nightstand and turned to glance at her a final time before he headed out the door. "Alyson . . . "

"Shut up, Mitchell. You know why I do it. I don't need another lecture."

Defeated before he began, he slammed the door behind him. Alyson sighed. Men were fools, all of them. Give them a good time and sooner or later they all started to fall in love with you. Fuck him. If she wanted to spend her last days as messed up as she could be, that was her choice. If she overdosed, then the end would be here that much quicker and she would be out of this hellhole. She wouldn't have to wait for the creatures to find a way in and rip her apart; she wouldn't starve to death like the rest of the assholes in the hospital.

Only Laura, Jack, and the medical staff had access to the hospital's stash of pharmaceuticals, and if fucking people like Mitchell—who could get the keys from Jack every once in a while—got her the shit she needed, hell, it was only sex right? She wished she was brave enough to steal a gun or get one from Mitchell, brave enough to stick it in her mouth and pull the trigger. The drugs made her feel good though, and they weren't anywhere near as messy. She knew that, given time, the drugs would do the job, and she was content on most days. With thoughts of slow suicide floating in her head, Alyson fell asleep in the darkened room.

"VINCE, let it go," Laura said, fighting the urge to give up and storm out of the room. Somehow the meeting had spiraled out of her control and had turned into a schoolyard spat as Vince and Jack resurrected one of their long running arguments.

"Laura, I know Jack and Mitchell are close, but come on! The guy's a freakin' murderer. I just don't feel comfortable with him having access to so many key areas, much less the damn arsenal he has locked up in his quarters. I'm sorry, but it's the truth. The guy gives me the creeps."

"Mitchell paid for his crimes," Jack argued. "When I hired him he was already out on parole. He's saved my ass more than once since I met him. I trust the man with my life, and he's been instrumental with helping me keep things straight around this place."

"Face it, Jack, he's your muscle. A thug who'd put us all to the wall and blow our brains out if you told him to. God knows what he does when you're not out there with him."

Suddenly the door to the conference room burst open. Jack's instincts kicked in and he drew his sidearm, barely stopping himself from putting a bullet through Daniel's face.

Daniel stood in the doorway, wide-eyed and out of breath, staring at Jack's gun. "Sorry," he said, holding up a hand as if to block a bullet. "I . . . I just made contact with someone who can help us."

Laura fell into her chair. "What? Who?"

"His name is Martin Kier. He's military, holed up in some kind of huge bunker about a hundred miles south of the city."

"Jeez, a hundred miles." Vince whistled.

"How many in his group?" Jack asked, getting right to business.

"Just him. He's the only one left alive there."

"One man? A hundred miles away? How can he help us?" Laura was confused, but she knew there must be some reason for Daniel's excitement or he wouldn't have butted in on the meeting. He seldom left the radio room.

Daniel caught his breath and pulled up a chair at the table. "According to Martin, he's the sole survivor of the base, yes, but the compound was built to house a couple of hundred people: scientists, military, high ranking officials. It's essentially a giant underground fall-out shelter, but it was being used as a research lab before the plague hit. There was a staff in place, working on various projects when the dead virus—or whatever you want to call—broke out. The base closed itself off automatically, trapping them all inside.

"Unfortunately, the virus had already breached the compound, despite its safety protocols. A war like the one in the city was fought down there, inside the complex. Unlike the military up here, they won. It was costly, but they did win. The virus mutated, though, and became airborne or something. I didn't really understand all of what Martin was saying. It was a bit over my head. He made it through it all though. Now he's just sitting around with years of stockpiled supplies: food, meds, weapons, even fuel!"

"Still, I don't see how that helps us," Jack interjected.

"I'm getting to that part. Martin is a pilot and it's a military base. There are two helicopters there, both of them for military transport. He could easily reach the hospital by air and either bring us some of the stockpiles or take a few of us at a time to the base. It's just a matter of deciding what we want him to do."

"You've asked him about all this?" Laura asked, unwilling to accept that such a miracle could simply fall into their laps.

Daniel calmed down a bit. "Well, no. I haven't asked him to fly us to the base, but he offered to bring the supplies we need without any prompting on my part."

Vince placed his hands on the table. "That seems odd. If he's willing to share all this stuff, wouldn't it be easier to move us there rather than have him haul it all out here? Could he even realistically make that many trips? And why waste so much if he just brings part of it and decides to stay here when he lands on the roof?"

"I don't know," Daniel admitted, "but I trust him. I could hear the sincerity in his voice. He has to be lonely out there. I would be. Maybe all the stuff that happened down there is haunting him and he just wants out of the place."

Laura nodded. "Okay, Daniel. If you trust him so much from one conversation, I'll buy into his desire to help us, but how do we handle this?" She looked to Jack and Vince for their input.

"Have him fly over a run of supplies," Vince replied. "It couldn't hurt if he's truly alone. There are nearly fifty of us. Numbers will be on our side even if he's lying. Hell, a transport full of soldiers is something we could handle as long as we know when they're coming. And if he's telling the truth, we get the stuff we need and we get to meet him face-to-face and check him out for real. Then we can decide what to do from there."

Jack nodded, agreeing with Vince. For once, the hippy had a well thought-out and sane suggestion.

"We're agreed then," Laura said. " Daniel, go invite our new friend over for a visit. Jack, I want you and Mitchell to prepare for any of the darker things that could come from this."

"We've got one surface-to-air missile left from the armory raid before the hospital was completely surrounded," Jack informed her. "It'll do just great if things go south."

"What about me?" Vince asked. "Don't I get a part in this?"

"Yes, Vince, you do. I want you to make a list of the order we'll leave in if this Martin is for real and we opt to move to his base.

Decide who's best suited to make the trip first, and who needs to stay here until everyone else is safely there."

"That's it?"

"No. I want you to inform everybody as soon as possible. Not everyone may want to leave the hospital, and you'll need to know who wants to stay. You can also prepare people for what's coming, good or bad." Laura stood up. "Well people, let's get to it."

CHRIS sat rocking Natalie, an empty bottle of formula below his chair. She cooed, gazing up at him with her beautiful green eyes, so much like her mother's. Chris wrapped her blanket tighter around her tiny body as his mind raced with Vince's news. He couldn't believe it. Salvation had come to them out of the darkness. Hope was with them after all.

The base had to be huge. Full of tunnels and open spaces, protected by thick metal walls, concrete, and the earth itself. No more fear that the dead would find a way in. Natalie would be safe. She could grow up without living in fear. She would have places to play, big spaces where he could let her run alone. For years to come she would have a life more normal than he could have dared to hope for. When Vince asked if he and Natalie would be willing to go, Chris hadn't hesitated in the slightest.

"Everything's going to be okay," he whispered to Natalie as she fell asleep in his arms; for the first time in a long while, he meant it. He only wished Rebecca had lived long enough to see her daughter enjoy a better life.

NIGHT fell over the city, embracing the hospital in its darkness. Thousands upon thousands of zombies surrounded the building, wandering mindlessly and biding their time, waiting for their prey to emerge.

According to Vince's poll, not a single person—other than Alyson—refused to gamble on the new home that fate had offered them. Jack couldn't blame them for risking it all. In the hospital you could see the dead if you bothered to look out, and you could hear their hungry voices calling up to you. Sometimes it seemed that the dead were using a form of psychological warfare against them, though Jack knew it was impossible. The creatures were just drawn to this place because they could sense the warm blood and flesh entombed in its walls. *Entombed*, he thought. It was such a perfect word to describe their situation. All of them, including him, were dead in the long run. They just hadn't fallen down yet.

After helping Jack prepare for the guest—or guests?—who would arrive in the morning, Mitchell returned to Alyson's quarters. She lay naked and uncovered on the bed, so drugged up she wasn't even aware of his presence, her eyes distant, her mind drifting somewhere far away. He considered taking her just because he could. If she remembered later when she came to, he could always pay her, but in the end Mitchell dismissed the idea. He stood at her window, listening to the moans of the dead below. Their cries seemed louder tonight, more desperate.

On the bed, Alyson rolled over onto her stomach. Mitchell turned and took in her naked form, lusting after her despite the session they'd shared this morning. Physical release distracted him and kept him sane—if anyone in the place *could* be called sane. It was his escape, *his* drug. Alyson's red hair was the fire that cleansed his soul.

He loosened his belt and walked toward the bed. For a while he would join Alyson in heaven. It would help pass the time until dawn.

TWO

AS the sun rose from behind the distant mountains, Daniel waited on the hospital roof, smoking one of the last few cigarettes to cope with the excitement and stress. Laura and Vince stood by his side, flanked by Jack, Mitchell, and two of Jack's hospital guards. The men all held assault rifles, except for Jack, who shouldered their sole missile launcher, ready to fire the instant anything went wrong.

They heard the helicopter before they saw it, the roar of the engine drowning out the soft, distant noise of the dead below.

Daniel had brought a portable radio. He switched it on. "He's coming," he said to Laura, stating the obvious as the small helicopter made its way toward the hospital.

Vince watched it through a pair of binoculars. Jack studied it through the missile launcher's sight.

"He's alone!" Jack barked over the *whump-whump-whump* of the helicopter's blades. "Or looks to be."

Daniel's radio awoke in his grasp. "Joseph Hospital, this is Martin Kier approaching your position. Do I have permission to touch down?"

Laura nodded at Daniel, then motioned for the others to stand down and clear the space for the bird to land safely. She thanked God that Vince persuaded everyone else to stay inside. The excitement over Martin's arrival had reached a fever pitch. If it hadn't been for Vince's convincing nature the whole group of survivors might have been on the roof. It was chaotic enough with just the small group she had.

The helicopter landed and its engine shut down. The man who called himself Martin Kier took off his flight helmet. He stared at them for a second, appraising them through his thick, dark glasses before stepping out of the helicopter. Martin wore green military fatigues, and he never removed the heavily tinted glasses as he came to greet them. He looked to be in his mid-twenties, well built and of average height. His midnight-black hair grew slightly longer than the mandatory military cut. The man moved with feline grace as he offered his hand to Jack. "Hello."

Jack didn't take Martin's hand. "You can call me Jack. The lady in the lab coat is Dr. Laura Smith. We're the leaders of this group. That chain-smoker over there with the radio is Daniel."

"Whoa." Vince shook Martin's hand and introduced himself. "I'm one of the people in charge here too. We're damn glad to see you. Sorry about Jack. Being a rude, hard-ass is his reason for living."

Martin smiled, or attempted to. The expression looked awkward and out of place on his lips. "I brought the food and gear you requested."

Vince waved at the helicopter dismissively. "Don't worry about that now. Good old Mitchell and the guys can unload it. I bet you're tired from your flight, and we have a hell of a lot to talk about. Let's go inside and get you a drink." Half joking, he added, "You brought coffee, right?"

Mitchell and Jack's men unloaded the supplies as Martin followed the others into the stairwell. Daniel tossed aside the cigarette he was smoking and stayed behind to scope out the helicopter, get a feel for the controls. He wanted to be ready in case something happened and he needed to fly it.

Glancing around the cockpit, Daniel saw the standard controls of a military bird. He'd only flown traffic copters before the plague, but the difference didn't look too drastic.

Vince led Martin and the others down what was usually the quickest route to the conference room, but the hallways were clogged with refugees. They all wanted to see the man who had restored their hope. Vince hurried past them as quickly as he could, dragging the others with him as if by sheer force of will. With each person they passed Martin's muscles tensed underneath his clothes, as if he expected the group to attack. Vince kept glancing at the twin side arms strapped to Martin's hips, praying no one spooked the stranger enough to make those weapons leave their holsters.

On the trip down, Martin only paused once to really take in the people and the surroundings. It was when Chris, carrying his daughter Natalie, nearly bumped into them outside the conference room. Martin's eyes went straight to Natalie and stayed on her as if he didn't register Chris's presence.

Finally, he looked up at Chris. "Is the child yours?" Martin asked, awed.

Chris nodded, unsure of how to respond.

Martin's eyes drifted back to Natalie. "You must be very proud."

Before Chris could reply, Vince shoved Martin into the conference room. "You can meet folks later, Martin. We really need to talk right now, okay?"

Martin glanced at Vince and saw the man's fear naked on his face. "Yes, you're right," Martin agreed.

Vince closed the door behind Jack and Laura as they entered.

After he finished familiarizing himself with the helicopter, Daniel caught up to the group outside of the conference room. Martin could hear him talking with Chris in the hall, but he took a seat at the table anyway. Laura sat at the head of the table, facing Martin, and Vince and Jack sat on either side of him.

"So you made it, Mr. Kier," Laura began. "There were those among us who thought you wouldn't show, or that if you did you'd only bring death and trouble with you. It seems they might have been wrong."

Out in the hall, Chris clutched Natalie close to him. "Did you see the way he watched my daughter? It wasn't right."

Daniel said, "Come on, Chris, he's military. He may be one of those guys who are freaked out by kids. No offense, but I am too." He laughed.

"No. It was more than that. He looked at Natalie like she was some kind of alien."

Daniel put a hand on Chris's shoulder. "Everything's going to be okay, Chris. He kept his word and came alone just like he said he would. I think he's been alone for a long time, as long as we've been cooped up in this hospital. Solitude will do that to a person. It can affect people in a lot of ways. He's been through as much, if not more, than we have. He was just happy to see breathing people again, I'm sure."

Chris shook his head. Cradling Natalie in his arms he walked off, leaving Daniel to frown after him.

Martin met Laura's eyes across the table. "I brought only what you asked," he said, then changed the subject. "You have children here. This place is not safe."

"Beggars can't be choosers." Vince's joke hung in the air like the stink of sour meat. No one laughed.

"It's been safe enough so far," Jack informed Martin coldly. "We're all supposed to be friends here. Why don't you put your weapons on the table, Mr. Kier."

Laura blinked at the gall of Jack's request. To her surprise, Martin unsnapped his belt, placed the weapons on the tabletop and slid them toward Jack, who took them eagerly.

"Mr. Jack, isn't it?" Martin asked. "If I wanted to harm you, you'd be dead by now. Having me relinquish my weapons does nothing to change that fact, though I am willing to do so if it will put you more at ease."

"Were there children in the base you're from, Mr. Kier?" Laura asked before Jack had a chance to defend his manly pride.

"No. I had never seen a child before until just a few moments ago. Today is a day of new experiences for me."

"What about your family?" Laura asked. "Were they killed by the virus?"

"Yes. My fathers all perished from the disease."

"Fathers?" Vince asked.

"The men who gave me life," Martin said, a quizzical look on his face, as if he had said nothing peculiar.

The room fell silent. Jack wondered if Martin was insane, but both Vince and Laura caught what Martin meant, or were able to guess at it.

"They were doctors?" Laura proceeded cautiously, hoping she was wrong.

"Scientists." Martin's face was impossible to read.

"Do you mind if I ask how old you are, Martin?" Laura was on the edge of her seat with nervous energy.

"I am slightly over thirteen months old." Martin attempted a friendly smile to assure her that he was not offended by such an odd question.

"Jeez." Vince shook his head.

Jack stood up. "Thank you very much, Mr. Kier. I think that'll be all for now. If you'll just wait outside, we need to discuss some things privately before we continue."

Laura said, "Sit down, Jack. Now."

He hesitated, considered disobeying her order. Finally he took his seat.

"Martin," Laura said, "you were one of the projects at the base, weren't you? It's how you survived whatever happened there, isn't it?"

Martin felt both relieved and worried that his attempt to pass for a normal person had failed. "Yes, Ma'am. My first name was X2114, but I named myself Martin Kier after two of my fathers who died. I was created as an experiment in human genetics. It was an attempt both military and scientific in nature. Though I may be different from you and immune to the dead virus, please understand that I am human. My fathers told me so."

"Martin," Laura began, but this time Jack put her in her place.

"Oh for God's sake!" He slapped the table. "This is insane! And you're full of shit! Who in the hell are you? I want to know: were you really living in that base, or did you just break in after everyone was dead and set yourself up as a king? Were there some people left? Did you kill them off yourself so that everything would be yours? Is that how it went down?"

"I have told you the truth." Martin's face was stone. Laura and Vince could see him struggling against what must have been an implanted urge to defend himself from Jack. At that moment, Laura knew Martin meant what he claimed: he was human—or he wanted to be. If he was just a weapon the military had created, Jack would have been long dead.

Laura tried to warn Jack, but he whirled on her and Vince. He couldn't believe they were buying this horseshit. Without another word, he stormed out of the conference room.

"I'm sorry," Laura said, shrugging her shoulders. "Jack isn't always like that, I swear. Some things are hard for him to accept."

"His response was what I had expected from all of you. I must confess, I didn't think you would find me out so soon."

"Martin," Vince said, "what were you created for?"

"I was created as a weapon. The military took over the project not long after it began. I was originally supposed to be the first cloned human being, but the military made sure I was much more."

"Then why didn't you react like a weapon when Jack threatened you?" Laura wondered. "Surely you were designed to defend yourself with lethal force. I can't see the military settling for anything less."

"The project may have been taken over by the military, but it was originally civilian in nature. My fathers taught me about humanity even as the military tested and honed my offensive capabilities. I believe my fathers hoped what they were teaching me would make me useless to the army and allow them to continue with the project without the army's interference."

"Okay," Vince said, dragging out the word. "I don't suppose it matters much now. You're here and you're not like the flesh-eating monsters outside, so I guess that makes us allies."

"Where do we go from here?" Laura asked them both.

"Daniel expressed to me your desire to leave this hospital, but it may not be wise for you to travel to my base. It was infected with a mutated strain of the dead virus, and despite the base's automated safety measures and my personal efforts, I cannot promise that you wouldn't be exposed to the new airborne pathogen."

"We have to try something, Martin," Laura argued. "We can't stay here forever, even if you continued to bring us supplies. The people here are coming apart at the seams. It's not just about surviving anymore. It's about starting over. And I don't think the virus has mutated in the way you believe it has. If it had, you would've carried it here with you, I'm sure. Its gestation period is usually only a matter of minutes, not hours."

"How can you be sure?"

"I can't be, but none of us have changed since you came and that's a good sign. I just believe it's unlikely. If everyone here remains uninfected by the time we're ready to send the first few members back with you, then we at least know the virus wasn't altered enough for you to carry it here. The first group that goes can check out the base and make sure it's safe before we transport the others."

"What about Jack?" Martin asked.

"Jack will come around in time," Vince assured him.

Laura shook her head. "I wouldn't be so sure of that. Not until he sees proof that you are what you say you are, Martin. Just try to stay out of his way until then."

"And the others here?" Martin asked.

Vince laughed. "I'll introduce you around while Laura and I decide who your first passengers will be. Don't worry. Jack's Jack, and most people aren't like him."

"Thank you," Martin Kier said, nodding. He hoped Vince was right. He'd come to help this group of fellow survivors, not kill them in self-defense. Perhaps what disturbed Martin the most was that, after seeing the child, he was not sure he could bring himself to execute them, even if they chose to eliminate him first.

MITCHELL headed down the corridor to Alyson's quarters, tired from unloading the supplies and pissed that he always got stuck with the grunt work. As much as he needed Alyson at the moment to take away the stress, he nearly went back the way he had come when he saw Jack marching toward him. He could feel Jack's anger like it was a physical force. He stopped dead in his tracks, clutching his fists just in case.

Jack walked right up into his face and looked him dead in the eyes. "Get the guns. It's time."

Mitchell's mouth dropped open. He'd always known Jack walked a thin line with the other members on the tribunal and had hoped one day Jack would take command of the hospital by force. He never thought it would happen though; it would start a civil war, and Jack wanted the group to survive more than anything. It was the driving purpose, perhaps the only purpose, in his life.

"Jack, are you sure about this?"

Jack grabbed Mitchell and flung him against the wall of the corridor. "Get the damn weapons! Get the others too. Laura has gone too far this time. I can't sit by and watch her take us all to hell."

Mitchell forgot about Alyson. He could get off later after things were put right. He darted down the passageway back the way he'd come.

Jack smiled after him. *Maybe today*, he thought. *Maybe today is going to be a good day after all.*

As Jack set his plan for a coup in motion, Vince called a meeting in the hospital's cafeteria. His voice echoed over the intercom throughout the building, urging everyone to attend and meet their new guest. Vince wasn't worried about low attendance. Even the dejected like Alyson and Chris were curious about Martin and the new sense of hope his presence had bought. In fact, Alyson was the first to arrive in the cafeteria where Martin and Vince waited.

Out of habit, Martin stood at attention beside Vince, who'd plopped into one of the chairs. Alyson approached them and smiled at Martin. "Hello, stranger," she purred, flicking her long red hair out of her face with a slight shake of her head.

"Hello," Martin answered. A good number of the base's staff had been female, but none of them had ever acted in such a fashion toward him. He realized her movements were designed to initiate mating, but he could neither explain nor understand the feeling inside of him as she drew closer to kiss him on the cheek.

"Back off, Alyson," Vince said. "Martin isn't human." He saw the hurt in Martin's eyes and immediately cursed himself for being so tactless.

"What?" Alyson squeaked, retreating a few steps.

Vince hated his poor choice of words even more. "That's not what I meant," he said, trying to explain himself to both of them at once. "Martin's a person just like us. I just meant give him some space, okay?"

"A person like us?" Alyson asked. "What in the hell is that supposed to mean? Why would you say shit like that?"

"I am a bio-genetically engineered weapon capable of evolution and independent thought," Martin explained.

"Oh," Alyson gasped. Neither Vince nor Martin could tell if she believed him, but she did seem calmer and she continued to look Martin over. "I'd let you be one for me."

More people started pouring into the room, and Martin locked onto Chris and his newborn daughter as they entered. "I came here to help," he announced to the crowd.

Vince grabbed his arm. "Wait. Wait until everyone's settled and then explain. That way you only have to do it once. It's easier, trust me." Vince stood up, putting a hand on Martin's back, and Martin deferred to his wisdom.

AFTER Laura had left the conference room, she'd returned to her quarters. She had faith that Vince could introduce Martin and convince the group that he wasn't a threat. Jack's reaction had upset her, but there was nothing she could do except give him time to calm down. In his current state, she knew reasoning with him would be out of the question, it would only make matters worse. Anyway, she had more important matters to deal with. She could feel another attack coming on, and she wanted to make sure she was alone when it hit.

She took off her lab coat, slumped onto the edge of her mattress and rolled up her sleeve. When she finished, she opened the drawer of the small desk beside the bed. Inside was her private mini-pharmacy from the hospital's stores. Unlike Alyson, about whom she'd heard rumors, none of her stash was narcotic in nature. It was composed entirely of treatments for her cancer and its symptoms.

She measured out a dose into a syringe and shot up, praying the treatment would stem off the attack. Exhausted both physically and emotionally, she reclined on the bed and closed her eyes, wishing she could bring herself to dream of a better tomorrow.

VINCE waited as long as he felt comfortable for the group to gather in the cafeteria. Almost everyone was there and settled in by now. Only Laura, Jack, and a few of the man's cronies were absent.

When the room finally grew quiet, Vince spoke. "As you all know, the man beside me is Martin Kier. He's the person we made radio contact with recently. And yes, his story is real. He arrived this morning by helicopter and brought us a delivery of supplies from the military installation he's been surviving in since the plague started."

Murmurs of excitement rippled through the crowd.

"There are a few things you need to know. The base may not be a viable spot for us to relocate to. We are making plans to send a small task force to ensure it will be safe for all of us." Vince could see the hope dying in the crowd. "Please, don't be discouraged. It's just a precautionary measure, nothing more. We have every reason to believe the base will be suitable for our needs."

Voices erupted from the crowd. *Who goes first? How will we know the base is safe? How soon does the task force leave?*

Vince struggled to regain control. "Four people including the doctor will go with Martin on his way home. They'll stay in complete and constant radio contact with us, and we should know if the base is all right in a matter of days. As to when they will be leaving, that hasn't been established yet. We need a bit more time to prepare."

"What is it we should know about Martin?" Chris asked, his tone so hostile and unforgiving it cut clearly through the others. If he was supposed to trust this stranger with his daughter's life, he damned sure wanted to know everything about him. Especially with the way the man had stared at her when they'd first met.

Vince didn't want to answer Chris's question, considering the way the informal meeting was headed. Disclosing the problems with Martin's installation had changed the mood of the crowd from hope to something approaching heartbreak and anger. But Vince knew he had little choice now. Chris had put him on the spot, and there was no way to back out.

He shot Martin a troubled glance, but the man—or whatever he was—was too new to such subtle human warnings to catch it.

Martin stepped forward boldly, looking out into the sea of faces. "My name is Martin Kier. I have come to help you in any way that I can. However, you should know I am not human in the normal use of the word."

A new wave of murmurs ran through the gathering, and everyone looked to Vince to see his reaction. He nodded, and shouts filled the room, ranging in tone from anger to utter confusion.

"Wait!" Vince yelled. "Wait! Just hear him out, okay? He's not crazy."

"No," Martin said as the room fell quiet. "I am a biogenetically-created weapon, created by your own government in secret. I am the prototype for what was to be a new breed of soldier, which would end the need for this country's men and women to die in battle. I have survived the undead nightmare we live in just as you have, though I was left alone. Everyone from my creators to my guards perished. Until your Daniel contacted me, I believed the human race to be extinct. I was made to serve you, and now I can do my duty. I will see you all safely from this place, this I swear."

At that precise moment, the doorway to the cafeteria crashed open, and Jack, Mitchell and their small band of cronies entered. All of them were armed. "Cut the shit, Mr. Kier," Jack said. "Don't believe a word he says. He's either insane, or worse, the first of a military assault on this building."

"Jack . . . " Vince held up a hand and tried to reason with him, but Jack hit him in the face with a loaded revolver. The blow knocked Vince to the floor.

"That'll be quite enough from you today, Vince. You and Laura may buy into his crap, but not me. I'm not going to stand by and let him destroy everything we've worked for."

Martin seemed to vanish. One second he was standing beside Vince, the next he was twisting Jack's arm behind his back. The gun clattered from Jack's grasp and his arm snapped as Martin turned him like a shield toward Mitchell and the others. Jack cried out until Martin slapped a palm over his mouth.

"Stop this madness!" Martin shouted. "I have no wish to harm any of you, but I will if you force my hand."

Mitchell blinked, trying to process what had just happened. He motioned to the rest of the men to hold their fire.

Jack managed to shake off the effects of the pain. He turned his head to look at Martin, who removed his hand from Jack's mouth.

"How did you . . . " Jack began.

"I am what I say I am," Martin replied. "Do you yield?"

Jack nodded and Martin released him as Vince fought to calm everyone down. Jack's betrayal he could deal with later; right now, he had a riot to prevent.

HOURS later, Jack sat with his arm in a cast, facing Laura and Vince. His men had been disarmed and confined to their quarters.

"Where do we go from here, Jack?" Laura asked, shaking her head in disappointment.

Jack didn't even bother to look at her. He stared off into space.

"How could you do this to us, Jack, and at such a critical time for us all?"

"Forget him, Laura," Vince said. "We'll confine him like the others."

"And how do we do that?" Laura snapped. "His goon squad represents about half of the men defending this place. The other half is busy watching them, except for Daniel and Gregory. Who's going to keep an eye on those things outside? Much less make up the team to go check out Martin's base."

"Take it easy, Laura." Vince laid a hand on her shoulder, trying to comfort her as she doubled over into a coughing fit. "Hey, are you okay?"

In a voice devoid of compassion, Jack said, "She needs her medicine. She's dying of lung cancer, you idiot."

Vince saw Laura's surprise, as if she believed no one knew her secret; she couldn't deny it though, couldn't even speak she was too busy wheezing. Vince wanted to believe Jack was lying, but Laura's shock told him otherwise. "Where is it, Jack? Where's her medicine?"

"She keeps it hidden all over the place. Try the back of the cabinet over there."

Vince darted to the cabinet, jerked it open and began throwing its contents onto the floor in a desperate search for the meds. He found an inhaler and helped Laura use it.

"How did you know?" she asked Jack as her breathing began to stabilize.

"I know a lot of things, Laura. For example, I know you're going to kill us all if you don't deal with our new guest. Even if he is what he claims to be, that just makes him more dangerous. We have to kill him now before it's too late."

"Vince, would you please see to it that Jack gets locked away like his men?"

Vince smiled, leveling the barrel of his .38 at Jack. "It'll be my pleasure."

With the help of Martin and one of the hospital's remaining defenders, Vince escorted Jack and his goons to one of the hospital's larger waiting rooms and locked them inside. The room made a poor makeshift jail, but at least it only had one way in and out. The guard sat in a chair facing the door, a fully loaded AK-47 in his hands.

With the matter of the prisoners settled, Vince refocused on assembling a team to escort Martin to his base in the morning, and Laura held a second meeting to restore some order and sense of peace to the hospital. Jack's treason—and it couldn't be called anything less—had woken everyone up to how quickly things were falling apart.

ON the roof of the hospital, Alyson stood with an empty syringe at her bare feet. She had finally found her way out. Martin couldn't save them. No one could. The world was dead and the only thing left to do was die. At least she would be going out happy. She giggled and danced as the night wind caressed her naked flesh. She could feel them already, the fingers of the dead running over her skin, the teeth of the dead taking chunks of her into their mouths. She spun on the roof's edge like a ballerina and raised her face as rain began to fall and wash over her. The water trickled between her breasts and slid off her shapely thighs. The end, the real end, was finally here. She hoped Mitchell had found peace with it as she had, then dove off the roof, gliding like a wounded bird toward the street below.

The dead ate her splattered remains.

One of them, a woman wearing a tattered wedding dress, stood from the feast and stumbled through her brethren toward the hospital. One of her legs was broken beneath her bloodstained gown. It barely held her weight.

She looked up at the hospital, catching the scent of living flesh above. She opened her mouth to scream as the hunger burned hotter inside her, but sprayed blood and stale bile instead. The corpse woman staggered, fell to her knees and thrashed about as her body rippled and spasmed, leaving red patches upon the street until at last she lay still.

The other dead close by quit howling and turned to look at her. Her eyes sprung open once more, only now they glowed a pale blue in the darkness. Had a living human been able to see her face, they would have sworn she smiled.

The woman pushed herself up, and without a single stagger, she walked to the nearest zombie and vomited blood into his face.

DANIEL sat in the hospital's stairwell, watching the dead. His head hurt from one too many beers. He'd finished off his entire stash, but it had been worth it. It wasn't every day he got to see an asshole like Jack get what he deserved. Sure, it had really messed things up around the place, and he was pulling watch instead of sleeping because the person who was supposed to be out here was locked up with the rest of Jack's men, but oh well.

Daniel wished for an aspirin, which, unlike his beloved cigarettes, were nowhere near running out. The damn things were all over the place, but he couldn't leave his post to get one.

He turned his attention back to the dead, hoping to see one of the idiots fall off the broken stairs below.

Daniel's breath caught in his throat. His knuckles went white as he clutched his rifle.

The dead had stopped howling. They weren't pushing and shoving each other or trying to jump across the gap in the stairs. They were all just standing there, staring at him with glaring blue eyes.

A sudden warmth filled Daniel's jeans and trickled down his legs. "Oh hell . . . " he whispered and raised his rifle. As the dead saw him taking aim, they opened their mouths in unison and screeched . Daniel dropped the rifle. It fell, spinning toward the ground floor below as he jumped to his feet and raced up the stairs.

Vince, who had been coming to check on him, was nearly smashed in the face by the stairwell door as Daniel came bursting out.

Seeing how freaked out Daniel was, Vince grabbed him by the shoulders and slammed him into the wall. "Are they on their way up? Answer me, damn it!"

Daniel shook his head wildly and managed to stutter the word "No."

Relief washed over Vince. "Then what the hell is wrong?"

"The dead are fucked up, man! They're just really fucked up."

Daniel broke free and darted off without looking back.

Vince turned to the stairwell door and knew he had to go down there, had to see. He drew his .38 and checked the chamber. Pistol in hand, he entered the stairwell.

It hit him then, sinking in, that the dead were silent. He stepped onto the stairs and peered over the railing into a sea of cold blue eyes. The dead stood motionless, as if they were all locked in some sort of waking dream.

Vince carefully backed into the hall and then broke into a run. Laura had to see this. Maybe she'd know what was going on; he sure as hell didn't.

DANIEL had run all the way back to the makeshift communications room.

In an effort to stop shaking, to take his mind off those dead blue eyes, he switched on the radio and listened to R.E.M.'s "What's the Frequency, Kenneth?" as he went to work trying to boost the hospital's signal. His head bobbed to the music as his fingers danced through the wiring of his radio. A cold cup of black coffee sat at his side. He took a sip, grimacing at the bitterness and almost spit it out when the incoming signal light lit up.

He shut off the music and tried to tune in the radio, but remembered he'd just taken it apart. The light had to be a glitch, but something told him to check anyway. He opened the channel and smiled as static crackled on the airwaves. He reached again for his coffee, laughing at himself for being so foolish.

"You are ours," said a voice on the radio, a single voice that sounded like a billion souls speaking at once. "We are coming."

Daniel spilt his stale coffee on his lap and cursed. He had to be imagining this. The radio wasn't working—*couldn't* be working.

"We are coming," the voice said again. "Your flesh is ours."

Static crackled loudly as the channel closed itself.

Daniel leaned into his chair, wide-eyed and shaking, wondering if he had gone mad.

THREE

LAURA stood by the window as Vince and Martin watched her. "Something is certainly going on down there. I've never seen the dead just stop like this."

"Really?" Vince asked sarcastically.

"I don't understand it," Laura said. "It goes against everything we know about their behavior."

"What the hell do we do about it?" Vince asked. "And I swear to God, if you say some shit like 'let's just enjoy the silence,' I'm going to throw you out that window."

"It's got to have something to do with the virus. It's changed, mutated somehow."

"How could it do that?" Martin wondered.

"Oh my lord," Laura blurted. "It's you. You and your helicopter."

Vince stepped away from Martin, aiming his .38 at the man.

"I did nothing," Martin said, completely unafraid of Vince and the weapon pointed at him.

"You didn't have to. You brought the airborne strain of the virus with you. It does exist, and you're not only a carrier of it, you've spread it all over the city when you flew in. The airborne strain must have altered when it encountered the original, altered itself in some way where it affects the dead rather than the living, changing them into something completely new."

Martin nodded. "Please understand there is no way I could have known my presence here would cause this. I am sorry."

"Laura?" Vince asked, keeping his gun trained on Martin.

"Put the gun down, Vince. What's done is done. The only question is what's happening to the dead. They're changing, that's clear, but into what?"

"We've got to get out of here, Laura. Staying around to find out is just asking to get our butts gnawed off."

"Agreed, but Martin's helicopter is the only way out. It's not going to carry everyone."

"I know that, damn it! Let's just grab who and what we can and go. Right now."

"I'm not leaving," Martin informed them. "Your Daniel is also a pilot, I believe. Have him fly you out of here. There's a map to the base inside the helicopter. My purpose is to save as many as I can, and I will make sure the hospital doesn't fall until Daniel can come back for a second group of your people."

Laura tried to argue, but Martin cut her off. "We must prepare. There is a storm coming, and even I cannot fight so many alone."

JACK paced back and forth in the waiting room. Most of his crew slept on the couches, but Mitchell was still awake and staring out the window.

"What are you looking at?" Jack asked.

"The dead. They're bringing ladders and rope into the building. Fucking ladders and rope."

Jack laughed. "You're shitting me."

Mitchell was pale as he looked up at Jack. "I wish I were."

The door to the waiting room opened. Martin stood in the doorway. "You may kill me now, or you can help save all those who may be saved. The choice is yours." He tossed a shotgun into Jack's hands and raised his arms to the sides, presenting his chest.

Jack stared at him, gritting his teeth. "You brought this, didn't you?"

"Yes," Martin answered painfully.

"Fuck you." Jack pumped a round into the shotgun's chamber. "Let's go kick some dead ass."

Martin grinned, and twin auto-pistols like something out of science fiction appeared in his hands.

THE door to the stairwell opened as the first stream of the undead poured into the halls. Martin, Jack, and Jack's men stood in the hallway like old-fashioned minutemen. They hadn't had time to build any sort of barricade.

As the dead raced towards them, Jack screamed the order to fire. The hallway echoed with gunshots and howls as the men tore the first wave of the dead to shreds. The hospital's defenders held their ground for a few seconds until they were forced to reload. Martin, in an effort to buy time, charged into the ranks of the dead. His guns blazed, each shot perfect, splattering rotting brain matter everywhere.

Jack and the others held their fire as Martin tossed aside his empty weapons and dove deeper into the midst of the enemy. He bent his hands downward at the wrists, and blades shot out from beneath the sleeves of his uniform. He sliced the closest creature's skull open with a single swipe and plunged the other blade into another monster's face. He yanked the blade free as the thing leaked blood from between its eyes and collapsed.

Martin gave Jack the signal and dropped to the floor, rolling away from the mob. Jack's shotgun thundered, and Mitchell opened with his AK-47 on full auto; the other men hit the dead with everything they had. The bodies piled up throughout the hallway as Martin rejoined them, but more of the dead raced to take the place of the creatures who had fallen.

"We can't hold them forever like this!" Jack shouted. "Our ammo isn't going to last forever.

"Fall back," Martin ordered. "Fall back and reload."

Not all of the dead followed them as they retreated. Many chose the easier route and headed off down the hall in the other direction.

DANIEL locked himself in the communications room when the gunshots started. He frantically searched around in his pockets. "Oh God, where is it?"

He finally grasped the butt of the cigarette buried in his coat pocket and pulled it out. It was his last one, the last one he was aware of in the whole hospital. He'd been saving it for a special time, for when he really needed it. He ran it under his nose, inhaling the scent of unlit tobacco, the scent of heaven.

He dug out his lighter and flicked it, but it didn't ignite. He flicked it again and again, pausing only to bang it against the wall desperately.

Disgusted, he threw it down along with the cigarette and slumped against the wall. Tears slid down his cheeks. His sobs were quiet at first, but soon he wept openly, alone in the darkness as he listened to the howls of the dead and the gunfire on the floor below.

VINCE held tightly to Laura's hand, almost dragging her with him as she tried to keep pace. He had already sent someone to find Daniel and get him up on the roof, but Laura insisted they find Chris and Natalie before they headed up to the helicopter. Vince had no choice but to go along with her; she wouldn't leave without the child, and wherever they managed to escape to, they would need Laura's skills for as long as she could fight off the cancer. Besides, given time and the proper tools Laura might one day put an end to the dead virus once and for all.

Vince wondered if she'd be able to make it the rest of the way to Chris's quarters, but ever the fighter, Laura gasped for air and pushed on. Her strength amazed him and gave him hope.

They found Chris's door barred. Laura struggled vainly with the knob.

"Move!" Vince screamed, and she stepped aside as he kicked open the entrance.

Chris glanced up at them as they made their way inside. He sat rocking Natalie, hugging her tightly to his chest. "Save her," he said, crying. "Someone's got to. She doesn't deserve to die like this."

"Okay, Chris. Okay." Vince helped him to his feet. "We're certainly going to try."

DANIEL selected a heavy wrench from his tools and tested its weight. It would have to do. Like an idiot, he had dropped his gun in the stairwell.

He cranked up the stereo, and Michael Stipe's voice blared; the room rattled to the tune of "The Great Beyond." It was one of

Daniel's favorite songs, and somehow it seemed to fit. The music covered the noise of the dead as they tore the door off its hinges.

Daniel adjusted his glasses and stood his ground. Two dead things rushed into the room. He swung the wrench and clobbered the first one in the head. It lurched sideways and fell with a crash into one of Daniel's worktables. Its left eye dangled from its socket as the thing thrashed about on the floor.

The second intruder came at him too fast, and he couldn't get a good swing at it. It grabbed him, strained against him, tried to sink its teeth into his flesh.

Daniel threw the thing off and darted for the door. He nearly collided with a third creature in the hall. He gave a quick hard kick to one of its knees, then fled, not bothering to look back as the creature toppled to the floor.

As he rounded the bend in the corridor, a voice cried out. "Daniel!" One of the hospital's defenders, a man whose name he couldn't remember, was running after him. Daniel skidded to a halt as the man caught up.

"We need to get you up to the roof!" the guard said. "You need to fly the helicopter!"

Shit, Daniel thought.

Vince, Harold, Laura, and any other survivors were all counting on him. Counting on him to fly a type of helicopter he'd never even sat in until today. He remembered the time he'd spent going over its controls and knew he could do it, even if just barely. It would be enough.

The guard shoved a rifle into his hands as they raced toward the roof. The weapon brought Daniel no comfort. If they encountered a large pack of the dead on their way, it wouldn't make any difference whether or not they sent a few of the creatures back to hell. They'd be overwhelmed and that was that.

They rounded another corner and jerked open the door to the stairs that led to the roof. A decaying woman in a bloodstained wedding gown leapt out at them, slashing the guard's throat with her long decorated nails. Blood spurted from the wound with every beat of his heart.

Daniel didn't have time to take a shot at her, so he barreled into her, pushing her back inside the stairwell and over the railing. She hissed, still groping for him as she fell into the darkness below.

Daniel glanced back at the guard's corpse, wishing he could remember the poor guy's name. Then he shut the door to the stairs and sprinted up to the roof.

MOST of the hospital's defenders were dead and had switched sides in the battle. Mitchell had disappeared in the fray, leaving only Martin and Jack to hold back the dead long enough for Vince and Laura to escape.

The dead had them cornered now two floors below the roof, backed into a waiting room with no way out. Martin was fighting the creatures hand-to–hand, holding them at the door while Jack tried to reload. A purple blood-like substance oozed from numerous wounds and bites covering his body. He punched one of the things in the head, which flew off and landed on the floor to be trampled under countless feet.

Jack raised his gun and shot a creature that had made it past Martin. The blast hit it in the chest, knocking it to the other side of the room.

'It's no use Jack!" Martin wailed as a wounded dead thing, its lower spine shattered, sank its teeth into his thigh.

'I know," Jack whispered, letting his shotgun clatter to the floor. He pulled a bandolier of grenades from his backpack, which he had swiped from a fallen friend, and without hesitation he popped the string's pin and ran into the swarm of undead. "See you in hell, Martin!"

The waiting room burst into a ball of flames, showering the street below with shards of glass and chunks of debris.

THE building seemed to shake as Vince bounded up the last steps to the roof. He lost his footing and would have fallen over the railing had Chris not grabbed him.

"What the hell was that?" Laura asked.

"Jack," Vince answered curtly as he shoved her ahead of him. "There isn't going to be a trip back, Laura. I'm sure Martin did all he could, but I think we're it. We're the only ones who are going to make it out of here alive."

Laura nodded sadly as they opened the door to the roof and came face to face with the barrel of a massive, cannon-like gun. Mitchell lowered it and grinned. "It's about time someone made it up here."

Daniel stood with him, waving at them with a trembling hand. Laura embraced him, happy to see their pilot alive.

Chris cradled Natalie in his arms and headed straight for the helicopter. "Come on! We've got to get out of here before the dead catch up with us!"

Vince met Mitchell with a knowing look. "You're not going, are you?"

Mitchell shook his head. "There's no place for someone like me left in this world."

"I wonder if there's a place left for any of us," Vince agreed. He laid a hand on Mitchell's shoulder for a moment, then darted to join the others.

Mitchell watched as the helicopter whirled to life and lifted off from the hospital's roof, streaking away into the sky. He swiveled the machine gun on its tripod until it pointed toward the stairs, and he waited for the dead to come.

THE QUEEN

THE air stunk of filth and human waste. The summer heat heightened the smell, but Scott had long grown accustomed to the stench. Sweat glistened on his sunburned chest and shoulders. He reached up, running his fingers through his short brown hair. They came away wet and covered in grime. He couldn't remember for the life of him when he'd last been allowed to bathe. There was a large tub of water in the center of the pen where the prisoners were kept. Scott eyed it, not yet thirsty enough to expose himself to the germs and bacteria it contained.

Eleven other men shared the small pen with him. Most of them sat around, lost in their own thoughts like he was. Buck and Hank played cards with a tattered deck for which they'd been able to bribe the guards. Hank had traded a section of flesh from his left thigh in order to get it.

The bandage he wore had yellowed, and Scott guessed that soon Hank would succumb to infection and die. He had seen a lot of men die over the three weeks he'd been trapped here. The guards didn't seem to care, as long as they had one or two healthy males.

The women that had been taken alive were treated much better than the men. Scott had never been inside their actual quarters, but he knew it was inside the breeding center, out of the sun. It had plumbing and was kept clean and free of disease. Unlike the pig slop the men were fed, the women were given real food. It all made sense in a sick kind of way. The dead guards needed the women to make babies, more "cattle" for the pens, whereas they only needed one man to knock them all up.

Of all the men in the cage, only David stood at the fence, peering through it at the hills beyond the compound. He was a newcomer to the breeding center and still hoped that someone would rescue them. He dreamed of escape. It was a dangerous thing. Scott knew there was no way out other than death; it was just a question of how one died and ended up on the other side of the fence.

If someone perished in the pen while the guards weren't around, Scott and the other prisoners made damn sure the corpse didn't get back up, even if it meant bashing its head with a stone until they were covered in blood. The newly risen dead weren't always as evolved as the guards, and they often went on a feeding frenzy. Stopping that from happening was worth the lashing. The men took turns so that no one was overly punished or outright put to death for the deed. It was Scott's turn now, and he figured it wouldn't be long before he was bashing open Hank's skull.

The guards mostly stayed inside the compound proper. Whatever force had reanimated them had also greatly reduced their rate of decay, but hadn't stopped it. Being outside in the heat of summer was unhealthy for them in the long run.

Scott watched as "Chief Hole in His Neck" peeked out of the compound door for the hourly check on the pen; the dead man had gotten his name because his throat was torn open and his rotting windpipe dangled out. He was one of the few guards who couldn't speak, but he held a high rank among the dead and was easy to get along with if you stayed out of his way and didn't cause trouble. The dead man's gaze lingered only for a moment on David, who still stood at the fence, then the mute guard popped back inside, closing the door to the air-conditioned compound behind him.

Scott tiredly pushed himself to his feet, wiping his hands on the pair of tattered black jeans he wore. David didn't notice his approach.

"You've got to stop doing this," Scott warned.

David jumped at the sound of his voice. His bloodshot eyes stared at Scott in shock. "Doing what?"

"Hoping," Scott answered. "If you don't, they'll likely have you for dinner soon. It makes them nervous when one of us shows any bit of spirit left. Just be thankful you're not one of them already and get over it."

David started to respond, but Scott had already turned his back to the newcomer and was headed towards his spot, where he planned to sit and wait for the cool of the night.

2

THE dead were getting closer. Riley ducked farther down in the brush, which grew on a hill above the gravel road. Two jeeps, flanked by a number of creatures on foot, crept their way up the mountainside. The whole scene was very troubling. Just how desperate were the dead getting for food if they were sending hunting parties this far out, and did it mean that all the cities had fallen at last?

The hunting party had stuck to the road so far, and Riley doubted they would stray into the woods, but his cabin was only a few miles north of the road. He counted eight of the things, including the drivers, all heavily armed. He couldn't face a force of that size by himself, and even if he miraculously took them all out, more would come in search of their brethren, and likely in greater numbers. Then they would surely find his place.

Riley kept still and waited for them to pass by. When they were well out of earshot, he began to sneak back the way he'd come.

As he reached home and emerged from the trees, he saw little Brandon playing in the tall grass surrounding the cabin. The boy's face lit up when he noticed his father. He dropped the stick with which he'd been hacking at the wild flowers and ran towards Riley with his tiny arms open. Despite his worries, Riley couldn't help but smile as he swept Brandon up from the ground and clutched him tight to his chest.

"Where's Mom?" Riley asked, cutting off his son's litany of questions about his scouting trip.

Crestfallen, Brandon motioned towards the cabin, keeping one arm propped on his father's wide shoulders. "She's getting ready to cook dinner."

Riley frowned and placed Brandon back on the ground. The last thing they needed were smoke signals pouring out of the cabin's chimney today.

Brandon followed as Riley walked onto the porch and stuck his head inside the kitchen through the open front door. "Hi, honey, I'm home," he called out, trying to hide his concern from Brandon.

Hannah looked up from the vegetables she was chopping and greeted Riley with a smile, which died on her lips as she saw the fear in his eyes. "It's time isn't it?" she asked.

Riley nodded. "We both knew this day would come sooner or later."

She moved to take Brandon's hand. "How long do we have?"

"I don't know. An hour, a week, there's just no way to tell. They may never find this place, but they're close enough for us to be better safe than sorry."

Hannah leaned down and kissed her child on the forehead. "Brandon, honey, would you please go play in your room for a few minutes? Mommy and Daddy need to talk, okay?"

As the boy marched off deeper into the cabin, Hannah got back to her feet and turned to face Riley. "Where are we going to go?"

He shrugged. "I have no idea."

3

IT had been a tough decision but ultimately Riley had chosen to leave the truck. It was in great shape, perfect for off-road travel, and he had stored enough fuel to fill it up twice. But the dead controlled the roads now, and the truck was too risky, even out here in the wilderness. It was better, Riley knew, to set out on foot. They would travel slower and they wouldn't be able to carry as much, but it would be far safer. On foot, they could stick to the trees and stay clear of the roads; they would be nowhere near as noticeable should they come across a group of the dead.

Hannah prepared some rations, and the family divided the load of food and water, with even little Brandon carrying a canteen of his own. Riley also let him carry a hunting knife, though Hannah had protested. The knife would be of no use against the dead as Brandon didn't have the strength or the skill to drive it into someone's skull, but it made the boy feel safer and that was what mattered to Riley.

Hannah carried an old-fashioned .30-.06 rifle, which once belonged to her father, and she also strapped a .38 revolver to her hip. Riley carried two holstered .45 automatics, an M-16 he'd bought illegally before the world fell apart, and numerous spare magazines for all three weapons in his backpack.

Leaving this place wasn't easy for any of them. They'd been up here alone for a full three months since the dead first began to rise. In a lot of ways, it felt more like home than the house they'd lived in for years before they fled for the high country.

They made their way into the woods, and Riley watched a tear slide down Hannah's cheek as she looked back at the cabin. It cut into his heart like a blade.

They still had no idea where they were headed. There was no logical place to head for, so Riley and Hannah had merely decided to set out east for the coast and hope for the best. If nothing else, maybe Brandon could see the ocean once before they all died.

Riley swore to himself the dead would never take his family alive, even if he had to kill them himself.

4

IT was feeding time in the pen. The sun had long sunk beneath the surrounding mountains. Two of the dead guards emerged from within the compound, carrying a large bucket filled with slop as runny as cream corn. With the help of a third guard, they emptied the bucket over the fence onto the ground of the pen. The human prisoners pounced on it like hunger-maddened animals, scraping it up from the dirt with their bare hands.

Scott and David did not participate in the fight for their evening meal. David remained at the pen's far side, staring at the roadway that lead up to the breeding center. Scott sat Indian style on the ground with his arms across his legs, palms open towards the stars. His eyes were closed, his breathing slow and steady. Scott would find leftovers later, or he would fight with the flock at the morning meal. He doubted if David had any thoughts in his head about food, and he didn't care. Let the newcomer starve if he wanted to. There were worse ways to die.

All that mattered to Scott at the moment was finding a shred of peace. Meditation could take him away from the horrors of this place.

Earlier in the day, he'd told David to stop hoping, that it was a lost cause, but now he wondered: wasn't he himself seeking hope by leaving the pen, if only in his mind? He sighed and opened his eyes. The guards were already headed back inside the breeding center and the frenzy among the men for the slop was dying down. Scott slowly got to his feet, ignoring the taunts of his fellow inmates that he'd missed the meal.

This time David saw him coming, then turned back to the fence as Scott reached his side. "How dare you tell me to stop hoping?" David whispered. "Hope is all that's left to any of us now."

Scott accepted the stinging words as if he deserved them. He nodded towards the road leading out of the compound. "What exactly is out there that you want so badly? There's no place left to go. The dead are everywhere. In here, we know we're not going to be cut open and chewed on."

"What's the point of being alive if you can't live?" David shot back.

"Hank and Buck, those two rednecks over there, would argue with you that we are living. They get fed, have their friendship, and once every couple of days they get to have the orgy of their wet dreams with the ladies inside."

"But would you argue with me?"

"No," Scott answered. "No, I would not."

David grinned. "Then what are we going to do about that?"

Scott offered his hand, and the two men shook. "I'm Scott. Scott Burgess."

"And you can call me David."

"I know." Scott laughed. "Well, David, it looks as if we have a lot to talk about."

5

STEVEN placed the half-full bottle of whiskey atop his desk. All he wanted in the world was the feel of its fiery embrace as the alcohol slid down his throat, but he couldn't bring himself to open the bottle. Too many people depended on him. He hadn't asked for this job, but the *Queen* was his ship. She was all he ever loved in his life, and when the time came he'd go down with her. He knew every inch of her like the back of his hand, and yet she'd changed so much over the last few months he barely recognized her.

Once upon a time, she'd been a gleaming beauty of magnificent white hulls, a floating paradise where dreams of love and adventure thrived. Now her hull was spotted with makeshift plates of armor and the scars of battle. Gun emplacements lined the length of the main deck on all sides. Where once she'd held hundreds of vacationers, she now contained barely one hundred refugees, tired, frightened and desperate.

Someone knocked, and through the open door of the captain's quarters Steven noticed O'Neil standing in the hallway. In one fluid motion, he swept the bottle off the top of his desk and into the drawer where it belonged.

O'Neil shifted uncomfortably. "Sorry to disturb you, sir, but I have the inventory of our supplies that you asked for."

"Of course." He motioned for O'Neil to take a seat across the desk from him. "And how do things look?"

O'Neil slumped into the offered chair. "Not as bad as we thought. The last dock we raided gave us enough fuel for another two weeks or more."

"And it only cost us the lives of six men," Steven added bitterly.

O'Neil continued with the report. "Our ammunition stockpiles for small arms are holding up remarkably well, and Luke assures me that the new torpedo tubes he set up on the forward hull will work if we need them. Our only real pressing concern is food. Even with a rationing system in place and the reduced number of passengers and crew onboard, we'll be out again in less than a week. The priority of the last raid was fuel for the *Queen*, so we didn't have time to stock up like we needed."

"They came crawling out of the woodwork," Steven chuckled.

"I'm sorry, sir?"

"The dead, Mr. O'Neil. Regardless of where we put into port, they're always there, waiting. We never have enough time."

"Yes, sir. I don't like the thought of touching land again anytime soon."

Silence lingered in the room for a moment before O'Neil finally said, "Well, sir, what are we going to do?"

"Pray," Steven answered. "Pray our little hearts out . . . And while we're at it, bring me a map of the area we're in now. Going back ashore is really our only option, isn't it? Since the damn fish are just as dead as the rest of the world. Besides, even if they weren't, you know we couldn't catch enough to feed everyone aboard this ship. It's just not possible with our limited equipment and resources."

O'Neil left in search of a map, leaving Steven alone once again in the darkness of the room.

6

NO stars lit the sky. Thick, dark clouds let loose what seemed a never-ending shower of rain. Brandon slept peacefully under the small tarp Riley had set up for him. Hannah rested against a tree, drenched to the bone. Her long red hair clung heavily to her neck and shoulders. Riley leaned over and put his arm around her. To him, she was beautiful no matter the circumstances.

"How far do you think we made it today?" she whispered, trying not to wake Brandon.

"A pretty good distance despite the weather," he assured her. "We're safe here for the night, I think."

Hannah's .30-.06 rested beside her, propped against the same tree. "Riley, do you think there's anyone else left?

"Sure, honey. Sure. There's got to be. If we've made it this long, it just makes sense somebody else, somewhere, has made it too."

"It's not fair," she muttered with a fresh wetness sliding down her cheeks. "Brandon doesn't deserve this. He should be in school or playing video games. Think of all the things we took for granted, Riley, things that Brandon will never know except from our stories. If there are other people out there, we have to find them for his sake and start over somehow."

Riley listened to the rain as it bounced off the leaves of the trees around them. "Hannah," he said softly, "I'm sorry."

"Sorry, Riley? It's not your fault that the dead woke up or that we're living through the end of the world. If it weren't for you, Brandon and I would be dead. I'm grateful for the time we had in the cabin. How many other people even had a chance like that? To pretend things were going to be okay? Those months were like heaven. It's just . . . it's just Brandon." She nestled her face into Riley's chest and sobbed hard against the muscles she found there.

Riley's arms encircled her. "I swear, Hannah, if there is a place to start again, we'll find it or die trying. We've just got to hold it together for a while longer. Rain or no rain, we'll start moving again in the morning." Riley shut his eyes and thought only of his wife's body pressed against his until dawn.

The clouds broke as the sun rose. Riley checked over their weapons to make sure the dampness hadn't damaged them as Hannah and Brandon made a game of packing up and preparing to get on the move. The three shared stale granola bars for a quick breakfast and drank water from their canteens, then set out in the direction of the sun.

7

SCOTT didn't like David's plan. In fact he loathed it, thought it was insane. He had no better ideas to offer, however, so he went along with it. They'd carefully selected which guard to make their offer to, and the chance to go through with it had arrived. The guards were out in full force today, as it was time for the prisoners to be rounded up for a breeding session. Chief Hole in His Neck was in command, flanked by six more of the dead, each carrying some type of fully-automatic military weapon. His subordinates opened the gate to the pen and led the prisoners out.

Scott, having been a captive for weeks, knew how things worked. He gave Hole in His Neck the sign that he wanted to make a trade. Hole in His Neck studied him, then motioned for his men to leave Scott behind.

When the others were all outside of the pen, Hole in His Neck stepped inside. Scott could swear he saw the hunger burning in the dead man's eyes.

"Screw it," Scott mumbled, hopefully too quiet for Hole in His Neck to hear. He cleared his throat and said, "David and I don't want to go inside today."

A look of utter confusion settled on the guard's features. A human male who did not want to get laid was beyond his understanding.

Scott saw the look and misread it. "David's the new guy. The one you just brought in."

Hole in His Neck signed the question "Why?" He wondered if Scott had lost his mind, and he toyed with the idea of dispatching the human then and there. He needed more help tending to the women's needs anyway; a new dead body walking around would help with his duty roster.

Scott gritted his teeth, steeling himself for what he was about to say. "Look. We're gay, okay? We just want to be by ourselves for an hour to breed in our own way. Just this one time," he added hastily.

Hole in His Neck smiled. A sick wet sound came from his exposed windpipe as he tried to laugh. He shook his head and shoved Scott towards the gate.

"Wait!" Scott urged. "You haven't even heard what I'm offering in return."

Hole in His Neck paused. It was not permitted to feed on the prisoners unless they broke the rules or offered non-vital pieces of their meat freely. Scott had been anything but a normal prisoner, and Hole in His Neck admitted to himself that he enjoyed the way Scott was begging for such an unnatural and shameful act.

"You could send one of your people with us, to make sure we don't escape. I'm only asking for an hour."

Using gestures, the dead man asked what he would get in return and indicated that it had better be worth such an affront to the rules.

"My legs," Scott said firmly. "Both of them, all yours. I don't need them to breed, and if I die from you taking them, you can stick me out here so you'll have a permanent watchdog over the others until I rot away to nothing from the heat."

Hole in His Neck held up his fingers, saying two guards would go with them, not one. Then he added that this would be the only time, one way or another.

Scott breathed a sigh of relief as the commander of the watch went to fetch David and the guards who would take them to the woods. Maybe, just maybe, this was going to work after all.

8

BULLETS sparked and pinged off the asphalt as Riley ran for cover. He half fell, half rolled behind the carcass of an abandoned truck. The spray of bullets followed him, thudding into the truck's frame.

Hannah and Brandon were nowhere to be seen. Riley had been cut off from them when the jeep-full of dead soldiers appeared out of nowhere.

Riley cursed himself for leading his family here. There shouldn't have been a road at all, not this far out in the country, much less a major one littered with the ruins of cars and trucks. The only things that should have been up there were trees and dirt trails. Riley didn't have the faintest idea where the road led, but it had seemed safe. Figuring they didn't have time to follow it in the woods until they could cut around, he chose to walk it. Now he was paying the price.

He heard the crack of Hannah's .30-.06 somewhere in the distance. *Damn the woman!* he thought. If she and Brandon had reached the trees, they should've just kept going; they shouldn't have stopped to save him.

Left without an alternative, he leaned around the end of the truck to see what was happening on the road. One of the dead stood several yards away, focusing its AK-47 on the tree line. Riley's military training took over, and he seized the chance. His M-16 opened up, sending a stream of rounds into the dead thing's chest and up its torso until, with a wet popping sound, the corpse's rotting head burst like a melon, spewing brain matter onto the road below its feet. Its body spun, headless, and dropped. Riley was on his feet and running for a better vantage point before the body hit the ground. He'd only seen three of the things, and he figured he could handle them as long as he knew Hannah and Brandon were safe. But that was the problem, wasn't it?

Riley felt fire tear into his shoulder, and the impact knocked him down. His rifle went skidding away from him. Out of the corner of his vision, he saw the dead man who'd shot him. The thing charged forward and lowered its rifle, to which was attached some kind of blade.

Riley didn't move, waited to the last possible second and grabbed for the weapon as the thing tried to spear him with it.

Close combat with the dead was extremely dangerous. A bite, or sometimes just a scratch from their nails, was enough to infect a person with the lethal virus, or evil spirit, or whatever it was that gave the dead life.

Taking his opponent by surprise, Riley ripped the weapon from its hands and sent the creature sprawling to the pavement beside him. It rolled at him, biting and clawing for his flesh. The thing never saw him draw the .45 automatic. He blew the brains out the back of its head.

"Hannah!" Riley screamed, praying for an answer.

In the distance, the monsters' jeep roared to life. Riley scrambled for his gun, then stopped and let out a whoosh of breath as the vehicle retreated. The road fell silent.

Blood stained the front of his shirt, leaking from the wound on his shoulder, but he didn't feel it. He bolted, his legs pounding beneath him, to where he'd heard the shot from Hannah's rifle. He skidded to a halt as he reached the tree line and saw Hannah in the dirt. His heart felt like it stopped beating as she looked up at him, revealing the tears on her cheeks, the blood on her hands. She was kneeling over Brandon, who lay in a growing puddle of red.

Spots engulfed Riley's vision, and Hannah watched him collapse.

9

SCOTT and David put on a show for the two guards accompanying them outside the breeding center. They held hands and acted eager to reach a place in the hills where they could be together intimately. The guards led them about a mile and a half from the compound before the group stopped and one of the dead men pulled out a stopwatch from its pocket. "This is as far as we're going," the guard informed them, and he started the watch. "You better get to it. The clock is ticking."

"You're going to watch us?" David asked, horrified. "That wasn't part of the deal."

"Tough," the other guard grunted. "Get to jerking each other off or whatever so we can get back."

"What's the matter?" Scott laughed. "Are you horny too? Wanna join us?"

The guard blinked his single eyelid while the other laughed at him. Scott sprang forward, grabbing the laughing guard's head and twisting it around so fast the neck broke with a sharp crack. It wouldn't kill the dead man, but breaking his neck would immobilize him and leave him helpless.

The remaining guard raised the barrel of its weapon toward Scott, tightening its finger on the trigger, but David tackled the dead man; they went down in a mess of tangled limbs as the guard's rifle blazed away.

Scott instinctively ducked out of the line of fire and snatched up the rifle of the guard he'd killed. He whirled to see David lying atop the other guard, his intestines scattered everywhere. The burst from the thing's weapon must have disemboweled him.

Scott squeezed the trigger of his rifle and held it, emptying the clip into David's corpse and the guard below. Done, he tossed the rifle aside. Neither David nor the guard would be getting up again.

He felt a pang of loss and guilt over David's sacrifice, but he didn't have time to think about it—the whole compound must have heard the brief battle. So Scott sprinted into the trees and didn't look back.

10

O'NEIL and Captain Steven studied the map spread out on the table before them. Steven stabbed at a point on the map with his finger. "We'll put in here."

"South Carolina?" O'Neil asked.

"Why not? This port here is out of the way in terms of the old commercial traffic routes, and it's close enough for us to reach it within two days."

"It'll still be guarded. If nothing else there'll be those things all over the docks. I don't like the idea of taking the *Queen* that close to land again."

Steven smiled. "We're not. Not this time. We'll sail in just close enough for the lifeboats to make it ashore."

O'Neil looked at the captain and blinked, completely baffled.

"Stealth, Mr. O'Neil. It's something we haven't tried before. If we go in at night instead of all guns blazing, the *Queen* herself may still face an attack, but the dead may not notice our smaller boats until we've had time to do everything we need for once." Steven saw the way O'Neil was glaring at him. "Yes, it's more of a risk to the raiding party if the dead do notice them, and it'll mean less supplies brought back overall because we won't be loading straight onto the *Queen*, but I'm willing to take the gamble in hopes that it will save us some lives. If it works, it'll give the raiding party a better edge than they've ever had before, and, well . . . if the *Queen* does become engaged, I think she can handle herself. We have before, and we'll do so many more times, I'm sure."

"Sir," O'Neil said, "I think you should know most of the crew and the people onboard still just want us to take some little island, put down some roots, and finally get off the waves."

Steven grinned. "No, our mobility is what's keeping us alive, Mr. O'Neil. Perhaps you should remind these people that if we lose it, we've lost the war."

O'Neil changed the subject, avoiding an argument. "How many men will be needed for the lifeboats in this plan of yours?"

"I was thinking about sixteen, total. That should give them the firepower and the free hands they'll need."

"But who's going to lead them?" O'Neil asked.

11

SCOTT hadn't stopped moving for nearly twelve hours, pushing his underfed and exhausted body far beyond its limits. He nearly fell into a tree, grabbing its bark to keep his balance, but finally he dropped to his knees and vomited into the wet grass.

So far he'd seen no signs of his pursuers. When he'd first started running, it had been like something out of a nightmare. Jeeps full of the dead had come roaring out of the breeding complex. The first two hours of the chase had been the roughest, ducking in and out of the trees, zigzagging his path, eluding both those chasing him and the normal patrols in the area. He hadn't seen or heard a jeep or dead man in the past seven hours though, and he couldn't force himself to go any farther at this point. He needed rest desperately.

Scott wiped the vomit from his lips and rolled over onto the ground, stretching out. The noise of a rifle chambering a bullet snapped him out of his thoughts.

A woman stood over him with the barrel of a .30-.06 aimed at his chest. She was covered in blood that wasn't hers. Long red hair was matted to her face and shoulders by sweat, blood, and dirt. She appeared healthy and well fed, but every inch as tired as he felt.

"Hello?" Scott greeted her weakly.

"Are you a doctor?" she asked in a voice filled with both anger and deep sadness.

Scott's mind raced. What the hell was he supposed to say? "I know a little," he answered quickly, lying very still so that the woman didn't feel threatened.

She took a step away from him. "On your feet. My husband and son are hurt. They need help."

"Okay." Scott pushed himself up, despite how much his whole body ached.

The woman led him about a fifth of a mile east. He knew instantly something wasn't right, even before they entered her makeshift campsite. He could see a young boy gagged and tied to a tree, straining against the ropes; the body of a man lay stretched out nearby.

Scott wondered if the woman had kidnapped the child—until he saw the massive gunshot wound on the boy's chest and began to realize just how much trouble he was in. He forced himself not to stare at it as it twisted under the ropes, tearing its flesh as it tried to get free.

Scott knelt down beside the man, who was alive, just barely.

"Can you help them?" the woman pleaded, the barrel of her rifle still aimed at Scott.

He doubted very much he could fool the woman into letting her guard down. She was too on edge. "Why did you gag the boy?" he asked, hoping to lead her mind back to Earth.

Fresh tears rolled down her cheeks. It was clear she couldn't rationalize her behavior without admitting her son was dead. "He . . . he was just gibbering. Saying horrible things. I couldn't take it anymore."

"Was he really your son?"

"Yes," she answered, not bothering to correct the word "was."

"And this is . . . ?" Scott placed a hand on the man's arm.

"Riley. He's my husband, Riley."

"He's going to die just like your son did," Scott said, staring down the madness in her eyes. "He's lost too much blood. There's nothing we can do for him out here."

"Liar!" The woman's finger tightened on the trigger as she shoved the barrel of her .30-.06 closer to Scott's face.

"Whoa!" He raised his hands high in the air. "Careful there! I'm sorry, lady. I just call them as I see them."

The woman hesitated, lowering the rifle's barrel slightly. Scott grabbed for the weapon. Too bad for him, Hannah was faster.

12

HANNAH smashed the butt of her rifle into the man's face as he took a swipe for it. He fell backwards, cursing and bleeding from his nose. The things he'd said had cut through her illusions like a razor, exposing the truth: her son was dead and her husband was dying. She'd be damned if this filthy punk was going to take her dad's rifle too.

She snapped the rifle's butt back up against her shoulder and braced it. The weapon barked as the shot smashed open the skull of the thing which had once been her son.

The man cringed away, as if she were more dangerous than ever. He raised a bloody hand to stop her from hurting him. "Please."

"What's your name?" Hannah asked.

"Scott." After a second, he added, "Ma'am, I don't mean any disrespect, but your husband just quit breathing. I don't suppose you'd be kind enough to shoot him too?"

"Riley!" Hannah cast her rifle aside and threw herself over her husband's corpse.

Its eyes shot open.

"Watch it!" Scott pulled her off the body and shoved her aside as the dead man sat up and reached for his arm. Scott pulled a .45 from the corpse's own holster and gave it a reason to lie down again. The shot seemed to echo in the air.

Hannah turned her face away from the gore, sobbing, though she had no more tears. Scott made no move to comfort her.

He popped the magazine out of the handgun and took stock of the number of rounds left, then snapped the magazine back inside the gun. He also sorted through a backpack, which appeared to have belonged to the child. Whoever this woman was, her family had been well supplied.

He opened a granola bar from the pack and tore into it, unable to control himself. Scott couldn't remember the last time he'd had real food, and it tasted like heaven, stale or not. "Where are you from?" he mumbled through a full mouth.

Hannah ignored him.

Scott finished the granola bar in a second bite. "How have you managed to stay alive this long?"

"What does it matter?"

"Well for one thing, you have food. You're well armed. Hell, I even saw some antibiotics in this pack. If you're from some kind of settlement or shelter that survived, I'd sure as hell like to know about it."

"Where are you from?" Hannah shot back.

"Trust me lady, you don't want to know." Scott snickered and ripped into another ration bar. "I've been locked up by the dead in a camp straight out of Hell."

"A camp?" Hannah was stunned. "Why didn't they kill you?"

"Where have you been, sister? How do you think the dead get their food these days? There aren't enough of us left out there for them to just round up and slaughter for dinner anymore. They're trying to breed us like cattle so that they'll always have food."

Hannah stared at him in horror.

"Yeah." Scott nodded. "It's all that and worse. I still want to know where you came from. You sure as hell weren't in a camp."

"My husband and child are dead."

"I'm sorry." Scott twisted the top off of a canteen and helped himself to some water. "Seen a lot of people die. One of my friends died just so that I could make it out of there. It looks like your husband died trying to take you to greener grass too. Better get used to it, people dying. That's how things are with the dead ruling the world. Speaking of which . . . " Scott closed the canteen. "We need to get moving. Staying in a single spot for a while can be suicide. Who knows who or what heard those shots."

13

LUKE was anything but your typical engineer. Long black hair with spots of gray hung over his purple flannel shirt. He sat crouched on the knees of his worn blue jeans, fiddling with a homemade torpedo casing. He heard O'Neil enter his workshop, but made no move to stop fine-tuning his current project. "I'll have two more live ones by tomorrow morning," he said.

O'Neil sat on Luke's unused workbench. "Why do you always work on the floor?"

Luke smiled. "The freedom," he answered simply. "It helps me think."

O'Neil grunted. "Whatever works, I suppose. As long as you don't blow a hole in the bottom of the ship."

"You didn't come here to talk about my work habits, Mr. O'Neil. What's up?"

"The captain's planning to raid a port in South Carolina tomorrow night. I've got the usual crew ready, and I'll be in command of the operation. I thought I'd stop by and see if you'd come up with anything new."

Luke glanced back at O'Neil. "If you're talking about understanding the dynamics of what makes the dead get back on their feet with hungry stomachs . . . " Luke pushed his glasses back up the bridge of his nose. "No, I haven't. That's Doc Gallenger's area, not mine."

"I thought you were helping him."

"Sure, when I have the time. You might have noticed I have been rather busy lately, what with keeping this old girl running and designing these new toys for the captain."

"It's not that I don't trust that Gallenger's doing his best, Luke, I just thought—"

"What? That having nine degrees in everything from pathology to physics makes me superhuman? That I am supposed to be able to wave a magic wand and save your ass? I wish." Luke shrugged. "I ain't God, ya know."

"I didn't say that you were. God has a social life," O'Neil teased.

"You want me to go with you tomorrow?"

"Hell no! Steven would have me shot if I let you off the *Queen*. You're the only real brain we've got."

"So you say," Luke said. "There are plenty of people on the boat who could do what I do around here."

"Maybe, but not one of them could do it all." O'Neil got up from the bench. "Just promise me you'll get to helping Gallenger, okay? We need a way to stop the dead more than we need the weapons to keep running."

As O'Neil turned to leave, Luke muttered, "Be careful out there, you idiot."

"I always am," O'Neil responded with a flash of his teeth, then he was gone.

14

SCOTT figured Hannah was whacko after what she'd endured, with every right to be, so he let her brood as they walked. The woman insisted on traveling east to the coast, so that's where they headed.

Scott had managed to get a few hours of blessed sleep while she kept watch, and he counted himself lucky she hadn't killed him while he dozed. When he woke up, they buried her family and moved on.

"What the heck is that?" Scott asked as he noticed a building ahead of them.

Hannah paused. "It's a cabin," she said, and then continued towards it.

"Whoa. What are you doing?" Scott grabbed her by the arm. "We don't know if anyone's in there."

"There's not. Not anyone alive anyway."

"How can you be so sure?"

Hannah pointed through the trees. "The door's been busted open. The windows are shattered. And that appears to be dried blood all over the outer walls."

Given little choice, Scott followed her into the clearing in front of the cabin. Several bodies, all dead from head wounds, littered the grass.

"Looks like somebody put up a good fight," Scott commented.

Hannah headed straight for the main door, which dangled by a single hinge. She stepped past it and into the building.

A body missing its legs and arms watched her enter. Old blood stained its mouth and chin. Hannah was sure its tongue had been cut or bitten out; otherwise the thing would have been screaming obscenities at her.

She glanced about the remains of the simple room. Someone had taken shelter in this place, seeking safety in the wilderness just like her own family had done, only these poor people must have been discovered before they could run.

Hannah jumped as a gunshot sounded behind her, sending the limbless monster on its way to Hell.

Scott shrugged as she glared at him. "It was creeping me out, okay?"

The pair carefully searched the place for more of the dead or anyone left alive. They met back in the cabin's main room, alone.

"We'll take what we can," Hannah said. "Food, ammo, whatever, but we're not staying."

Scott was too delighted to be put off by her air of superiority. "You're not going to believe what I found out behind this dump!" He smiled. "Come on, I'll show you!"

15

THE cabin had been a godsend. Scott couldn't believe their luck. With their stock replenished and their stomachs happily full of canned corn and dried tomatoes, they journeyed east again, much richer. Hannah still carried her .30-.06, which she never set down for a second, but now she also carried a functional AK-47 assault rifle. Scott himself had added a pump-action twelve gauge to his arsenal. Their best find, however, had been the bike. It allowed them to continue traveling off–road, yet much faster.

Scott held onto Hannah's waist as she throttled the small bike's engine at over forty miles an hour. She jerked the handlebars from side to side, dodging trees, and Scott wasn't sure but he thought for the first time since they'd met he saw the slightest smile on her lips.

"If you don't mind if I ask," he yelled over the bike's roar, "hy the hell are you so set on going east?"

Much to his surprise, Hannah answered him. "I want to see the ocean one last time before I die!"

Scott mulled over this revelation for a second. "Works for me!" he shouted, and Hannah charged down a tiny hill.

16

THE *Queen* sat in the harbor, motionless and far from the docks. No organized attack had been launched against her yet. Henry O'Neil admired her from a distance as his lifeboat drifted toward the shore. There were four boats, each carrying an equal share of the raiding party.

O'Neil's heart pounded in his chest. A long time had passed since he'd been on shore. He'd fought numerous battles aboard the *Queen* and occasionally ventured onto a dock to hold the hordes of the dead back for returning raiding parties, but this was different. He was excited and scared shitless at the same time.

An African American man named Roy sat across from him, loading a shotgun. O'Neil didn't know Roy well, but he knew him to be a veteran of raids.

The plan was simple. Land on the beach near the warehouses along the dock, hit the shore running, and stock up on whatever nonperishable foodstuffs they could get their hands on; they would then steal one of the boats that lined the port and ferry the goods back to the *Queen*. This operation would cost them most of the remaining lifeboats, but if they could steal some decent motorboats, it would be more than a fair trade.

Jennifer and Jason also shared O'Neil's lifeboat. The twins were inseparable. Jennifer was the warrior of the pair. Muscles bulged from underneath the jumpsuit she wore. In addition to the rifle and sidearm she carried, she hefted a machete. She was something of a legend among the *Queen*'s raiders, and her confidence made O'Neil feel safer.

Jason, by contrast, lacked muscle. He was the party's medic and an assistant to Dr. Gallenger. The young man's brow was creased in thought as he checked over his medical kit.

O'Neil held no official rank, having come aboard the *Queen* after the plague started, yet he was second only to Captain Steven; everyone treated him with respect. He hoped he lived up to it out here where it mattered most.

The lifeboats reached the sand of the shoreline. O'Neil screwed a silencer onto the barrel of his pistol and stepped onto solid ground. His land legs were clumsy, but as he raced after the others toward the docks, he got the hang of it.

The party split up and headed for different warehouses while one group went in search of a getaway boat. There was no sign of the dead, but O'Neil knew it wouldn't be long.

Within minutes they located a pair of small motorboats, the only ones around that appeared functional, and soon after, men brought the first load of canned and freeze-dried foods. That's when the shit hit the fan.

One of the raiders screamed, "They're coming!"

Before O'Neil could shout orders, the dead charged forward from the town, and the docks were suddenly ablaze with gunfire.

17

THE would-be raiders quickly found themselves pinned down and outnumbered. "It's a trap!" someone shouted, and O'Neil cursed the idiot. It wasn't a trap, it was probability: the creatures were everywhere these days.

Jennifer threw O'Neil off his feet as a bullet whizzed past. "Better keep your mind on the fight, sir!" Then she raised her M-16 and swept their enemies with rounds.

O'Neil hated the dead. Why couldn't they be the lethargic automatons driven purely by instinct like in the movies he'd seen as a kid? *Life freakin' sucks*, he thought. Pushing himself up, he took aim at a creature with a hole in its chest and a butcher knife held above its head. With a single shot from his pistol he dropped the thing to the ground.

The dead were attempting to flank the raiding party and cut them off from the boats. O'Neil knew if that happened, they were all screwed, so he bolted for the docks. He saw Jennifer wrestling with a dead woman who'd made it past their wall of fire. Jennifer's rifle was gone and she struggled to bring her machete into play. She never got the chance. The dead woman lashed out with a straight razor, and Jennifer's throat sprayed blood.

As O'Neil reached the boats, Roy was there waiting for him.

"We've got to get the food back to the ship!" O'Neil shouted.

Roy nodded. Most of their party was already dead or dying, and they couldn't risk trying to save the others. Too many people on the *Queen* depended on them, and if they failed, a lot more would die.

"What the hell is that?" Roy yelled, pointing.

O'Neil turned to see a dirt bike zigzagging towards them through the midst of the battle. Two human shapes rode it, one clearly a woman at the handlebars.

"Fuck that," O'Neil said, bringing up his pistol to take a shot at her. If the dead thought they could crash a suicide bomber on a damn dirt bike into the motor boats, they had another thing coming.

Roy struck O'Neil's arm, knocking his pistol downward so that he fired harmlessly into the wood of the dock.

"Why the—" O'Neil started, but Roy cut him off.

"Those ain't dead folk!"

O'Neil glanced at the bike again as Roy fired up the boat with the most cargo. The motorcycle skidded to a halt a few yards from O'Neil, and the passenger—a haggard young man with lashing scars covering his bare back—jumped off. "Going our way?" he asked.

O'Neil ignored the young man's joke, gazing into the green eyes of the woman who drove the bike.

"Get in!" Roy screamed from below, and O'Neil watched this woman, this angel, dart by him and leap into the boat.

"I think he means you too!" the young man said, grabbing O'Neil as he jumped into the boat; the stranger laughed as they crashed to the deck together.

Roy kicked the motor into high gear and left waves in their wake. The docks and the nightmare faded behind them as a few desperate shots thudded into the sides of the boat and the dead howled in vain.

18

"WHO are you people?" Scott asked. "And what was all that back there about?"

The redneck-looking black man answered, "I'm Roy and this is Mr. O'Neil. We're from the *Queen*."

The man identified as O'Neil just kept staring at Hannah as she asked, "What's the *Queen*?"

"*That.*" Roy pointed out over the water.

"Holy shit," Scott muttered. The *Queen* was a ship, and a damn big one from the looks of her. She was as long as a battleship, but certainly not military; or at least she hadn't started out that way. Her overall hull, tarnished white, was spotted by the odd piece or plate of armor welded on. Jury-rigged gun emplacements ran the length of her decks from port to stern. She'd definitely seen better days, but even with the tiny amount Scott knew about ships, he could tell she had a lot of power left in her.

Roy piloted the motorboat right up to her side. Heavily armed men and women threw down cables from the deck to haul up the supply crates. "Too bad we can't keep this baby," Roy said mournfully. "She's a fine little boat in her own right."

"We're keeping her fuel," O'Neil said as he finally snapped out of the haze he'd been in. "Make sure you drain her tanks before you go up." He caught one of the ropes raining down around them and handed it to Hannah. "Welcome aboard, ma'am," he said with a smile that lit up his face.

She and Scott scurried up the rope into the crowd of people waiting on the *Queen*'s main deck. Both were overwhelmed by their welcome. Hannah couldn't remember the last time she'd seen so many people alive.

O'Neil pulled himself up behind them and was barking orders at the crowd before his feet even hit the deck.

"Let's get loaded up quickly, people," he yelled over the chaos. "We need to get out of here before the dead get it together and come sailing after us."

19

A yeoman named Pete led Scott and Hannah to their quarters, two Spartan bunkrooms side by side on the same hall. "I know it's not much," Pete apologized, "but here you're going to be safe."

Scott was still trying to absorb it all. "You mean you guys have really been sailing around out here since it all started?"

Pete nodded. "The *Queen* was at sea when the dead woke up. We haven't put to port yet except to raid places for food or supplies. The captain figures we're safer on the waves."

"Have you heard from anyone else, other survivors like yourselves?" Hannah asked.

"I hate to say it, ma'am, but . . . well, no. Benson, our communications expert, stays at it around the clock though. We've never come across more than a few at a time. We're always glad to see new faces, and I'm sure you'll fit right in among the crew. Either of you have experience sailing or know anything about ships?"

Hannah and Scott shook their heads.

"No worries," Pete said, waving his hand. "I know we'll come up with something for you to do. We try to pull our weight on this ship." He looked them over again and stopped. "I'm sorry, you probably want to get some rest. I'll leave you to it. Just one quick thing: the captain will want to meet you tonight. He likes to welcome everyone aboard and see if you know anything about what's left out there. You'll be having dinner with him in about five hours. I'll be back to get you and show you around."

Pete shook Scott's hand again and bowed to Hannah, then he was gone. Hannah and Scott looked at each other, as if asking whether they really wanted to be alone. Silence lingered in the air until Scott finally made a move. "See you at dinner then." He stepped into the room he'd been assigned and shut the door behind him.

He plopped onto his bunk and fell instantly into a deep sleep. His dreams were dark, but his exhausted body didn't care.

20

STEVEN shook his head in disgust. "We lost fourteen hands and gained two. We can't keep up this rate of attrition. Perhaps you're correct, Mr. O'Neil. Maybe we should think of finding an island and starting over."

O'Neil couldn't believe what he was hearing. Captain Steven was agreeing with him after refusing for months to even consider the possibility.

"There is an island not far from here, sir, the one I've told you about. I think it was called Cobble or something like that. It was just a tourist trap before the plague. You could only reach it by boat or helicopter. I doubt we'd find much resistance there, and it's in a temperate zone so we could grow a wide assortment of food stock between the winters." O'Neil grew excited as he let out all the details he'd been plotting. "I bet there's even a fuel depot there, at least for the smaller boats. We could leave the *Queen* just offshore, and she'd be well within reach if we needed her again."

Steven smiled at O'Neil's passion. "Sounds like you've really thought this out. All right, Mr. O'Neil, we'll try it your way. As soon as we can be sure those creatures from the docks aren't pursuing us, go ahead and plot a course for this island. And have those two new folks brought up here. I'm eager to hear news of the mainland."

"I think you'll find the new woman rather captivating, sir," O'Neil commented.

Steven pulled a cigar from his desk and lit it up with an old fashioned wooden match. "Do I detect a bit of personal attachment in your voice, Henry?"

The younger man blinked. The captain rarely called him by his first name. Most people didn't. It put him on edge, though he knew the captain was only teasing, trying to provoke a response. "No, sir. I just . . . I thought you'd like to be prepared is all."

"Oh," Steven snickered, "I see."

Hannah lay on her bunk, staring at the ceiling. She'd tried to get some sleep, but she couldn't stop thinking about Riley and Brandon. Brandon would have been so happy on this ship. The *Queen* would've been like a paradise to him, the adventure of the high sea and children his age to share it with. It would have been like something out of a story book. And Riley . . . she missed Riley so much. Without him, she felt hollow, incomplete. A piece of her soul had died along with her family, just like the world had died long ago. She'd adjusted to the world's destruction, but the pain of her own loss stung at her heart.

Someone knocked on the door of her quarters. Forgetting herself, she reached for her .30-.06 and slid a shell into its chamber as the door opened.

"Whoa," Pete said, raising his hands and taking a step back. "It's okay."

Hannah lowered the rifle. "I'm sorry," she said. "Old habits die hard."

"Better them than me," Pete joked uncomfortably. "The captain is waiting for you to join him for dinner."

Hannah followed Pete out into the hall where Scott was waiting, clean-shaven and dressed in new clothes. His whole appearance was different on many levels. He actually looked handsome and, if possible, smugger than he usually was. "About time you got up, sleepy head," he said to her as the trio made their way up to the captain's quarters.

Captain Steven and O'Neil greeted Hannah and Scott as they entered. Hannah looked the captain over. He was in his later forties, his hair mostly gray, yet he possessed strength not only in his short, burly frame but in the very grain of his character. He looked like a man who'd seen Hell firsthand and who'd beaten it back by the sheer force of his will. The necessary introductions were made and Pete and O'Neil seated everyone at the table.

"Will there be anything else, sir?" O'Neil asked.

"No thank you." Steven reached for a napkin to drape across his lap. "That will be all."

O'Neil and Pete left the quarters, closing the entrance behind them.

The table was set with real china dishes and regal silverware, but it was the food that held Hannah and Scott's attention. There was glazed salmon, freshly baked bread, spicy brown rice, stuffed crabs, and a bowl full of red apples placed alongside a salad of cabbage and chopped carrots. The captain must have noticed their hunger. "Please, help yourselves."

Scott wasted no time in loading down his plate with everything in reach, plus a double portion of stuffed crabs.

"I assure you, we don't eat like this all the time," Captain Steven informed them. "We can't afford to. Most of our meals are of much simpler fare, but tonight it seemed fitting to have this feast, not only to welcome you, but to celebrate a much needed change in the *Queen*'s plans for the future."

"The future?" Scott mumbled through a mouthful of fish and bread.

"Yes," Steven continued. "The future. I refuse to sacrifice more lives just to keep us on the sea. It's time we found a new home and try to reclaim some of what mankind has lost to the dead."

"Do you really think that's possible?" Hannah butted in. "The dead are everywhere. No matter where you go, they will find you eventually."

"But their numbers are dwindling too," Steven explained. "Their bodies rot. Time takes its due. We only have to last a couple of years, perhaps, before we outnumber them once more. Then we can truly retake the world, as it was meant to be."

"How can you know the dead are dying? Have you discovered what brought them to life to begin with?" Hannah argued.

"Our crew may be made of refugees, Hannah, but some are rather extraordinary people. We have two medical doctors on this ship and one real scientist who've been studying the plague since the moment they came aboard. We still don't know the nature of the force, or whatever it is that reanimates the dead, but we do know it doesn't stop the decay of their flesh; it merely slows it. So in time, nature itself will destroy our enemy's ranks. But enough of this. I want to know about you two. Who are you? What did you do before the dead walked?"

"Do you really want to know?" Scott asked, suddenly forgetting about the food.

Steven nodded.

"I was a professional killer," Scott said. The table fell silent, but he continued. "I worked for the government when I started out, then went freelance. I couldn't guess at how many people I put bullets in before the CIA caught me. When the plague started I was rotting away in a federal prison, and that's where the dead found me, alone, unarmed, and locked up behind bars.

"Obviously, they didn't kill me. Maybe I was so starved by then I didn't have enough meat on my bones to be worth their trouble. Who knows? So they took me to a new kind of prison that they had created. It was called a breeding center, a place where they herded us together like cattle and bred us for food."

"Well," Steven ventured, "I, uh, don't suppose it matters now what you did in those days. You're one of us now, and I hope you will make the most of this fresh start." He turned in his chair to address Hannah. "And what of you?" he asked.

"I . . . " Hannah began, and her voice cracked, "I was a mother."

21

AS the days passed aboard the *Queen*, Hannah found work in the ship's daycare. Over the last few months, the ship had picked up a couple of infants and nearly a dozen children who either had no parents at all or whose parents held jobs which occupied much of their time aboard the ship. Hannah found happiness in her work with the kids. She even got along with her sole co-worker Jessica, a young woman barely out of her teens, but Hannah didn't know how Jessica ever handled the children by herself. She was a hard worker but lacked the emotional connection with her wards that Hannah developed instantly.

Jessica, without resentment, let Hannah take the lead, and the children took to Hannah's new lessons in crafts and educational projects with zeal. Hannah, despite herself, began to let go of her past and embrace her future. The memories of Riley and Brandon would always be with her, but she felt hope swelling in her again. These children needed her, and she could offer them so much more than just busywork to keep them safe and out of the way.

Scott, on the other hand, was assigned to the *Queen*'s group of raiders and defenders, which was now sorely diminished. He worked closely with O'Neil, whom he grew to hate more and more with each passing day. O'Neil took a more military approach to organization and training, whereas Scott taught the men "dirty" tricks they needed to know to stay alive, discipline be damned.

It wasn't long until Scott met Luke, and the eccentric genius and the occasionally psychotic former hit man became fast friends. They'd attended some of the same schools in the old world and both had done work for the government on Black-Op projects, though Luke's involvement was purely from a research and development standpoint. Scott wasn't anywhere near Luke's level, but he was sharp and he was a fast learner, fast enough to keep up with Luke when he droned on about his various theories.

As the sun sank beneath the waves, Scott and Luke relaxed in matching lawn chairs atop the highest point of the *Queen* above the command center. Scott sipped at the glass in his hand, admiring the potency of the drink Luke had whipped up this evening. It had the punch of whiskey without the burn.

"What was it like?" Luke inquired.

"What?"

"To kill people for money, man. How did you cope with it?"

"To be honest, I just never thought about it. A job's a job, ya know? Besides, it's not that much different than things are today. Everybody has had to kill somebody to stay alive and keep breathing, whether it was by a bullet through the brain or watching someone you care about throw away their life so that you could get away."

Luke leaned forward and sat up on his chair. "So what do you thnk about Captain Steven's new plan?"

"I don't think it matters, Luke. We're all living on borrowed time. Whether we die out here on the waves or settle down and wait for the dead to come to us, they will get us eventually. We lost the war the moment they started thinking like we do." Scott sat up and looked over the railing to the water below. "You're the resident genius. You tell me: have you ever figured out what brought the dead back to life?"

Luke shrugged. "Not really. It sure wasn't radiation or a virus like something out of those old B movies, though their bites are infectious just like in those films. Nothing about the dead makes sense. They shouldn't be able to move, let alone reason like they do. Sometimes a body will reanimate with partial memories of its life before death, and other times it's like there's a whole new entity in the host body. They're all hungry for us though, memories or not. It doesn't matter if they know your name and who you are—they'll eat you anyway."

"So where does that leave you, since science has failed and can't explain it?"

Luke's face flushed. "Science hasn't failed, Scott. Just because I don't have an answer today doesn't mean there isn't a plausible, quantifiable explanation to all this. It just means I haven't found it yet. I don't believe in spirits or Judgment Day. There is a sane reason for the plague, and I will find it. I'm sure."

"And you'll just keep searching for it, huh?"

Luke laughed. "Damn right I will. As long as I have to."

22

STEVEN bolted onto the bridge of the ship. The whole area was a mass of activity. His crew darted about, double-checking the data they'd just gotten.

"It's true then?" Steven demanded as O'Neil approached him.

"I'm afraid so, sir," O'Neil said grimly. "There are five vessels closing in on our current location, as if trying to surround us."

"Jesus." Steven scanned through the stack of reports O'Neil handed him. "Look at the size of them."

O'Neil nodded. "Some are military in nature for sure. This one has to be . . . " O'Neil pointed at a blip on a nearby radar screen. "We think it's an aircraft carrier, and the two flanking it from the east and west are most likely destroyers. It looks like they've finally got us where they want us."

"Nonsense, Mr. O'Neil," Steven said. "We've been in tight spots before. We'll get through this one too." He weighed their options in his head before he continued. "Can we out-maneuver them and make a run for it?"

"We can try. I don't think the largest one can match our speed, but if the two flanking the large ship *are* destroyers, they'll be able to overtake us even at our top speed."

"Change course and burn the engines at their maximum," Steven ordered. "And in the meantime, sound the alarm. I want to be ready if we do have a fight on our hands."

"Aye, sir," O'Neil replied. He punched a button and sirens squealed throughout the *Queen*.

A state of panic broke out on the ship. The raiders, who were also the *Queen's* defenders, Scott among them, rushed to their battle stations. People and families ran for their quarters, locking the heavy doors of their rooms against the growing terror outside.

The daycare was in chaos. Hannah and Jessica tried to calm the children and the parents who showed up demanding their kids. Hannah had left her .30-.06 in her quarters, but she concealed in her jacket a .38 revolver she'd looted from the ship's armory, thanks to Scott. Weapons weren't permitted in the daycare center, but right now Hannah was damn glad she'd been breaking the rules. She'd watched her own son die helplessly and had sworn to herself that these children would not share his fate.

In the sickbay, Dr. Gallenger prepared for the wounded to start arriving, in case the coming battle couldn't be avoided. Luke, meanwhile, darted through the corridors of the *Queen*, attempting to reach the main decks with a short, black metal tube gripped tightly in his arms.

O'Neil and Captain Steven watched from the bridge as the destroyers crossed the horizon and came into view. The ocean itself seemed to shake as the destroyer from the east fired its main guns at the *Queen*.

23

THE shot from the enemy ship hit the water off the *Queen*'s portside, sending waves crashing against the hull, though it didn't strike close enough to cause actual damage. The *Queen* lacked any sort of long-range weapon except for her jury-rigged torpedo launchers, which at the moment were facing away from the enemy vessels.

Captain Steven knew he had to do something. The destroyers were too fast to outrun, and at present the *Queen* was a sitting target for their guns. Closing with the two enemy ships for direct combat was a near suicidal option, but it was also the only one left.

"Bring us about!" he shouted. "Get us between them. Maybe they aren't stupid enough to take the chance of hitting each other with their main guns!" Steven turned to O'Neil. "As soon as you get a shot with one of the launchers, take it!"

Scott and the *Queen*'s defenders stood helplessly at their machine-gun emplacements as the *Queen* veered to engage the enemy. The destroyers were still not within range, but from the looks of things they would be soon. Scott shoved a belt of ammo into the massive weapon in front of him and began to pick a target for when the time came.

"Fire one!" O'Neil ordered.

A torpedo, dropped into the water, flared to life and raced towards the lead destroyer even as O'Neil ordered the remaining torpedo launched in its wake. Moments later, the first missile struck the destroyer just below the waterline, sending waves of fire and ocean spray up onto the decks of the military vessel. The second torpedo got lucky; it collided with something inside the destroyer, which turned the entire ship into a blazing wreck of secondary explosions.

Cheers went up on the bridge and the decks of the *Queen* as it angled towards the remaining enemy ship, which fired. This time the *Queen* was hit dead on. The blast ripped a hole in her side, killing many of her defenders instantly.

"Damage report!" Steven snapped, knowing full well that the *Queen* faced a new problem now—and not just the damage to the ship. Those killed or mortally wounded by the blast would soon reanimate.

"No damage to the engines!" O'Neil reported. "The hull breach is being contained. We're not taking on water!"

Finally, Luke reached the deck and positioned himself to get a shot at the enemy ship. He extended the black metal tube he was carrying and slashed out a section of power cables on the wall near him to hook into the weapon. He had spent all of his free time in the last few months refining the invention; he was fully aware of its capabilities. What he was about to do would cripple the *Queen* in some respects, and he certainly wouldn't survive, but it was worth the risk. He aimed the tube at the destroyer and pulled the trigger.

A beam of energy leapt from his weapon, striking the destroyer's ammo stores for the main guns. The energy melted through the destroyer's armor and reduced the ship to a ball of flames, which lit up the sea even under the midday sun. Luke, his weapon, and a large chunk of the *Queen* vaporized in the energy weapon's backwash. People screamed, both inside and abovedeck, as the *Queen's* engines blew from the surge.

"What in the hell was that?" Steven cried.

"I don't know!" O'Neil yelled over the chaos on the bridge. "We've lost main power, and the engines are burnt out. Power is out every-where on the ship. The backup generators are keeping the internal comm. system and the emergency lights working, but that's about it. We're dead in the water, sir!"

"Shit!" Steven whirled about to the officer at the radar station. "What about the other three dead ships?"

"I . . . I don't know, sir," the officer stammered. "It looked as if the big one was keeping back, maybe even changing course away from us before the screen went dead. The two smaller ones were still on an intercept heading. They should be on us in the next few minutes, tops."

Steven slammed his fist against the radar station. "Somebody tell Luke I want those fucking engines back on-line now!"

24

DR. GALLENGER got to his feet—or tried to. As he attempted to stand up, the fractured bone of his left leg tore through his flesh, and he hit the floor hard. He felt no pain as he examined the rest of his body, saw the piece of shrapnel protruding from his right lung. He had to get up. He could sense that his brethren would be here soon, and he was hungry. Hungrier than he'd ever been.

He deemed the shrapnel to be irrelevant, but snapped his broken leg back into place and used the materials scattered about the sickbay to fashion a splint. Then he did get up. He hobbled across the room to check on Nurse Jones and found her lying in a pool of blood.

Tilting his head like an animal would as he observed her, he watched her eyes flutter open, then dart this way and that as she realized she couldn't move. A huge medical cabinet had fallen on her and had broken her neck.

Taking pity on her, Gallenger picked up a piece of debris and smashed in her skull.

He found the remains of his desk and the .45 he'd kept in the drawer. Feeling suitably armed, he left the sickbay. Soon he would taste flesh for the first time.

EVERYONE on the *Queen* had been tossed about as the destroyer's shell had hammered into its hull. Hannah struck her head against one of the children's lockers in the daycare center. As her vision focused through the blood in her eyes, she became aware that she was still alive. She hurt too much to be dead. Her head especially. She also realized she was alone. She felt a twinge of anger at Jessica for leaving her for dead, but then realized she would've done the same. It was the kids who mattered, not them, and Jessica had probably taken them somewhere safer in the ship.

Hannah dug inside her jacket and produced her .38. She had no idea how the fight outside was going, but she knew Jessica would need help. Jessica, as the saying goes, was not the sharpest tool in the shed, and Hannah didn't trust her to see the children through this battle. She pulled herself up and headed out of the daycare.

"Jessica!" she screamed as she ran down the corridors, hoping the woman was still in earshot.

She rounded the corner of the passageway and came face to face with a dead man dragging his insides across the floor. He lunged at her, grunting, but she narrowly sidestepped his attack and shoved him as he went by her. He toppled to the deck and twisted about, already trying to get up and come after her. She popped off three rounds into his forehead, spraying his brains onto the wall.

Hannah stood a moment afterward, her breath coming in raged gasps; she tried to collect herself and calm down. The *Queen*'s machine guns chattered above—the fight hadn't been lost yet. She took a deep breath and set out in search of Jessica, though with much more caution.

THE two yachts had swept in quickly, managing to evade most of the *Queen's* defensive fire. Both of them came up along her portside, close enough for the dead to scale the *Queen*'s hull as they traded small arms fire with those left alive on her decks. The *Queen*'s gun emplacements were useless with the yachts so close. They couldn't be angled downward to engage the dead, so Scott had abandoned his post and began to spray the climbing dead with an AK-47 instead. One of the attackers, a middle-aged man covered in burns, lost his hold as Scott's rounds peppered his back, and he plummeted into the water.

While Scott was sidetracked, a creature hauled itself onto the *Queen*'s deck beside him—Roy's twelve-gauge thundered and sent it careening over the side of the ship.

Scott motioned his thanks to Roy, then returned his attention to the dead and loaded a fresh magazine into his weapon.

25

THE struggle for control of the *Queen* raged on. Her whole exterior deck was a war zone, and smaller battles filled her corridors.

"Sir," O'Neil said, trying to draw Captain Steven's attention away from the carnage below the bridge. "Captain, we can't hold her. The *Queen* is lost. We need to give the order to abandon ship."

O'Neil's words jarred Steven out of his own thoughts. Abandon the *Queen*? Had O'Neil gone insane? He turned to argue, but the door to the bridge opened and Doc Gallenger staggered inside. Before anyone could react, the good doctor's corpse raised the .45 in its blood-smeared hand.

The first shot slammed into Steven's shoulder. The second and third burrowed into his chest. Benson, the communications officer, took a round to his throat before O'Neil managed to draw his own sidearm and shoot the doctor in the face.

O'Neil rushed to Steven's side and squatted beside him.

"Leave me," the captain ordered, coughing blood onto his lips. "I'm staying with the *Queen*."

The other command personnel were fleeing the bridge as O'Neil stood up. Most of the *Queen*'s lifeboats were gone. Finding a way off the ship would be difficult, but not as difficult as surviving afterwards. The dead would be waiting.

In a corner of the *Queen*'s main deck portside, Scott and Roy were holed up behind one of the large metal cooling pipes and were running out of ammo fast. "Roy, you're a good man," Scott said, "but how would you feel about leaving all this and not looking back?"

Roy could see the gleam of an idea in Scott's eyes. "I reckon what's gotta be is gotta be. I'm guessin' you have something in mind to save our asses."

Scott grinned. "You could say that. Come on!" He charged across the deck through the ranks of the dead and the few humans left alive. Scott reached the railing and didn't stop. He hurled himself over the side and landed on the yacht below, completely surprising the five corpses still aboard it. With his AK-47 on full auto, he cut them down where they stood.

Roy followed him, but skidded to a halt at the edge of the deck. "Crazy mother fucker!" he shouted and took the leap. He landed on the yacht with the sound of snapping bones.

O'NEIL dispatched a corpse blocking his way in the corridor. If he'd counted his shots right, he had three rounds left in his pistol. It was beginning to sink in that he was royally screwed.

From outside, someone called his name. He jerked open the hatch to the exterior deck, and Hannah threw herself at him, wrapping her arms around his body. He hugged her back tightly, then forced himself to push her away, despite how much he wanted to hold her forever. He knew she didn't feel the same about him; they barely knew each other, yet she'd won him over the night he'd met her on the docks, had given him more purpose to his life than anyone or anything ever had. "The captain's dead," he informed her. "We've got to get off the ship if we want to stay alive."

A dead woman darted towards them through the open hatchway, a piece of glass raised like a knife in her rotting hand. O'Neil tried to get a shot, but Hannah was faster. She emptied her .38 into the woman's neck and face.

O'Neil moved to lead them outside onto the deck, but she grabbed his arm. "Wait! What's that noise?"

"Oh God no." O'Neil stuck his head outside and looked up at the sky. "It can't be."

An F-16 fighter roared over the *Queen*. Its wings wobbled; whoever was flying it certainly wasn't an experienced pilot.

O'Neil and Hannah stepped outside to watch the jet turn and streak back at the *Queen* on a collision course.

"Would this be a bad time to tell you that I love you?" O'Neil asked as they watched the plane race closer.

"No, I don't suppose it would." Hannah tried to smile weakly as she took his hand in hers.

26

SCOTT could still remember the death throes of the *Queen* after the jet had plowed into her, the way the flames had danced over her frame as she sank into the waves. The image haunted his dreams at night. He remembered Roy as well. The black Southerner had been as tough as they came, but with two badly broken legs and the meager amount of worm-infested food they'd found on the yacht, Scott had no choice but to kill him. So he shot Roy in the stomach with his own shotgun and dumped him overboard before he could reanimate as one of the dead.

Only a week had passed since their flight from the *Queen*, but it felt like months. He lay stretched out atop the cabin of the yacht and stared up at the stars. The engines were shot and he was thirsty. Sweat glistened on his bare chest in spite of the cool night air. He knew he wa s sick, whether from the rotting food he had been eating or just the fact that his body had finally suffered all it could take. If he could make it to land and get some medicine, proper food and a little rest, he might be his old self, but those things seemed like pipe dreams in the face of what the world had become.

He felt his eyes close, then forced them open to glance at the shotgun propped up on the deck near him. Scott started to consider *all* his options again as a gentle rain began to fall and the heavens wept.

THE WAVE

1

JEREMY lay shirtless, sprawled out on the wood of his deck and looking up at the Carolina night sky. The breeze, a gentle cool circulating through the warm air, carried the smell of his freshly mowed lawn, and the portable stereo beside him belted out the chorus to Rush's "Working Man."

He glanced at the bright green display of his watch. Almost two o'clock in the morning. The witching hour was long gone, but he felt pumped up and wide awake. He leaned over and hit the skip button on the stereo. "Fly by Night" replaced "Working Man," and he smiled.

His heart pounded in his chest. He couldn't explain it, but for some reason he felt on edge, eager. He lay back down and listened to the music.

Astronomy was not normally one of his interests, but tonight the sky seemed different, the stars hotter and pulsing bright. It wasn't something he could explain, just a feeling he couldn't shake.

He reached into the darkness beside the stereo and lifted a mug of sweet tea to his lips, arching his back a bit as he sipped.

In that moment, the world changed. A piercing light danced like lightning across the summer sky, and everything seemed to go white.

Jeremy dropped his tea, cursing as the cool liquid splashed over his naked chest. The light grew brighter and he had to shield his eyes. At the same time, the alarm of his wristwatch went off and the stereo erupted into sparks. Geddy Lee's voice shrieked upwards, almost deafening, the music growing louder and louder until it finally went silent. Beneath the deck, his car came to life. Its horn honked randomly as its headlights lit up and blew out, the shards clinking onto the gravel driveway like rain.

Jeremy screamed, and the light was gone. Spots lingered before his eyes, swirling purples and greens. His temples throbbed.

Fumbling blindly, he grasped the railing of the deck and pulled himself up. His vision cleared, but around him everything was black. The stars seemed to have vanished from the sky, and the lights in the neighborhood had blinked out, the houses on the distant hills invisible in the darkness. Even the normal specks of headlights moving along I-40 below the mountains were missing.

He stumbled across the deck to the sliding glass door of his bedroom and went inside, flipping on the light switch. Nothing happened. He flipped the switch twice more. No light.

Bumping his way from the bedroom to the kitchen, he managed to reach the island in front of the sink. He yanked open the top drawer and grabbed his plastic emergency flashlight. It didn't work. He bashed the light atop the island and shook it, but it didn't come on, so he tossed it.

He felt his way along the island to where the phone hung on the wall. As he guessed, it was dead. His cell was too.

An irrepressible fear began to grow within him. Sweat beaded on his sticky skin, mixing with the droplets of spilt tea. He stumbled back to the bedroom's large walk-in closet and found the shelves. As he pulled down his hunting rifle, his knees gave way and he dropped to the carpet. "Jesus Almighty," he whispered, "what the hell is going on?"

He shoved a bullet into the rifle's breech and jerked the chamber closed. Pulling his knees to his chest, he sank back against the closet wall to wait for dawn, his knuckles white as he held the rifle.

2

PITTSBURGH

"WHAT the fuck is going on?" Howard asked as he pushed his way into the crowded control room of the reactor plant. It seemed as if the plant's entire staff had gathered in the small space. There were no alarm klaxons, no red glow of emergency lights. Only a small fire burning in the metal trash can beside Gibbons' console. The flickering light seemed alien and out of place in the heart of the plant.

A wave of pleads, questions, and fear slammed into Howard as he entered.

"Shut up!" he ordered. "Shut the fuck up!"

The cacophony in the room dampened but did not end.

"Gibbons," Howard barked, pointing at the pimply-faced engineer. "What the hell is going on? Twenty words or less. Now!"

The young man's eyes went wide with terror in the pale light. "Everything has gone down, sir. Backups, outside lines . . . everything. The core will breach, sir. Without the cooling units functioning, it's just a matter of time."

Howard's mind raced. Backups? Everything? That was supposed to be impossible. This was his damn plant. Things like that didn't—couldn't—happen here.

"How long?" Howard asked.

"There's no way to know, sir. Ten seconds, an hour. Your guess is as good as mine."

Howard opened his mouth to yell at Gibbons, but a heat wave blasted him. His flesh melted and burned away as the reactor ruptured.

The meltdown was visible for miles around as the night lit up like an exploding star, and a mushroom cloud blossomed toward the heavens.

3

NEW YORK

THE freeway had become a war zone. Amy lay against her steering wheel, wondering how she had survived.

Even at this late hour, the freeway was crammed with traffic. When the light had appeared, a light more blinding than the sun itself, everyone's engine had died and stalled. Cars slammed into trucks, into each other. Vehicles hit the concrete sides of the freeway while some overturned on the median. Flames blazed in every direction, and explosions ripped through the night.

Some people bolted from their cars, ran from the freeway as if their lives depended on it, while others tried to help those trapped inside the wrecks.

Amy watched as the driver of an eighteen-wheeler jumped out of his cab and opened up on the crowd with some sort of rifle; another traveler shot him in the forehead, and he crumpled to the asphalt.

Amy sat in her seat, sobbing, too frightened to move. Irrationally, she wondered what her boss would say when she showed up late at the hospital. Her only injury was a scrape on her hand, sustained when she had rear-ended the silver Dodge Shadow in front of her and had reached out to brace herself.

She tried to turn on the car radio, but nothing happened. She tried again and again until the knob broke off in her hand. Finally her head sank to the steering wheel, and she started to mutter a prayer as people screamed into the night across the freeway.

4

WASHINGTON D.C.

PRESIDENT Clark sat at his desk, shuffling through the reports from NASA and other organizations about the energy wave that had struck the earth. Below them rested even more reports, these from the military and countless government and law enforcement agencies regarding the chaotic aftermath. Things did not look good for the human race.

Of course, things were even worse than what he was hearing. Ninety percent of all communications throughout the world had been lost, and even inside the city proper, news had been reduced to word of mouth. All forms of technology that required more than simple kinetic or combustion energy were essentially useless. The wave had seen to that. Even the backup systems and batteries were down, though already some were coming back online thanks to the available scientists and technicians.

The effects of the energy wave on technology appeared to be dissipating at an exponential rate, but it would still take weeks, perhaps months, for the world's more advanced systems to be fully restored. Fortunately, a few of the heavily-shielded military bunkers—like the one beneath the White House—had survived most of the wave's impact, otherwise the president's knowledge of the outside world would have gone from limited to nonexistent.

General McMahan kept insisting that President Clark flee the city and head for a more secure bunker in another state, and in fact the general was hard at work preparing a makeshift convoy from the civilian and military vehicles that filled the bunker, as well as the White House's garages and parking areas. Even though nuclear attacks by the former Soviet Union or any other nation were highly unlikely, judging from the state in which the wave had left the US's own arsenal, he claimed the city was not safe.

The droves of frightened people who wandered to the gates of the White House, pleading for assistance and looking for hope, disturbed McMahan and put him on edge, but he was even more concerned about those who had been driven mad by the wave, by some kind of electro-biological aftereffect on the human mind. Clark had asked the scientists about the madness, but their answers were vague; they assured him it would only worsen, and that few, if any, would be immune to the wave's lingering radiation.

So far, Clark had refused McMahan's requests to leave. He hoped his presence would comfort those citizens who had retained their sanity, give them hope that steps were being taken to resolve this catastrophe. The weight of the country and the world lay heavily upon his shoulders, and he could only hope his best efforts would be enough to ensure the preservation of humanity.

He set the stacks of papers on his desk and buried his head in his arms. With his eyes closed, he said a silent prayer to God to have mercy on them all.

5

JEREMY awoke as the first rays of the morning sun crept over the mountains and sparkled through the glass doors of his bedroom. He stirred inside the open walk-in closet and rubbed his neck. It hurt like hell from the way he had slept against the closet wall.

Looking down at the rifle in his lap, he felt like a fool. His nerves had gotten the better of him last night, and he wondered what the heck he'd been thinking. He bet the power was already back on—but what had been that strange light in the sky? Had he dreamt the whole thing? His memories seemed unbelievable and more than a bit crazy.

As he walked into the bedroom, he placed the rifle on the bed and glanced at the digital alarm clock atop his dresser. Its display was blank and unlit. So much for the power being back on. So much for a hot shower.

Jeremy changed into a tattered Rush T-shirt and a pair of fresh underwear and jeans. In the kitchen, he snacked on a muffin from the pantry as he tried the phone again. No luck there either.

As he ate, he vaguely remembered something happening to his car during the strange light, and he decided to inspect the damage.

The drive in front of the car was filled with shards from the exploded headlights, and when he tried to start the engine, nothing happened, not even a sputter.

He punched the dashboard and sat there for a moment, wondering what he should do. Luke Thompson lived just up the road from him, his nearest neighbor and friend. The old man was inflicted with terrible health problems, mostly from his age, but his smoking and constant drinking didn't help. He might need a hand. Besides, if his truck survived the light, he and Jeremy could head into town and find out what was going on. At the very worst, Jeremy was sure he would walk away with a smile and a free beer.

Luke lived only half a mile or so up the road, so Jeremy took his time, enjoying the green fields by the roadside. Summer was truly here, and even the weeds were vibrant and beautiful. He had moved down here a few years back and didn't miss the big city in the least.

As he started up the small hill of Luke's drive, he didn't see the old man sitting on the porch of the tiny shack that passed for a house. It seemed Luke was always there, whittling and waiting for passers-by whom he could harass in his own good-natured way.

Jeremy picked up the pace, nearly broke into a run. As he reached the house, he yelled, "Luke! You in there? Luke?"

The front door was open like always, but the outer screen door was shut. Three weathered, cracked concrete steps led up to the door.

Jeremy bolted up them. He swung the screen open and peeped inside.

The living room was a mess. Some things never changed. He grinned at the microwave dinner wrappers, empty beer bottles, and crumpled cigarette packs that intermingled with the piles of dirty clothes covering the couch and floor.

Jeremy stepped inside, seeing instantly that the old man's power was off like his own. "Luke? You here?"

He picked up an open pack of smokes from beside an overflowing ashtray on the TV stand and helped himself to one. He hadn't smoked since high school, but he figured now was as good a time as any to start again. Lighting up, he took a deep drag and coughed like a kid. He ground out the cigarette in the ashtray and headed toward the bedroom.

He prayed the old man hadn't passed away during the night. He and Luke weren't exactly close—Luke was too old-fashioned to let his feelings show with anyone—but Jeremy got on well with him. No one else could make you smile the way Luke could. Jeremy couldn't have asked for a better neighbor.

Out of the corner of his eye, Jeremy glimpsed someone or something outside, moving around the house. Not long after, the back door creaked open and slammed shut.

"Luke?" Jeremy picked up the ashtray from the TV stand and weighed it in his hand. Not his weapon of choice, but better than nothing; he imagined it would hurt like hell to have it smashed into your nose.

He went to call out again, but suddenly Luke came tearing at him from the rear of the house. The old man didn't make a sound, but his eyes were wide open, his face split into a snarl. He hurtled forward in a desperate rage, and Jeremy barely dodged him, dropping the ashtray in the process.

Luke crashed into the TV stand and went down onto his hands and knees. His muscles tensed, as if he were going to lunge to his feet and attack again, so Jeremy kicked him in the stomach, knocking the wind out of him and throwing him onto his back. Jeremy dropped on the old man, pinned his withered arms over his head. "Luke, please, it's me! Jeremy!"

Luke raised his head and snapped his teeth like a mad dog, incredibly strong somehow. Jeremy, forced to let go, rolled away from the old man, but not quickly enough—fingernails raked a long gash in his arm beneath the sleeve of his Rush T-shirt. Jeremy gritted his teeth, and then Luke was on him again.

Before he even realized what he was doing, Jeremy snatched up the ashtray from the floor and brought it down on Luke's skull, crunching bone. Luke went limp and fell over.

Feeling sick, his whole body shaking with adrenaline and disgust, Jeremy dropped the ashtray; blood and gray hair had stuck to the glass. There was no doubt that the old man was dead. His scalp was caved-in and bleeding.

Tears welled up in Jeremy's eyes as he unconsciously rubbed the wound on his arm. He fell onto the couch and sat there, staring at the dead television set in a daze.

6

HOURS later, Jeremy placed an empty beer bottle on the TV table. The beer had been warm but good. You could always count on old Luke to stock his fridge with the essentials.

Thinking of Luke caused Jeremy to lean over and vomit on the floor in front of the couch. It was the same place Luke's body had lain not long ago, before Jeremy dragged him into the bedroom and covered him with a bed sheet. The image of blood soaking through the thin white cloth made Jeremy retch again.

He rocked back and forth on the couch, replaying everything in his mind. Luke hadn't been himself. He had been more like an animal. Jeremy wondered if any part of the old Luke had been left inside. He doubted it, and he tried to convince himself that he'd done what he needed in order to survive. It had been kill or be killed, simple as that. But still, it didn't feel that way.

He cursed himself for being so weak.

Whatever had happened the night before was worse than a simple power outage; he realized that now. The light hadn't been just a dream. Something was terribly fucked up with the world—and he should have been doing something about it. The day was half gone and he still hadn't tried Luke's truck. By now he could have been in town, hunting for help and maybe finding out what had happened last night. Yet he sat there, stealing a dead friend's beer. Because what if the folks in town were like Luke? What would he do?

He had no idea, but he did know he couldn't stay here, and there seemed no point in going home. There was nothing there for him.

After a brief search, he found the keys to the truck hanging in the kitchen, but before he started towards town he needed to do one more thing.

Holding a dishcloth from a kitchen drawer, he walked to the bedroom and looked at the corpse snuggled inside the sheet. Inwardly, he said a final goodbye to the old man as he built up the courage to step around him and open the connecting door to the storage room. Half a dozen rifles hung on a rack on the far wall of the room, and a glass case below them contained Luke's collection of handguns. Not all of them were real—some were just replicas—but they had been Luke's only real passion in life, aside from sitting on his porch, drinking and smoking.

Jeremy wrapped his hand in the dishcloth and smashed open the locked case. He inspected each gun carefully until he found one that was both real and loaded. It was an old-style .38, which he tucked into the back of his pants before lowering a .30-06 from the rifle rack. Although he didn't know where Luke kept the ammunition for the handguns, Jeremy knew where he stored the ammo for the rifles and he stopped to load the weapon and dump the leftovers into his pocket.

Outside, he slid into the cab of the ancient, beat-up vehicle and turned the ignition. The engine rolled over on the first try and roared to life.

Jeremy glanced at Luke's house one last time, then left a cloud of dust in his wake as he sped off into the distance.

7

AMY pinched her arm so hard she bled. *Wake up!* she thought. *Oh please, God—wake up!* The last few hours were a blur of death and running, but apparently this wasn't a dream because it persisted.

She sat in the back of a van with her legs curled up beneath her. Across from her sat a boy of no more than twelve; Jake or Jack or something like that—she couldn't remember.

In the driver's seat, a man named Dan drove, his eyes fixed on the road ahead. His black hair was streaked with gray, though otherwise he appeared to be in his late twenties or early thirties.

The van jolted as it hit something in the street. Amy hoped it was a pothole, nothing else.

Sitting next to Dan, the woman, Katherine, held a 12-gauge shotgun in her lap, watching Amy and the boy intently. No one spoke.

There had been another man with them earlier who had gone crazy. Without hesitation, Katherine had splattered his head all over the wall, and she'd made Dan stop so she could kick the body outside. Amy could still smell the blood, and she had no doubt whatsoever that Katherine would kill all of them in an instant if she had to.

All day, they had driven south through the city in search of a safe place to get help, in search of others who didn't have what Dan called the "sickness." The van was both a blessing and a curse. It gave them the means to outrun any problems they encountered, but it also drew problems to them: the sound of the engine attracted the crazies. Already Katherine and Dan had been forced to fight them off half a dozen times. The noise also attracted the unwanted attention of other survivors, the kind willing to kill for the working vehicle. Thank God they had met up with that type only once and had been able to flee without a real fight.

Amy didn't really know where Dan was taking them. She hoped *he* knew. But after all she had suffered and seen, she wondered if there was such a thing as a safe place anymore.

Her stomach growled. There was food in abandoned establishments and stores throughout the city; the trouble lay in stopping to get it. They had learned that fact quickly and the hard way. The diseased were good at hiding and they seemed to be everywhere.

Amy fished around in her jacket pockets and retrieved half of a candy bar she'd looted the one time they had stopped earlier that day. The boy watched her hungrily but said nothing. She broke off a large chunk and offered it to him. He snatched it from her and sat back, chewing it and smacking his lips. Katherine watched but showed no signs of caring. *She must be hungry too*, Amy thought, *but she doesn't show it like we do.*

"We'll be there soon," Dan muttered, more to himself than to his passengers. "We'll get help. You'll see. Everything will be fine."

Amy hoped he was right. She knew that Dan was on the verge of a breakdown and wasn't at all lucid, but nonetheless she hoped.

8

PRESIDENT Clark stood on the White House lawn. He could hear the howls of the poor souls outside the massive walls encircling the yard. General Wiggins's soldiers lined the barrier, shooting any of the things that were smart enough to devise a way over.

Early last night, people had begun to flock to the walls, seeking entrance and refuge. They were all long dead or changed by now, no longer human at all by his definition. They were monsters, soulless automatons who wanted nothing more than to rip his throat open with their bare hands. He could no longer force himself to feel pity for these creatures, but he did mourn for the people they once were. They had been *his* people after all, his nation, and they had trusted him. This is where he had led them.

He had refused Wiggins's pleas to leave the night before, hoping that his permanent post would give people hope and help calm the rioting and looting. At least in D.C. He'd been wrong—he saw that now. The city was dead, his presence pointless.

He wondered if he had waited too long to take Wiggins's advice. The White House walls were surrounded by the creatures, six or seven rows deep, pushing and clawing to get inside. Hundreds had been crushed in the stampede, too many to count. It was as if all of Washington was out there.

Some of Wiggins's men were working around the clock to convert the vehicles inside the interior parking area into an armored motorcade, a convoy capable of piercing the ranks outside the wall.

Def-con installation IV was where Wiggins intended to head. Originally built to provide shelter from a nuclear holocaust, it was the closest functioning base, set deep in the mountains of North Carolina. Perhaps there they could find the answers to this mess and end the nightmare. With luck, they could build a new start for the world.

Clark jumped as a firm hand grasped his shoulder from behind.

"Everything is ready, sir," said General Wiggins. "We're just waiting for you."

Clark nodded absently. "What the hell are we going to do, General?"

"Survive, Mr. President. My job is to get you out of here to Def-Con IV, and I'm going to do it."

Wiggins led Clark to where the convoy had assembled just inside the southern gate. Five cars and two trucks comprised the fleet, civilian but covered in makeshift armor. Three of the cars no longer had roofs. They had been cut off to accommodate large .50 caliber emplacements, the kind normally mounted on the rear of army jeeps equipped for field duty. Bulky wedges of steel, shaped like battering rams, were welded onto the grilles of both trucks. The whole convoy looked like something out of that Mel Gibson flick about desert dwellers fighting for gas after the collapse of society. Clark didn't know whether to break into tears or roll on the grass laughing.

"You ready, sir?" Wiggins asked, escorting the president to the second truck in the line. "It could get a bit hairy out there."

"I am as ready as I will ever be, General."

"Then let's get the show on the road," Wiggins said, laughing. He opened the door for the president, then walked off toward the lead truck.

As Clark watched him go, he couldn't help but think of the people they were leaving behind: Dr. Buchanan, most of the civilian staff. The convoy could only hold so many people, and Wiggins had allotted most of the space to military and security personnel. Clark gritted his teeth; Wiggins had no right to jeopardize so many lives just to protect him, but to the general and his soldiers, it was their duty. The United States lived on as long as the president was alive, and in a way Clark was forced to admit they were right.

Besides, he almost thought Dr. Buchanan preferred being left behind. The scientist had claimed the energy field trapped in Earth's atmosphere was changing. Apparently, the aspects of the energy that had crippled mankind's technology would soon pass—"Two to four days, tops," Buchanan had said—but that was the only ray of hope; the energy field showed no other signs of decay. Buchanan surmised that the energy was permanent, or close enough not to matter.

And worse, his most recent data showed that only eight percent of the world population was immune to the biological effects of the field. When Clark asked why most of the White House staff was as of yet unaffected, Buchanan answered that some humans possessed a greater tolerance than others and that the bulk of the White House personnel had been sheltered inside during the wave. He guessed they would be normal until they were outside long enough to absorb the same amount of radiation as those who'd been openly exposed to the light.

That was why he seldom came out of the underground bunker; that was why he wanted to stay behind. The good doctor didn't want to find out whether or not he was immune. He just wanted to stay sane for as long as he possibly could.

A contingent of Wiggins's men still guarded the fences, and Clark watched from inside the second truck of the convoy as they opened fire into the creatures outside the southern gate. The things dropped in waves, but others moved up to take their place. The guards were sure to run out of ammo before the city ran out of creatures, but Wiggins would've known this and would have planned for it. Surely enough, within seconds Clark heard the thumping sound of grenade launchers being fired from the lawn. Explosions sounded outside the gate, and the lead truck shot forward, crashing its way into the mob. It plowed through the creatures, crunching some under its wheels and bouncing others off its armored plating.

Then the whole convoy was moving outside the gates. The M-60s mounted in the open cars blazed, and small-arms fire crackled over the howling creatures. Clark's truck bounced as the driver turned out of the yard too quickly, hitting the curb as he swung around to follow the other vehicles.

Inside the cab of the lead truck, Wiggins smiled. Everything was going as planned. The convoy cleared the horde, and the open road lay before them.

"Sir, what's that?" his driver asked.

Wiggins squinted. A lone creature had walked out of a building and was crouching in the road ahead as if waiting for them.

The damn thing had a rocket launcher held firmly against its shoulder.

"Oh shit!" Wiggins screamed, reaching over to claw at the wheel, the driver too stunned to react in time.

Light flashed from the launcher's barrel and the rocket streaked into the cab where Wiggins sat.

Clark heard the explosion as he watched the lead truck erupt into a ball of fire. Adrenaline surged through his body, and his knuckles went white from his grip on the armrest.

The car immediately behind Wiggins's truck crashed into the flaming wreckage so fast it overturned. Like a chain of falling dominoes, the convoy grinded to a halt. The creatures behind them were catching up, and more poured out of the side streets and alleys. They were everywhere.

One soldier manning a M-60 in the car behind Clark was torn in half as a dozen psychos attempted to pull him from the vehicle. His intestines left a trail of red on the car's paint as the upper part of his torso disappeared into the angry horde.

"Mr. President!" the soldier beside him shouted as a grotesque, drooling face pressed against Clark's window.

"Jesus!" Clark threw his arm against the inside of the glass to lend it extra support, hoping it would hold. "Take us back! Take us back now!"

The driver threw the truck into reverse and gunned the engine, backing straight into the brick wall of an apartment building. Clark was thrown forward from the impact, and his window shattered. Hands pulled him through the small opening into the street, dirty, bloody hands with jagged fingernails. He swam in a sea of biting teeth as his flesh was ripped and shredded, and in the distance black smoke rose from behind the White House's open gates.

9

AS Jeremy drove through the streets of Canton, he stared in shock at the mayhem around him. The whole town looked as if a war had been fought there. The Pigeon Center Market was a mess, its doors broken open, glass shards glittering everywhere. Other places were burnt to black rubble. Here and there cars were stranded in the road, some wrecked, others abandoned, their doors left open from when their occupants had fled. Some of them, unfortunately, hadn't fled far.

There weren't many of them—Jeremy could go for minutes at a

time without spotting one—but when he did, he always looked away. The bodies were horribly mutilated, torn or hacked to pieces. Some even appeared as if they were partially eaten by a pack of animals.

Jeremy had seen only three survivors since he'd driven into town. Two of those had been crazy like old Luke, and he'd avoided them as best he could. The third, he thought, may have been normal, but as Jeremy's truck approached, the man ran into the depths of the paper mill. Jeremy got out and called after him, but didn't dare go into the dark, winding corridors alone, even with the rifle and handgun.

The Ford's radio was broken, and everywhere Jeremy went, the power remained off. He knew little more than he had back at Luke's.

On the edge of town, he pulled the truck to a stop at the Exxon station and killed the engine. The sun was setting, and long shadows stretched across the pavement from the pumps. He climbed out of the Ford, leaving the .30-.06 in the seat, but he pulled out the .38 and didn't bother to conceal it. He knew better than to try the pumps themselves, so he walked towards the station.

The place was eerily silent. Like at the Center Pigeon Market, the doors were shattered, and Jeremy's boots crunched on glass as he entered. The smell of rotten meat made him gag.

In front of the first aisle, the cashier lay on the floor with a gaping hole in her chest; it looked as if someone had shot her point-blank with a shotgun. Urine, tinted red, pooled around her corpse, and the summer insects buzzed about her, laying their eggs in her gray flesh.

Jeremy covered his mouth as he moved deeper inside the station. Displays were overturned; coolers were left open or shattered, the aisles ransacked, and about the only thing left untouched was the cash register. Money had become just green paper again, useless. From what he'd seen in town so far, people took what they wanted or died trying.

Jeremy searched the store and loaded a bag with everything useful he could find: a jar of peanut butter, a lighter, a few warm beers and some bottled water, a crushed loaf of bread. There wasn't much left in the store, and it took a lot of effort to find even those few things. He also managed to find the store's first-aid kit, buried under a pile of junk behind the main checkout counter. All in all, he considered himself very blessed.

He unloaded his treasure into the truck and went back to the storage shed behind the station. He shot the lock off the door and took a jug and a siphon cable from inside. Maybe he couldn't get gas from the pumps, but there were more than enough vehicles waiting out there; it wouldn't be a problem.

As he returned to the truck this time, he saw them coming down the road: five men and three women in tattered clothing. Their eyes seemed to glow yellow in the fading sunlight.

Jeremy threw the siphon and jug into the truck's bed and leapt inside the cab. As he locked his door and cranked the engine, the people broke into a run. He floored the gas pedal and squealed out of the parking lot without looking back. He drove for over ten miles before he stopped to get gas from a Buick, which lay stuck in a ditch by the roadside.

As he waited for the jug to fill with gas, he wondered where he would go. If Canton was like this, he couldn't imagine what Sylva must be like, much less Asheville. He thought hard about where he might be able to find help. Where the hell was a close enough place that might still be normal? He slumped against the side of the Buick in defeat, watching the road and tree line for any sign of movement.

It popped into his head then like a bomb going off. All his life in Canton, he heard stories about a military base up in the mountains. For the life of him, he couldn't remember what it was called. Hell, he didn't even know if it was real, but he knew roughly where it was supposed to be, and if anyone could get through this mess okay it would be the army.

He snatched up the jug and yanked the siphon cable free of the Buick as he ran for the truck.

10

NEW York was a distant memory, something from a previous lifetime. Amy shook her head to clear her thoughts. In her sweaty palms, she clutched a M-16 rifle she had stolen from a long-dead looter; she and Katherine were hiding behind a stack of crates on the dock.

Dan, God rest his soul, had driven them through the worst of it before he'd finally flipped out; Katherine had put a bullet in his skull. The boy, Jake, had died too. Apparently he suffered from some kind of asthma, and without his meds neither Amy nor Katherine had been able to help him. But all of that was the past now, clouded and murky like a fading dream.

Right this second, they had other things to worry about. Amy glanced over at Katherine, crouched several feet away. There was no question of who was the leader. Katherine, Amy had discovered, was an ex-cop, and she was good at what she did.

On the other side of the docks, a pack of human-creatures milled about, sniffing the air, occasionally turning on each other even as they stalked their prey.

Coming to the docks had been Katherine's idea. They'd noticed them from the interstate, and she had suggested they could find a boat and set out to sea, maybe find an uninhabited island and start over, just the two of them. Even with their limited supplies, it sounded like a great idea. Traveling by sea was much safer than any road on the mainland. Out there, the creatures could never reach them.

Of course neither of them had planned on running into a pack of the creatures. Their new hope had blinded them, had made them careless, and now they were trapped, cut off from both the van and the boats.

She and Katherine would have just killed them—they were both well armed with gear they'd found or lucked into along the way—but the pack was over two dozen strong and this was their hunting grounds. Lord only knew how many still lurked in the buildings.

Hiding from them had become the only option, and even that had made things worse, giving time for more creatures to show up as the women waited for the first ones to wander off.

Amy could see the strain on Katherine's face. She couldn't recall when either of them had last slept. Sweat glistened on Katherine's tanned skin, and her glance said that this was it, the end for both of them. All that remained was deciding how they would die: either hide here and pray, or go out fighting to reach the van. Amy already knew what Katherine would choose, even as the ex-cop stood up with her shotgun and blew a hole in the nearest creature's chest.

Amy wanted to leap to her feet and help her friend, but she refused to believe that all their suffering had been for nothing. Deep down she wanted to live, and she was forced to admit that Katherine's pointless exit strategy was just macho bullshit.

Amy, still hidden behind the crates, watched the creatures charge toward them as Katherine pumped a round into her weapon and shot another psycho in its stomach, loosing its intestines onto the dock. Despite her bulging muscles, Katherine appeared helpless in the face of the horde closing in around her.

With tears in her eyes, Amy turned away as the things reached Katherine and tore at her with their nails and teeth. She tried to block out the screams for help as she crept towards the edge of the docks and eased herself into the water below.

Amy let the currents carry her into the dark beneath the planks, hoping the things would be too occupied with Katherine to search for anyone else. As far as she knew, they had not seen her.

Katherine fell silent, and Amy began to weep.

Hours later, when the sun had set and the docks had grown still, Amy hauled herself out of the water. None of the creatures had stuck around. Even Katherine's body was gone, leaving only smears of blood where she'd fallen.

Dripping wet and wrinkled from the water, Amy stumbled to the van, her muscles aching from hours of keeping her afloat. She carefully checked the vehicle to make sure nothing was waiting inside, then slid into the driver's seat. She clawed the extra set of keys out of the glove box and shoved them into the ignition. The moment the engine roared to life she knew the creatures would come pouring out.

She turned the key, and her heart froze as the van sputtered loudly without catching.

Amy tried again as she noticed movement on the docks and in the shadows of the buildings; the night came alive with the sound of hungry howls.

This time the engine turned over and she peeled out towards the main road, laughing hysterically as the van lurched over a speed bump, onto the interstate.

Despite the wreckage and abandoned cars littering the roadway, Amy found her foot getting heavier and heavier on the accelerator. Adrenaline rushed through her exhausted body as she swerved this way and that, dodging obstacles. She felt free, as if she were losing her mind, and it was okay. It would have been so easy to just keep going faster and faster until her reflexes couldn't keep up and she died in a fiery crash. It would be a better death than being ripped apart like Katherine.

Amy reached to click on the radio, knowing she would only find static across the dial, but something flickered in the rearview mirror and caught her eye. The van almost collided with what was left of an overturned eighteen wheeler as she jerked upright in her seat.

Slowing down, Amy studied the police car that had come up an exit ramp behind her to give chase.

"What the hell?" She knew it wasn't possible. Everyone in the world was either crazy from the effects of the wave, dead, or on the run like she was. Yet seeing the car's flashing lights brought back feelings of hope. Maybe her flight was over and the officers would look out for her and take her somewhere safe. Maybe somehow in this city people had survived and organized.

She brought the van to a stop as the police car pulled up beside her.

Amy was in the process of rolling down her window as she glanced into the car. A man in a tattered uniform with yellow-tinted eyes stuck a .38 out his window and aimed for her head.

"Oh God!" Amy snapped around to the steering wheel and rammed the gas pedal to the floor. The officer's shot slammed into the van's side just behind her door.

"Oh God, oh God, they're not supposed to be able to drive!"

In the rearview, she saw the thing's partner trying to lean out the passenger-side window to shoot at her.

He's going to blow out my tires, Amy thought. There was no way she could outrun them, not in this van, not with the roads the way they were. But the creatures could die—they were just people driven crazy by the wave—so she did the only thing she could think of.

Making sure her seatbelt was fastened, she hit the brakes. Tires squealed as the van came to a halt—and the police car smashed into its rear.

Despite her seatbelt, Amy was thrown forward. Her forehead struck the steering wheel and her world faded to black.

SHE came to with a start. Something wet trickled down her face. Amy wiped at it and her hand came away covered in a warm, wet red. Her head was pounding, but otherwise she seemed okay. She reached over and dug a .45 from the glove box and unsnapped her seatbelt. When she opened the door, she sprawled out onto the road, unable to keep her balance.

The police car was still there, a mass of broken metal wedged into the van's rear. The driver was clearly dead; pieces of windshield glass jutted from his face, and his head dangled at an unnatural angle.

Amy pulled herself to her feet and stumbled closer, holding the pistol ready. When she got close enough to see inside the car, she noticed the other officer's bottom half resting in the blood-soaked passenger seat. The top half of his body was nowhere to be seen.

She slumped to the ground beside the car. It was only a matter of time until more of the creatures came out of the night around her, but both the van and the car were totaled. She needed a plan. She couldn't just sit there and wait to die, regardless of how much she hurt or how tired she was. Her eyes were heavy with sleep and it fought to wrap her in its embrace. She shook herself awake, and her head throbbed from a fresh burst of pain. Her only chance was to find a working car with the keys still inside.

She got to her feet once more and walked down the interstate to start her search.

11

GEOFF lay back against the tree trunk, perched high above the ground on a narrow branch, an unlit cigarette dangling from his lips. He massaged the corners of his tired eyes with his finger, then blinked several times to clear his vision.

Below him, a kid moved slowly up the mountain trail. Normally Geoff would have radioed the base to let them know and to get orders on what to do. Fuck that: *normally* he wouldn't have been out here, risking his life to do the job of the base's malfunctioned external sensors.

He hoisted his rifle to his shoulder and peered through its scope. The kid was in his later twenties and was dressed like a punk in ratty jeans and a T-shirt of some stupid rock band. Geoff could have dropped him right then and there, problem solved, but something kept his finger away from the trigger.

The last few days hadn't been a cakewalk, even for him. He wondered how the punk had managed to survive, much less come so close to finding the base. Maybe Geoff had seen enough death over the last few days, or maybe he was just getting old; either way, the kid got to keep breathing.

He carefully took the cigarette from his lips and slipped it back inside the pack, then stuffed the whole thing into his jacket pocket. "Ah . . . shit," he whispered to himself and started down the tree.

The birds were singing in the forest and the sky above was a bright blue filled with sunlight. The world went on as normal, oblivious to the hell mankind was going through. Geoff found that funny.

He reached the bottom of the tree and vanished into the woods without a trace.

JEREMY paused on his way up the trail. He shrugged off his backpack and opened it, hunting for the map he'd picked up from the remains of a local tourist trap. He knew the base wouldn't be on the map, even if it did exist, but he wanted to check the other landmarks to make sure he was still headed in what he believed to be the right direction.

He didn't hear his stalker step onto the path behind him until an arm snaked about his neck.

Jeremy choked and fought against his attacker's grip until he heard the gun cock beside his ear.

"Stop it, kid, if you want to live to see the sun set."

Jeremy stopped squirming. "Look, mister—"

"Shut up, kid." The man released his hold and shoved him forward. Jeremy whirled around and almost broke into a smile when he saw the man's green camouflage uniform.

"I'd tell you to go home," the man continued, "but I guess none of us really have one anymore . . . "

The man, Geoff, was in his later fifties, and gray hair covered his head. His eyes were bloodshot and it looked as if he hadn't shaved in days.

With cat-like grace, he scooped up Jeremy's backpack and slipped it onto his own shoulder. Muscles rippled and bulged beneath his uniform. "So I suppose I'll have to take you back with me."

"To the base?"

"To what's left of it, kid."

As they made their way together through the woods, Geoff told Jeremy what he knew about the wave and about what had happened at the base, which he referred to as Def-Con IV.

Apparently, the energy had been some kind of shockwave from somewhere far beyond the space known to mankind, perhaps from some interstellar war, or from an alien species' failed experiments with dark matter. It didn't really matter where it came from.

The light was merely a side effect of the energy reacting with Earth's atmosphere. A portion of the wave's main body had been trapped in greenhouse gasses, and like a super and perpetual EMP on a global scale, the wave and its lingering remnants caused technological failures throughout the world, dampened or disrupted to the point of uselessness. Only basic things worked now; things like electricity and nuclear energy were out of the question until the field dispersed, which it was continuing to do a bit more every day.

The alien energy field also produced a type of ambient radiation, which scientists believed would still be there in a thousand years unless they found a way to deal with it. This radiation was what caused the rampant "plague" of madness across the globe. It broke down the neural pathways of the human mind to their most basic core, leaving human shells full of only instinct and violence, unless you were immune, and very few people in the world were.

At first, Def-Con IV retained contact with a handful of similar bases here in the United States and in the United Kingdom—for the first day they had even been in touch with the president and the White House—but they'd slowly lost contact with those bases one by one as the radiation plague and other problems took their toll. For all Geoff knew, Def-Con IV could very well be the last holdout of humanity in the world.

During the first few hours of the chaos when the wave had reached the earth, the base had opened its doors to the locals who had come seeking shelter. Very quickly, the staff of the base learned firsthand of the secondary biological effects of the wave as those same locals succumbed to the radiation.

A mini-war broke out inside the compound. It was a hard fight, but in the end Def-Con IV's staff prevailed. Only Geoff and a handful of staff survived. Two were badly injured: one in a coma, the other in a wheelchair but healing. Geoff informed Jeremy that if he had come looking for salvation and hope, he'd came to the wrong place.

They went through the high barbed wire fence that surrounded the Def-Con complex, and Jeremy got his first good look at the site. Before the wave, it had disguised itself as an agriculture research facility. Inside the fence, there were only three buildings, two of them the size of toolsheds, but the third was fairly large and very much civilian in nature. Blooming gardens stretched beyond the buildings with flowers planted around their edges, and the rear fence was far beyond eyeshot.

"Pretty amazing, isn't it?" Geoff asked.

"What?" Jeremy asked, as if snapping out of a dream.

"That the gardens survived," Geoff explained. "Like I said, when the wave first hit, people were flooding up here in droves based on rumors and desperate hopes. Of course, all they really cared about was finding the base and getting inside. I don't think many of them headed out into the fields. Most of them poured straight into the garage." Geoff pointed at the larger building. "I guess they thought it had to be the base since it's the only real building up here. It's in pretty bad shape now. Most of the vehicles were stolen or damaged by the mob when we stopped letting people into the real base below."

"How do you get inside?"

Geoff laughed and led him towards the more battered of the two sheds. Its door was new and a sharp contrast to the aged and beaten wood around it. "I had a hell of a time fixing this back," Geoff said as he opened the door, barely concealing his pride. "Carpentry's a lot harder than killing people, kid."

The shed itself was completely empty except for a large metal plate in the middle of its unfinished floor. Geoff squatted and ran his fingertips across the hatch until his fingers felt a crease, the edge of a small lid that popped open to reveal a numerical keypad. He typed in an eight-digit code as Jeremy watched. Somewhere below the floor, a motor came to life and the plate rose up like a tilted manhole cover. Geoff motioned to the hole. "After you."

Jeremy slid down into a metal tunnel just wide enough and tall enough for two people (no more than six feet in height) to walk comfortably side by side. When they reached the large vault-like doorway at the end, Geoff typed a code into another keypad on the wall, and the door dilated from its center. Beyond lay another series of corridors.

"Welcome to your new home, kid. You can call me Geoff. I don't think I caught your name."

"It's Jeremy, Jeremy Davis."

Geoff grinned. "You live around here, Jeremy Davis?"

"Not really . . . Well, I guess I kind of did."

Geoff shrugged. "Didn't we all. Well, I guess it's time you met your new family."

The soldier led Jeremy deeper into the base.

12

NATHANIAL Richards punched a button on the control panel in front of him and watched as the test ran again. On the gigantic screen across the room, an image of a translucent wave struck the earth once more.

Troy, sitting nearby, reclined and propped his feet up on a dark, malfunctioned console. He had no idea what Nathanial's simulation meant, but from the way Dr. Sheena Leigh frowned in her wheelchair, and judging by the grim look on Nathanial's face, Troy could tell it was nothing good.

The wave shattered as it struck the earth, slowing from the speed of light to a dead crawl in space as its fragments dispersed, each taking a different trajectory. Then the screen went black.

"Run it again," Sheena ordered, leaning forward in her wheelchair.

Nathanial shook his head. "We've run it over three dozen times today alone, Sheena. There's just no way to know where the pieces are headed. Maybe if we waited until the wave's aftereffects dissipated in the atmosphere a bit more, we could link up to one of the satellites. Surely at least one of them had to survive. We could—"

"I said run it again," she interrupted.

Nathanial got up from his seat as Geoff and Jeremy entered the room. He didn't notice them, too focused on Sheena. "You run it again! I'm through for today. Until we get more data, we're just wasting our time."

"Ahem." Troy cleared his throat and pointed over Nathanial's shoulder at the newcomers.

Nathanial turned to face them, his features red with frustration. "Who the hell are you?"

"His name is Jeremy," Geoff responded with an edge to his tone. "He's not infected by the radiation, so you might as well just go ahead and welcome him aboard."

"I hope to God he knows something about astrophysics and computers because I fuckin' quit!" Nathanial stormed out of the room through an opposite entryway.

"That's Nathanial," Geoff informed Jeremy. "You get used to him. That guy over there slacking off is Troy. He's military like me."

Sheena rolled her chair up to them, and it was clear from the way her arms strained that she was not yet accustomed to her disability. "Do you, Jeremy? Do you know computers?"

He stared at her. Even wheelchair-bound, this tiny woman with flakes of gray in her black, pinned-up hair seemed tougher than Geoff. She met his stare, her eyes unwavering through her thick glasses. "Well?" she urged.

"Um . . . no, ma'am, I don't."

"What did you do before . . . ?" she let her sentence trail off.

"I was an artist."

Sheena cackled. "You sure know how to pick them, Geoff. What use is he going to be? And more importantly, who's going to give up their share of the food to feed him?"

Troy hopped to his feet and moved between the doctor and Jeremy, sticking out his hand. "Glad to have you along for the ride. I promise not all of us are as crazy as we seem."

Jeremy took Troy's hand and shook it firmly.

"Bring him to the lab later," Sheena ordered. "We need to make sure he's clean."

Troy winked at Jeremy. "Gotta go. Duty calls." Then he grabbed the handles on the back of the doctor's chair and rolled her out of the room.

"Who was that?" Jeremy asked as the pair disappeared down a corridor.

"That's our doctor and science whiz, Sheena. She was in charge here before things went to shit. She still thinks she is, most of the time."

A pale man, dressed in black and only slightly older than Jeremy, wandered into the control room. He wore thin, sleek glasses and carried himself with a flare of style. He stopped in his tracks when he noticed the two of them.

"Oh God," Geoff muttered, "not Ian."

"Good afternoon, Geoff," the man said with a soft British accent and a smile. "And who might this be accompanying you today?" He didn't wait long enough for a response, jumping back in as if hoping to interrupt any reply. "You don't actually have to answer that. I couldn't help but overhear your encounter with our resident witch doctor. She's rather narrow-minded these days, obsessed with death you might say."

"Death?" Jeremy asked.

Ian nodded, waving his hand effeminately as if dismissing Jeremy's concern. "You've heard about the wave, I'm sure. It broke apart when it hit the earth, you see, and our good doctor is worried that a piece of it will hit the sun. If it did, it could disrupt the fusion reactions inside the star like it did the energy sources here; it would start a chain reaction and act as a booster as well, causing even our tiny sun to become a supernova. The sun would simply explode. It would be the end of our solar system. Of course, given our limited resources at the moment, it's impossible to know where the fragments of the wave are headed."

Jeremy blinked, stunned to silence. Ian laid a hand on his shoulder. "Carpe diem, young man. Don't worry about the future, only be concerned with the time you have now."

"What brings you out of your private coffin, Ian?" Geoff asked.

"Coffee, my good man, Coffee. I was just on my way to the mess to brew a pot while we still have some left. Would you two care to join me?"

"I think we'll pass," Geoff said without giving Jeremy a chance to respond.

"Have it your way then." Cheerfully, Ian continued along on his quest.

"Come on, kid." Geoff literally pulled Jeremy out of the control room. "Let me show you to your bunk."

They rode a nearby lift down to the military living quarters, a row of twenty-four rooms lining a long corridor. According to Geoff, only three of the base's survivors lived down here: himself, Troy and the repair tech Wade. Nathanial, Dr. Sheena Leigh (when she could be pried away from her projects), and the base's communications officer, a woman named Toni, stayed on another level in the civilian section, whereas Ian made his home in makeshift quarters he'd set up inside the armory, despite all the available space. Ian had been the CIA liaison and was, in Geoff's opinion, the only complete psychopath left in the complex. There was also a woman named Lex, who was in a coma, Geoff explained. She was kept in the medical labs so Sheena could keep a close eye on her; they weren't sure whether she would wake up normal or be affected by the wave.

For the time being, Geoff assured him, Jeremy could stay with the "normal" people in the military quarters. The room he gave Jeremy was rather Spartan. It contained only a bunk, a small bathroom, and a single table supporting a computer tied into the mainframe.

"It's not much," Geoff said, "But it's a hell of a lot safer than living out there with those things."

A memory of Luke's deranged, hungry face flashed through Jeremy's mind and he shuddered.

"The creatures don't come around here much. It's rather secluded and very few people knew there was even anything up here in the mountains. We do get a few wanders now and again. Nothing we can't deal with so far. Besides, even if the things flocked up here in droves, there's no way they could get inside the complex proper."

Jeremy nodded as he shrugged off his backpack and placed it on the bunk.

Geoff headed for the door. "You look like you could use some rest, so I'll leave you to it. We'll worry about finding you a job tomorrow. Everybody here contributes somehow for the good of us all—except maybe Ian. We have to work together if we want to stay alive."

As the door slid closed behind Geoff, Jeremy slumped into the chair at the table and rested his head in his hands. It was true: he felt safer here than he had in days, and it was good to see people again, no matter who they were, but he still wondered if coming here had been the right thing to do.

JEREMY awoke to someone pounding on his door. He rubbed his eyes and climbed out of the bunk as a short, hideously muscled man entered the room. The man's bald head gleamed from the light shining through the open doorway behind him.

"Time to go, new boy. We've got work to do."

"Who . . . who are you?"

"Name's Wade. I keep things working around here, but today I'm going into town and you're going with me."

"What? I just got here. Why me?"

"You're not that dense are you?" Wade walked over and rapped his knuckles on Jeremy's skull. "Hello in there."

Jeremy backed away, and Wade glared at him.

"None of us other than Geoff have really left the complex since the wave. Hell, you lived through the shit out there. I need a guide, Jerm, and you're it."

"But I don't know anything you don't," Jeremy argued.

"Daylight's burning, new boy. Get your shit together or get out."

Jeremy had slept in his pants, so he pulled on his Rush T-shirt and reached for his .38.

Wade saw him. "Leave that piece of crap. Here." He shoved a .45 automatic into Jeremy's hand. "We'll stop and get you a real weapon on the way out too."

Minutes later, Jeremy sat inside the garage with Troy, Geoff, and Wade. He held an Uzi in his trembling hands and watched as Wade worked underneath the hood of a military issue jeep that had seen better days.

Troy held an M-16 and took continuous drags off a cigarette. "I still don't understand why you have to do this, Wade," he commented between puffs.

"You want to keep breathing?" Wade shot back, his voice muffled by the hood. "If I don't get the parts to fix the ventilation systems from where you idiots shot it up, we're all going to be headed out of here, and I sure ain't trustin' *you* to bring back the right gear."

Troy chuffed. "Next time a bunch of flesh-eating crazies get loose in the base, Wade, maybe you should have a talk with 'em, huh? Tell them not to get near anything important as we blow their freakin' brains out."

Wade popped his head out from under the hood. "Fuck you. You think I want to go out there into Hell?"

"Look, Wade." Geoff moved closer to the jeep. "Troy and I could do it. Just tell us what you need. You don't have to go."

"Yes, I do," Wade said. "Jeremy here'll be all the help I need; besides, the boy has to contribute somehow. Why not this way?"

Geoff raised his hands in surrender.

Wade tossed Jeremy the keys to the jeep. "Get in and crank her up."

Jeremy did as he was told, and the jeep's engine roared to life on the first try. Troy tossed aside his smoke and went to push open the building's main door.

"Catch you later, guys," Wade said. "We got some shopping to do." Then he motioned for Jeremy to get on with it, and they drove out of the complex and down the gravel road towards Canton.

"So just how bad is it out there, really?" Wade asked.

Jeremy glanced over at the burly little man. "Everyone I saw on my way here was dead, crazy, or both. The power's off everywhere."

"No shit, Sherlock. I knew *that*." Wade turned his gaze to the roadside for a moment, as if collecting his thoughts, then looked back at Jeremy. "There used to be one of those large chain hardware and electronics stores just on the other side of town. Did you see it on your way up here?"

"No. But I know where you're talking about."

"You think we can get in and out of it without getting our asses chewed off?"

"I don't know. Those creatures . . . some of them are pretty fast. If they're inside the store . . . "

Wade picked up the twelve-gauge shotgun from the seat between them and pumped a round into the chamber. "Shit," he said, "just another day in paradise, huh, Jerm?"

On their way through town, Jeremy had to floor it twice as the creatures poured out of the ruins of buildings and shops, attracted by the sound of the passing jeep, but he and Wade managed to get by without any real close calls.

When they pulled into the large parking lot of the hardware store, only two creatures were milling about. Jeremy parked the jeep directly in front of the store's Plexiglas entrance and grabbed his Uzi. He started to open fire on the creatures, but Wade smacked his weapon down.

"Don't do it. You saw how the ones in town reacted to the jeep. The noise will just bring more of them." He pulled a pistol out of the jury-rigged holster on his tool belt and screwed a silencer onto its barrel. As the creatures came snarling towards them, Wade dropped each one with a single shot to the skull. "Geoff taught me a few things," he explained, tucking away the gun.

Together they shoved open the store's heavy doors and stepped into the dark interior. "I'll just be a minute," Wade said, reaching for a buggy. "You stay here. Only shoot the fuckers if they get too close and you have to, okay?" Wade cocked his head to the right. "And keep the damn jeep running," he added as he went inside.

About seven or eight of the creatures now occupied the lot, but they hung back, almost as if they were waiting for something. It was really creeping Jeremy out.

Finally Wade returned with a buggy full of circuit boards he must have ripped out of PCs; Jeremy couldn't even begin to guess what the other odds and ends were for.

Wade tossed everything into the back of the jeep and hopped in. "Let's get the hell out of here before they decide they're hungry."

"No argument here," Jeremy said, switching the jeep into drive. He peeled out and tried to steer clear of the creatures.

As the jeep neared the exit to the interstate, a second pack of monsters came bounding out of the woods and made straight for them. Wade cursed and snatched up Jeremy's Uzi. He opened fire out of his window, and several attackers fell, but now the creatures from the lot were charging at them too, advancing from the other side as if trying to block them in.

"Fuck—hold on!" Jeremy thrust the gas pedal all the way down. The jeep struck the curb and bounced out of the lot onto the road.

Wade looked back at the shrinking figures still giving chase. "That was too fucking close," he muttered. "Way too fucking close." Then he clapped Jeremy on the shoulder and grinned. "Good driving, new kid. Glad I brought you along."

13

AMY opened her eyes. She didn't feel completely rested, but some sleep was better than none. Eighteen hours had passed since her flight from the docks. She sat up in the backseat of the Toyota, which she'd finally found after a nasty encounter with a creature on the interstate. She had used the car to flee the city proper and had driven for hours, out into what seemed like the middle of nowhere, nothing around but the road and the trees, the safest place she could find for a nap. So she had locked the car doors and had stretched out on her seat, hoping that if any creatures stumbled across her and tried to get in, the noise would wake her up in time to deal with them.

It had been worth the risk. She felt much better physically, but she was still haunted by the horror of her situation. She was alone. The car was nearly out of fuel and she was down to only five rounds left in her .45. She missed Katherine. Hell, she missed the world. But worse, she still had no long-term plan, no idea how she was going to survive, no clue where she was headed. She had fled south, but she didn't know how far. Virginia maybe? She wasn't sure. Amy figured it didn't matter. One state was just as dead as the next.

She needed to find others like herself who'd made it through the wave without going crazy, though she wondered if she were the last sane woman on Earth. The thought terrified her. And the creatures . . . If the cops who'd almost killed her were any indication, some of those things out there were getting smart. Not normal, but intelligent, and that made them a hundred times more dangerous. It was one thing to outrun or hide from a pack of mindless monsters and another thing altogether when they started shooting back and driving cars. What else were the things capable of now? Amy shuddered and pushed the thought from her mind.

Tenderly, she reached up to touch the wound on her forehead. It wasn't serious, but she was worried about infection. She had no water or food, much less medical supplies, and trying to locate some in a city or town was out of the question. Even if she had been well armed, she wouldn't have tried it on her own. So the big question was, what did she do now?

Using the car was dangerous. It attracted the mindless creatures and made her more noticeable to the intelligent ones as well. Going at it on foot seemed like an equally bad idea; she would have no way to outrun the creatures and she certainly couldn't stand her ground and fight. What the hell was she going to do?

Finally she made a decision: Amy unlocked one of the car doors and got out, leaving the vehicle behind.

Water had been the deciding factor in her choice. In the car, she would have driven right past the supplies she required so badly to stay alive, unless she stopped at a gas station or something of the sort, and then she would have to deal with the hordes of monsters she attracted. The way she reasoned it, on foot she might be able to find a stream or some kind of berries in the woods. So she walked off the road and headed into the trees, feeling her way carefully through the newly fallen night.

14

GEOFF met Jeremy and Wade on the road home about two miles outside the complex. "You done good, kid," he told Jeremy when he saw the parts they had gone after. He ushered them on towards the base, but stayed behind to take care of any creatures that might have followed them back. He promised to meet up with them later in the mess, and then he disappeared into the trees, becoming a part of the woods themselves.

THE inhabitants of Def-Con all sat in the meeting room. Sheena was allowed her rant on the importance of determining the various trajectories of the wave's fragments—not that they could change those trajectories should a piece be aimed for the sun—and when she finished, Wade stood up and informed everyone that the base's air system was fully repaired; he also updated the group on the life expectancy of the power core before giving the floor to the communications officer Toni.

Jeremy had not formally met her yet, so he watched the woman intently. She was tall and thin, in her late twenties or maybe early thirties. Her eyes were a bright green, and brown hair touched the tops of her shoulders. She spoke softly in a controlled, though almost shy, voice. Her efforts to reach anyone else in the government or military, or anyone on civilian channels and the small band frequencies, continued to meet with failure. Toni had no clue whether that meant they were alone in the world, or if the aftereffects of the wave simply hadn't cleared enough to get out a good signal.

Geoff was the last member of the staff to speak, and despite the bleakness of the other reports, his was the most unsettling. The number of infected wandering close to the base was increasing at an alarming rate. Geoff hadn't realized how much until today. No one blamed Jeremy's arrival or Wade's shopping trip, yet Geoff clearly thought these factors contributed to the problem. He wasn't concerned about running out of ammo in the near future or worried about the creatures penetrating the complex; he was afraid the army of infected would grow so large there would be no way out of Def Con without a bloody fight. Geoff did not suggest abandoning the complex, as no one knew of somewhere remotely safe to set out for, yet he made sure everyone understood the threat of being trapped here for the rest of their lives.

When the meeting was over, people broke up into their own little clusters to continue private arguments over what should be done. Geoff and Troy pulled Jeremy out of the room and led him outside toward the garage. The night sky was clear and sparkling with stars. Two creatures were straining against the fence, and when they spotted the trio, they howled and slashed their flesh on the barbwire in their attempts to get in.

"Didn't you just tell everyone to limit their trips up here?" Jeremy whispered.

"Yeah, but there are times and there are times," Geoff said, walking to the fence as he drew his pistol.

"Come on." Troy slid the heavy garage door open and led Jeremy inside. "Forget about them. They're not why we're up here."

Jeremy heard two faint popping noises in the darkness behind him. When Geoff caught up again, Troy closed the door and hit the interior lights. He waved his arm around like a game show hostess showing off a prize. "Welcome to paradise."

"The garage?"

Geoff tried to rub something red and wet off the front of his uniform. "It's not the place but what's in it, kid."

Troy returned from the rear of the garage with a large jug in his hand. "Ta-dah! This here is Wade's special home brew."

"It'll knock you on your ass," Geoff said, "that's for sure."

"But you could drink in the complex. Why come up here?"

"There's nothing like this down there." Troy turned up the jug to his lips and took a long swig, coughing as it burned down his throat like liquid fire. "And hell, Geoff here would go crazy if he couldn't see the stars. Mankind wasn't made to live in the earth."

"What he means is . . . " Geoff grabbed the jug from Troy's hands, "we'd go crazy if we were cooped up with those *suits* much longer. All of them except Wade are educated people, and me and Troy here are the last of the grunts. None of them take him seriously at all, and they only listen to me because I saved their asses when the shit went down and they know I'm the only one who can do it again."

Geoff offered Jeremy the jug, but he waved it aside. "No thanks. Isn't getting wasted up here dangerous?"

Geoff laughed. "Isn't breathing dangerous these days, kid?"

Jeremy didn't answer.

MANY, many feet below them, Sheena rolled her chair closer to Lex's bed and reached out to take the woman's wrist in her hand. Lex's pulse still felt steady, if somewhat weak. There had been no change in her condition for days.

Sheena looked Lex over and winced. Once, she'd been a vibrant thirty-three-year-old woman whose charm and laughter lit up the dark corridors of Def Con. Now her skin was a sickly pale color and her long blond hair had lost its luster. Sometimes Sheena found it hard to believe she was looking at the same person who'd been her assistant, friend, and lover for the last five years.

She leaned forward in her wheelchair and rested her head on Lex's chest. Tears glistened down her cheeks as sobs shook her broken body. She lifted her head, and her hand crept to the main power cord of the life support system. "I'm sorry," Sheena said, no louder than a breath; then she pulled the plug.

A sharp, piercing tone filled the room as Lex's vital signs flatlined. Sheena silenced the alarm with the flip of a button and turned out the lights. She wheeled herself out of the dark room without looking back.

"AMAZING *grace, how sweet the sound,*" Troy sang as the staff of Def Con gathered before the grave at the edge of the large gardens. Black-eyed Susans bloomed around the freshly dug dirt, their yellow petals straining to touch the sun.

To Jeremy, Troy's voice sounded like that of a weeping angel. But as beautiful as the sound was, it stirred the creatures at the fence into a fury. Jeremy tried hard to block out the raging and the thrashing.

There were more of them today. They numbered in the dozens, and Jeremy noticed Geoff's unease as the ceremony continued. The guard was armed to the teeth and clutching a fully loaded AK-47 in his hands. Everyone else seemed focused on saying goodbye to Lex, even Ian, though the CIA man didn't look well. A sheen of sweat covered his snow-white skin, and he fidgeted with his handkerchief.

When Troy's song ended, they all stood together, watching the bloodthirsty horde outside the gates until finally Geoff barked, "Okay! Everybody back inside—now!"

Jeremy wondered as he went if this would be one of the last times he would feel the sunshine on his skin.

Sheena kept the nature of Lex's death to herself. Some suspected what she'd done, while others didn't care, but no one confronted her about it. Lex's death affected them all, including Jeremy, though he'd never met the woman.

A somber air fell over the Def Con complex. On the surface, Geoff, Troy and Wade waged a quiet war against the growing tide of the infected. Ian kept more to himself than ever, rarely leaving his makeshift quarters in the armory. Only Nathanial seemed to actually improve since Sheena suddenly stopped riding him about collecting more data on the trajectories of the wave in space.

Jeremy at last found the time to introduce himself to Toni, and the two spent hours each day trying to enhance the base's communications gear to extend its range and the power of its signal. She was a very kind and warm person, Jeremy discovered, once you wormed your way around her defensive layer of shyness.

"Pass me the screwdriver," Toni called from beneath the control room's main communications console. Jeremy selected a Phillips head carefully from the toolbox and passed it over. He heard Toni work for a moment with the tool before she slid out and smiled at him.

"I think that does it. Anyone on this side of the country with so much as a handset should be able to hear us now."

Jeremy grinned and pointed at the top of the console. "So this little red light is supposed to be on and flickering this way?"

"What?" Toni pulled herself up and looked at the light. Her whole body tensed up and she barely seemed to breathe.

"Was it something I said? I'm sorry if . . . "

She whirled on him and threw her arms about his neck as he stood there, totally dumbfounded.

"Someone out there is trying to reach us!" She half giggled, half screamed as she slammed a finger down to transfer the incoming transmission to the room's speakers.

The broadcast was garbled by terrible static and interference, but they managed to understand a few words. "This . . . Freedom Station . . . Anyone . . . us?"

Toni held a hand over her mouth.

"Freedom Station," Jeremy repeated. "Holy shit."

Toni had already opened the channel and was responding. "We copy that, Freedom. This is Def Con, and you have no idea how happy we are to hear you."

"Repeat . . . Couldn't . . . " the voice replied.

"Go tell the others!" Toni told Jeremy. "I'll try to clean this up some and keep the channel open . . . Go!"

Jeremy dropped his toolbox and darted off, yelling down the corridors.

15

THE woods were quiet and a gentle rain began to fall as Amy made her way up the mountainside. The night had given way to a gray sky full of clouds. The rain was a warm one, however, and she welcomed it. She fished around in her pockets and brought out the last of the berries she had found during the night, plopping the whole handful into her mouth. They were wonderful, the food of the gods, but she longed for more and hoped she would come across another patch soon. She wasn't a nature person, having grown up in New York, but she knew some berries were poisonous and had to be careful what she picked.

Briefly, she entertained the notion of trying to shoot or catch one of the rabbits that ran rampant in the woods, but she had no idea how to hunt them. If it came down to it, she swore she would eat grass rather than waste the last five rounds in her weapon. She couldn't risk being defenseless if one or more of the creatures crossed her path.

Amy reached the top of the large hill, which, to a city dweller like her, was considered a mountain, and she looked down at the town below. The instant she saw it, she ducked into the foliage out of instinct. She cursed herself for being foolish. It was miles away. Nothing could see her . . . unless the creatures down there were the smart kind, keeping a watch with binoculars.

There didn't appear to be any kind of road or trail leading from her position to the town. It looked as if the forest stretched all the way to the city limits. The town's proximity meant she was much more likely to come across the creatures than she had thought, even if she kept to the woods and tried to cut around it. She took a moment to steel herself before heading straight for the town. She was going there, and she was going to find the things she needed. Maybe, if it was mostly deserted, she could find a home or some kind of building to hole up in and finally get some rest.

As the sun began to sink from the sky, she made it to the edge of the town. She hadn't bumped into any creatures, and that was a good sign. She didn't see any in the parking lot of the gas station either. It was the town's most outlying building. It was damaged a bit on the outside, a few bullet holes and shattered windows, but from what she could tell it hadn't been ransacked. It called to her with the promise of food and other wonders.

For over forty minutes she stayed hidden, watching for any sign of trouble or movement before finally creeping out of the trees. The sound of her own footfalls on the pavement unnerved her. She glanced around, making sure she was still alone.

As Amy approached the glass doors of the station, she breathed a sigh of relief. Not only did there appear to be no one inside, but its aisles hadn't been trashed. She started to open the door when she heard a gun being cocked behind her.

"You can put your weapon down now, ma'am," a voice with a heavy Southern accent ordered. She dropped the .45 to the pavement and turned to see a very large gun pointed in her face. She guessed it might be a Magnum like Dirty Harry used in the movies, but wasn't sure. The man who held it was young, much younger than she was. He barely looked out of his teens. A mess of thick blond hair covered the top of his head and he wore a pair of filthy overalls over a white T-shirt that had seen better days. His appearance would have been comical if not for the way his deep-blue eyes watched her with such dead seriousness.

"I reckon you ain't one of *them*," he said, "but you sure as heck ain't from around here neither. Everybody here is dead or crazy. I ain't seen anyone else alive for a while now, so just where did you come from? Who in the heck are you, lady?"

"Amy. My name is Amy . . . I'm from New York," she added hastily.

The man laughed. "New York? You're a long way from home." He lowered the huge pistol and nodded, as if to himself. "Welcome to Virginia, Amy. We'd best get inside. Most of them things are gone from 'round here, but there are still a few stragglers left, I think. Best not to take chances, ya know?"

He reached past and opened the glass door for her. She started to head inside again, but he stopped her. "Don't forget your gun," he said, grinning and pointing at the weapon she'd dropped. "You may need it."

She retrieved the pistol and followed him to the back of the station, where he unlocked a massive metal door and ushered her inside.

"Place used to be a restaurant or something," he said, closing the door behind them. "When Pop and I bought the place, we turned the freezer into a backroom of sorts. We kept the door though. It's solid steel. Nice place for an office if you get robbed or the world suddenly goes F-ing bananas."

Amy didn't laugh at his joke. She was busy eyeing the room. It was small and furnished with a singular desk and what appeared to be a makeshift bunk; food and other supplies were stacked all around the space and packed in the corners.

"You've been living here . . . since the wave, I mean?"

"Yeah," he said. "No place else to go." He sat on the bunk and stared at her. "Guess we have a lot to talk about, huh, Amy?"

Hundreds of questions flooded her head, but the first one she asked was, "You said most of the creatures are gone from this town. Where did they go?"

"You mean the crazy people? Don't know. A group of guys drove into town and rounded them up—only the guys weren't normal either. The crazies didn't attack them. It was pretty messed up. I hid and stayed out of their way. Didn't see much. All I can tell you is that they went south, all together in one big group with the weird guys leading them."

"What's your name?" Amy suddenly blurted; it had just sunk in that she was safe, at least for the moment, and in the company of another real human being.

"My real name's Joseph Hunter, but I prefer Joe." He stood up from the bunk, and from one of the boxes that littered the room, he produced a bottle of water. "I'm sorry, Amy. I bet you're awfully hungry and tired from the look of you. Why don't you help yourself to some food and get some sleep. I'll keep watch outside. I have some things to tend to anyway. We can talk later, okay?"

He held out the water and Amy accepted it, drank most of it in a single gulp. "Thank you, Joe."

He nodded and shut the huge door on his way out.

Amy ate a meal of Vienna sausages, Pringles and crackers, then stretched out on the bunk. A smile lingered on her lips even as she slept.

As the days passed, Joe told her the story of the town of Bloomington. Like everywhere else, it had been plunged into darkness and chaos the night the wave struck the earth. Joe and his pop made their way to the church that night with the other survivors, but the holy place hadn't offered them any protection. The crazies outside attacked it time and time again, whittling down its defenders and their stockpile of ammunition. Then people inside began to change, and the pastor ordered that they be shot.

Finally Joe and his pop got of the church while they still could and made it here to their place of business. As far as they knew, by that time the entire town was crazy except for them. He and his pop had taken shelter here in this backroom, listening to the changed ones pounding on the metal door and howling for their blood.
Eventually the crazies must have realized they couldn't get inside, so they left the station. After that, there had been a few close calls, a few firefights with the mindless kind that couldn't shoot back, a few narrow escapes when they ventured into town for things that weren't kept on hand. But they managed, Joe informed her.

When Amy asked where his pop was now, Joe lowered his face into his hands and quietly told her that the old man had changed. "I got him with his own damn shotgun," Joe told her. "Buried him out behind the station." It was the hardest thing he had ever done in his life, and it troubled him still.

Joe imagined before he met Amy that he, too, would go insane, if not from the wave's effects then from just the pain of being alone. He'd been extremely happy to find Amy on his doorstep. He believed she saved his life by showing up when she did.

She was grateful for him too, and she was happy in this place. In a matter of days, she had invited Joe to share the bunk with her instead of making him sleep on the floor. They needed each other desperately to feel alive, to feel hopeful when they looked in each other's eyes. Joe wrapped his arms around her after they made love at night, made her feel safe and allowed her to think that someday things would be okay again.

What Joe had said about most of the creatures leaving town had proved true as well. As long as they were careful, he and Amy could venture almost anywhere they wanted, for supplies or to just get some fresh air and stretch their legs for a while. Well armed as they were, they never encountered more crazies than the two of them could handle. All they needed was each other, and together they could rebuild a little piece of the world they had lost to the wave.

16

THE conversation with the Freedom had been cut short when its orbit had taken it out of range, but the survivors of Def Con had learned a lot during the brief communication. It wasn't the real Freedom Station they were speaking to, at least not the one known to the public. The station identified itself as the Freedom II, a military-oriented prototype based on the original Freedom's design; it had still been under construction when the wave hit. Hank, the astronaut with whom they spoke, explained that the original Freedom had been destroyed by the energy blast and that only the experimental shielding of the Freedom II had kept the station functional enough to save the crew and allow them the necessary time to make repairs. Still, only Hank and one other member of the eight-man crew were left alive, and they wouldn't last long: they were quickly running out of supplies and were down to one-quarter power. Hank and Toni arranged a time to talk again when the station's orbit brought it back into range, and they traded downloads of information regarding what they knew of the post-wave world.

Sheena was beside herself. Now she could finally get the data she needed firsthand to see whether the wave's worst damage was over with. Nathanial, Geoff, Wade and Troy were howling for a celebration. Only Ian seemed reserved.

"It's a lie," he informed the crowd gathered in the control room. "There is no Freedom II." His words cut their excitement like a knife.

"How could you possibly know that?" Sheena asked as Nathanial clinched his fists and almost charged the CIA man.

"Lies and cover-ups used to be how I made a living, my dear, or have you forgotten? I know more truth about what America has and hasn't done in the last five years than all of you put together. Trust me. There is no Freedom II, nor will there ever be."

"You'll have to excuse me, Ian, if I don't take the word of a self-professed liar over what my own ears just heard," Geoff remarked.

"I'm inclined to agree with Geoff," Nathanial said. "If Hank isn't on the Freedom II, where is he? Who is he? It just doesn't make sense for it not to be true."

Ian sighed as if confronting a group of school children. "He's one of them, the infected."

"Oh, now that's just bullshit!" Troy roared. "Those creatures up there can't tell their asses from a hole in the ground. Have you ever seen one, just one of them, try to climb the fence? They could, you know, if they could think to do it."

Ian sighed again. "Before we lost D.C., I received a packet of downloaded data on the infected from a doctor named Buchanan. Perhaps you've heard of him? He was the chief science advisor to the president. His reports in the packet disputed his earlier conclusions about the radiation and its effects. Yes, it turns some people into monsters, the majority actually, while some like us, for whatever reason, remain sane. Buchanan believed the possibility of a third group to emerge, a thinking, reasoning breed of those snarling killers up there . . . " He pointed at the ceiling.

"Fuck off, Ian," Wade said. "You never told us this before."

Ian ignored the mechanic and added, "You all heard what you wanted to hear just now, not what you actually did. Hope can be a powerful weapon if wielded correctly."

"Get out of here, Ian," Sheena ordered. "Go back to your damn coffin in the armory!"

Ian nodded and walked toward the control room's exit. "Just promise me one thing," he said. "Do not give them our location until you've had more time to study the transmission and its origins."

"You're too late on that one, Ian," Toni called after him as he disappeared around the corner. "I already did."

After a moment of silence, Jeremy said, "What if he's right?" Suddenly he felt everyone's eyes on him. "No, I mean it. He's damn weird, I'll give you that, but he was CIA. Toni, can't we trace the source of the transmission? Find out where it came from?"

"Yeah," she answered quietly. "We can, but it'll take a lot of work."

"It would go a lot faster if we had your help, Nathanial." Jeremy glanced at the computer tech.

Nathanial shrugged. "Sure. Okay."

"In the meantime, I think all the rest of us have stuff to be working on, right?" Geoff said. "Dr. Leigh, why don't you continue your study of the wave; the rest of you, suit up. We're going up top. There are about forty more of those things at the fence again and I, for one, want them gone."

TROY shielded his eyes as he stepped out of the shed onto the main grounds of the base. The cacophony of the maddened creatures washed over him like a tide. "Jeez, Geoff, where the hell did you learn how to count?"

Geoff stepped out behind him and followed Troy's gaze. There weren't forty creatures outside the fence. They numbered closer to a hundred or more. The heavy, reinforced poles that held the fence in place swayed under the massive force.

"Got some gas no one seems to be usin' over in the garage," Wade offered.

Within minutes, Wade had a jury-rigged hose running from the large fuel tanks. Troy and Geoff helped him drag it out and turn it on.

"Yee-freakin'-hah!" Troy bellowed as he held the hose's nozzle, spraying down the creatures and the fence alike. "Anybody got a match?"

Wade shook his head and held up a silver Zippo. "This was my favorite lighter," he said, looking at it sadly. Then he lit it with a flick and tossed it at the fence.

Howls and screams rose up as a burst of blue flame swept through the ranks of the infected. Geoff shut off the hose, and the three of them stood in silence. Black smoke drifted into the heavens, and it was all Troy could do not to vomit from the odor of burning flesh.

"I don't believe it." Nathanial slumped over his computer screen. "What the hell does it mean?"

He and Toni had been able to trace the source of the message supposedly from Freedom II. It hadn't come from orbit at all but rather somewhere in South Carolina—only a few hundred miles away from the complex.

"It means Ian was right," Jeremy said. "Someone out there, whether it's those creatures or not, knows we're here now. They know we're alive and sane. Worse, they know how many of us there are."

"Oh God," Toni said, suddenly sobbing, "I am so sorry."

"Hey." Jeremy took her in his arms, and she nestled her face deeper into his shoulder, wetting his shirt. "It's all right. You didn't know."

"So what do we do now?" Nathanial asked.

Jeremy gritted his teeth. "We get ready. We get ready for whoever or whatever's coming."

17

THE doors of the lift opened onto the armory level. Jeremy had never been to this part of the base before and was taken aback by the condition of the hallway. Unlike the rest of Def Con, this area hadn't been repaired since the battle after the wave. The lighting was poor, as many of the lights had been shot out or were flickering badly, casting eerie strobes along the corridor. The metal walls themselves were scarred by some kind of explosion, as if someone had set off a grenade. Spent shell casings littered the floor as Jeremy made his way to the end of the hall. The entrance to the armory was open. Ian emerged from an unnoticed side corridor behind Jeremy.

"How the mighty have fallen," said the agent.

Jeremy whirled around at the sound of his voice.

"Calm down, young man. I'm not some monster come to end your life."

"Ian, you were right about the Freedom II."

"I know." He walked past Jeremy into the armory. "Would you care for some music? I find Wagner particularly relaxing in times like these."

"How did you know so quickly about the Freedom, I mean?"

Ian took a seat in a folding chair between the racks of weapons, which lined the walls of the vault-like room. "Their shielding," Ian said. He picked up a cold cup of tea sitting beside the chair and sipped at it. "There was a project like what they described, but it never got off the ground. The energy expenditure to generate the kind of field they mentioned was impossible. The project was scrapped because of it."

Jeremy took a seat on the floor in front of Ian. "Why do you stay down here so much?"

Ian laughed. "I'm not immune to the radiation like the rest of you seem to be."

Jeremy's mouth dropped open.

"This is the most shielded part of the complex. I choose to stay here because I value my life. Even so, I am finding it harder each day to resist the urges rising inside of me. Very soon I think you may find yourself in a position where my disposal will become vital to your own survival."

Jeremy shifted uncomfortably.

"I assure you," Ian said, "you will have to do it. None of the others, not even our good doctor, even suspect that I am unwell."

He paused and set down his tea. "I don't have any magical answers about who the people onboard the fictional Freedom II might be. I'm not God, Jeremy. But whether they are looters, survivors like us, or reasoning versions of the creatures outside, they will be coming. Will they bring death or hope? I don't know. Personally, I believe hope died the second the wave touched our world."

"Will you help us get ready for them?"

"There's nothing I can do, Jeremy. I'm certainly not about to go up top again, and I don't think you can really ask that of me. Geoff is the military expert. He can handle it."

"And that's it? That's all you have to offer?" Jeremy shook his head. "Don't you care about anyone?"

"Yes," Ian answered, "I care about me, and either way, I am dying. Now good day."

Ian picked up a book and opened it to the chapter marked with a piece of ribbon. Jeremy didn't argue. He got to his feet and went in search of Geoff.

Something had to be done, and it looked like it was up to them to do it. His life and the world he knew had been taken from him once; he wasn't going to give up this place too—not without a fight.

18

"IT can't be done," Geoff slurred, dropping the empty jug to the garage floor. "This base was never designed to be a defensible position out here. It's a damn bomb shelter, kid, a really high-tech one, but still just a shelter."

Jeremy grabbed Geoff by the front of his uniform and tried to yank him to his feet. As drunk as Geoff was, he pulled Jeremy's arm behind his back with incredible ease as he stood. "Kid, it's all open space and fields up here. The fence is the only real obstacle to anyone who wants onto the grounds. If these things show up with welding torches and burn through the perimeter and the outer seal in the shed, then maybe they deserve to have us for dinner." Geoff released his hold on Jeremy and staggered out into the sunlight. "Jesus, kid, I just roasted a mob of people alive to save your ass. What more do you want from me?"

"Where are Troy and Wade? Maybe they'll listen to reason."

"Reason!" Geoff spun around to face Jeremy. "There ain't no reason left anymore, kid. Just death, death and the dying."

Jeremy drew the .45 from the holster on his belt and leveled it at Geoff. "Do you want to die so badly, Geoff?" He shook the gun. "I can make it happen, right here, right now."

Geoff's eyes narrowed, and he finally nodded. "Okay. We'll play it your way, Jeremy. We might as well go out fighting." He stumbled over and threw an arm around Jeremy's shoulders. "I just hope to God you or Wade can come up with a way to make a stand up here. I'm shit out of ideas."

Outside the fence, three new infected knelt, gnawing on the charred remains of their less fortunate brethren.

NATHANIAL Richards sat alone in the control room. He looked at his watch; two hours until the next message from the Freedom was due. It was far more than enough time for what he had in mind. His fingers danced over the keys of his computer and the complex was his.

He was not a man given to worry. Born to the CEO of one of America's leading pharmaceutical corporations and to a mother whose life revolved around him due to the constant absence of his father, he considered himself blessed. Nathanial never wanted for anything. Even in college, when the police had raided his dorm room and found his stash of narcotics, his father had swept in and made it all go away. What was a petty possession charge to a man who carried senators, bought and paid for, in his pocket? His parents had always been there to save him, and he had never doubted that they would come. But they were gone now. No more bailouts. Political power and money meant nothing these days.

Outside of his family, the only true friends Nathanial had ever known were computers. From the time he could type, machines were a part of his life. They gave him his own power and control, but the wave had taken even them from him. Oh sure, there were computers all over Def Con, but the web and cyberspace no longer existed. He'd lost everything. Nathanial was alone, and death was coming for him. The transmission from the Freedom II had fired his hopes that the old world would return, but now he knew deep in his heart that the people on the other end of the transmission were evil incarnate, and he wasn't going to let them take the last thing he had left: his soul.

Weeks ago, he had been forced to disable the base's self-destruct system to save himself and everyone trapped with him. The codes had been easy to break for someone like him, and they were even easier to manipulate now. Def Con itself would be his shield when the darkness came, a shield of fire and retribution.

His soul would remain his own.

WADE finished covering the last mine as yet another one of the infected emerged from the trees. He didn't waste the time or the ammo to dispose of it. Instead he broke into a run for the gates. As he passed through, Troy and Jeremy slammed them shut behind him. The psycho threw itself against the barbed wire, clawing at the fence and foaming pink at the mouth.

"That does it." Wade collapsed to the earth, out of breath. "We're as ready as we're going to be."

They had spent the last few hours littering the area outside of the fence with mines and barricading the doors of the garage. "As long as those things out there don't trip all the mines before our company shows, we should at least have a chance," Geoff said. He had drunk cup after cup of black coffee, trying to sober up while supervising the others.

"Don't worry," Troy said, patting his .30-.06, which was equipped with a sniper scope. "Me and my friend here won't let them."

"Guess all we can do is wait," Jeremy said. "It's almost time for the Freedom II to make contact again."

"You go on and be there with the rest of them when it happens," Geoff urged as Troy climbed to his position atop the garage. "Us three pretty much got things covered up here."

Jeremy nodded. He took one last glance at their work and then headed for the shed and the outer seal leading into the complex.

19

TONI was the first to join Nathanial in the control room. He looked haggard, as if he'd never left his station since the Freedom's first transmission. Jeremy and Sheena came in minutes later. No one asked where Ian was and Jeremy was thankful for it. He hadn't decided what to do about the former CIA agent's condition and didn't see any reason at this point to add the worry to the rest of their collective woes. "Everything ready?" he asked.

"We're set up to trace them the second they make contact," Nathanial assured him. They all watched the communications console as the figures on the time display flashed and changed to the appointed hour.

"Come in, Def Con. This is Freedom II. Do you copy us?

Over.""Go!" Jeremy shouted at Nathanial, and the computer engineer began the trace.

Toni hesitantly opened a response channel. "This is Def Con. We copy you, Freedom II."

Seconds ticked by in silence. No reply. Nathanial indicated that he'd managed to get a fix on the origins of the transmission. All the color had bled from his face. "It's coming from a point just two miles south of here and closing slowly . . . Sweet Jesus. They really are coming for us."

TROY saw the convoy first from his spot atop the garage. A line of pickups, four-wheel drives and jeeps bounced up the winding gravel road, growing ever closer. Troy counted thirteen vehicles in all, and numerous men and women on foot jogged along at their sides. The thing that bothered him, though, was the infected's lack of interest in the convoy. He knew for a fact that there were packs of the creatures still out there in the woods, but for whatever reason they were not attacking. It could only mean one of two things: either these people knew a way to control or ward off the creatures, or they themselves were so poisoned by the radiation in the atmosphere that the infected didn't recognize them as human.

Using hand signs, Troy gestured what he saw to Geoff and Wade, who were concealed in the remaining bushes just inside the fence. Then he said a prayer for them all and checked the chamber of his rifle to make sure it was ready.

"COME in, Freedom II. Come in," Toni repeated over the open frequency.

"Give it up," Nathanial suggested. "They got what they wanted: a definitive fix on our exact position. They're done talking now."

Toni's shoulders sagged with defeat. Her fears were confirmed, and in that moment she knew she was the one who had called this new terror upon them. She turned to look for Jeremy, but he was already gone from the control room.

IT was one of the joggers rather than one of the vehicles who stumbled onto the most outlaying mine. The explosion and the rain of pulpy, charred flesh brought the convoy to a halt. People began to pour out of the vehicles and leave them behind.

Troy swore under his breath. Whoever was leading the mob knew what they were doing. The working trucks were too valuable to lose, and by approaching the base on foot it would cut down the damage the mines could inflict on the transports.

The .30-.06 propped against Troy's shoulder had a pretty good range. He sighted one of the joggers as the moving mass of attackers began to pick up the pace. Troy put a round through his target's throat just as the mob reached the main section of the minefield. Explosion after explosion tossed dirt and body parts into the air, but the people just kept coming, without even pausing to tend to their wounded.

In the bushes, Wade took a deep breath and made his peace with God. The fastest of the joggers had already reached the fence. He saw one of them toss something at the barbed wire, and then his world went white.

Troy watched in horror as his friend was blown apart, along with a large section of the fence. The attackers flowed through like ants. He fired off a last shot with the rifle, then tossed the weapon aside and tried to scurry down from the garage roof.

Geoff remained hidden the whole time. He waited in the bushes as the attackers ran past on both sides. They moved like men but they weren't really human anymore. Their battle cries were the snarls of maddened dogs, and their skin was tinted yellow with sickness. He caught a glimpse of one's eyes. There were no whites left, just a sickening bloodshot mass.

Geoff switched his AK-47 to full auto and stood up, spraying the backs of the fifteen or so that had made it by him. They crumpled like weeds before a scythe.

A rifle cracked and a bullet ripped through the back of Geoff's shoulder. He whirled around and charged at the mob head-on, his rifle blazing and spitting empty shell casings. He made it a few steps before his bullet-ridden corpse toppled to the ground, rolling from its momentum.

Troy, down from the roof, saw the base's opening—Jeremy was trying to come out. Troy shoved him back down. "Lock it!" he yelled.

"But Geoff . . . "

"He's dead. Wade too." Troy climbed down and pushed Jeremy aside. He typed in the code, and something thumped hard against the hatch. A gun chattered and bullets pinged off the metal.

Both Jeremy and Troy ducked instinctively. "Shit!" Troy grabbed Jeremy and tugged him deeper into the base. "If they've got the gear with them to cut through between the outer seal and the inner lock . . . we've got an hour, maybe two, tops."

"How many are up there?" Jeremy asked. The look on Troy's face told him all he needed to know.

DEEP in the bowels of Def Con, Ian threw down the book he was reading and screamed. Spit flew from his mouth as his head shook uncontrollably. He leapt up from his chair and ran at the armory door, but his shoe snagged a nearly invisible tripwire he'd set in place the day before; the armory's lights turned red as its huge door slammed shut in front of him. Ian pounded his fists against it until the bones of his hands were shattered, and then he started to use his head.

☣

TROY and Jeremy burst into the control room, nearly scaring Toni to death. "What the hell?" Nathanial bellowed.

"They're cutting through the outer seal," Jeremy said, panting for breath. "The others are dead."

"Nat, are any of the exterior cameras still working?" Troy asked as he closed on the engineer.

"A few . . . not the one in the shed."

"Bring 'em online. I have a bad feeling our friends up there aren't just going to be sitting on their asses in the time it takes them to cut their way in here."

"Okay, I've got two cameras reporting operational. Both of them are a good bit away from the gates though."

"Put the closest onscreen."

The huge wall display flashed to life, showing a small group of attackers, who appeared to be reloading their weapons. In the background, other attackers stood watching something beyond the camera's field of vision.

"Can you pan around and see what those others are so interested in?" Troy asked.

"I can try." Nathanial worked at his keyboard, and the image flickered and bounced as the camera slowly turned. Three of the attackers stood outside the fence amidst a pack of infected. The creatures cowered around them like pets.

"I don't believe it," Troy said, rubbing his forehead. "Damn, those fuckers are smart."

Nathanial furrowed his brow. "Huh? I don't get it."

"They're rounding up the infected in the woods. When they cut through the seal, they're not just going to rush in here. There's no sense in *them* risking their lives. They'll let the mindless ones come in first, hoping they'll either overrun us or at least weaken our defenses."

"Aren't they all infected?" Toni asked.

Nathanial answered before Troy had a chance to. "Yes, but they're not the same. These new ones aren't at all like the ones we've had to deal with in the past. They're much more advanced, like they're evolving back into something much closer to what we are, just not as nice. And certainly not above using their lesser brethren as weapons or cannon fodder, or whatever you want to call it."

"Somebody should get Ian. We're going to need all the help we can get," Sheena suggested.

"No," Jeremy replied, "Ian's fine where he's at."

"We should at least warn him," Toni added.

"Ian's fine." Jeremy moved to take hold of Toni. "Trust me, he's where he wants to be."

"Jeremy." Troy motioned him over to a table in the control room. Troy ripped a map off the wall and spread it across the tabletop. "You don't have to die here. None of us do. There's a back way out."

"That's impossible!" Sheena snapped. "If there was another entrance I would know about it."

Troy ignored her and pointed to a spot on the map. "There's a tunnel inside the ventilation system here. Wade found it a few days ago. It's sealed up with an iron grate, but I think you can get through it. It opens into the back of the garage."

"The garage? Those things are all over the place up there," Nathanial pointed out.

"They're spread out pretty good though, and most of them will probably follow the normal infected in here once they get through the inner door. If you wait until they get into the base, by the time you get up there you'll at least have a chance."

"What's with all the *you* stuff?"

"Jeremy, someone has to stay here to slow them down and make them work for every inch of the base they take. That's me. I'm the only real soldier left."

"Troy—" Jeremy started, but Nathanial interrupted him.

"I'm staying too. So is Sheena. I'm not running, Jeremy, and Sheena can't. She'd just slow you down and get you killed."

Sheena nodded. "You and Toni go on," she ordered. "Make sure you take the time to gather up the things you'll need if you get past those things."

"No!" Toni cried, squatting beside Sheena's chair to embrace her.

Sheena didn't return the hug. "Go on. You've only got one chance at this and time's running out."

Jeremy pulled Toni to her feet and looked back at Troy. There was so much he wanted to say but the words wouldn't come. Troy smiled and shot him a mock salute. In spite of the tears burning in his eyes, Jeremy laughed. Then he nodded and led Toni out to gather what they would need.

20

THE outer seal clanged as it dropped inside the corridor below, and minutes later a well-placed charge blew the inner door off its hinges. The mindless ones flooded down the passageway and into the base. Troy waited for them in the only unblocked passage to the control room.

A man dressed in the tatters of a tuxedo came tearing around the corner, pink saliva flying from his mouth as he saw Troy and howled madly at him.

Troy raised the automatic shotgun in his hands and fired, cutting the man in two at the waist. A woman in a bloodstained jogging suit was next, and Troy splattered her brains all down the corridor. When the shotgun clicked empty, he snatched up his M-16 and retreated towards the control room, firing on full auto into the increasing tide as he went.

In the control room, Sheena struggled clumsily to ready the handgun Troy had given her.

"You're not going to need that," Nathanial told her as the gunfire on the other side of the door was replaced by the sound of Troy screaming.

Sheena looked up at Nathanial and understood.

Finally the door burst open and a woman with matted gray hair and a bleeding hole in her left cheek led the creatures inside. Nathanial stabbed at his keyboard one final time.

JEREMY kicked the grate loose and leapt down into the garage. A quick glance told him that the area was clear of the infected—both breeds. He turned and helped Toni climb out of the vent.

Only a couple of vehicles were left, and only one that he knew for sure still ran. He tossed his pack into the jeep. "Get in," he told Toni, "and hold on."

Apparently one of the thinking infected had heard the thunk of the falling grate from inside the garage and was now opening the large doorway to check it out. Jeremy ran him down as he tore out into the dying rays of the setting sun.

The few attackers who'd stayed up top were caught completely off-guard. Jeremy took advantage of their confusion and plowed through them. He spun the jeep's steering wheel, making a sharp turn toward the gardens and the rear fence. He was already deep in the fields when the first shots began to ping off the tail of the jeep.

He reached over and shoved Toni down in her seat. "Hold on!" he yelled as the jeep streaked towards the fence. He ducked under the dashboard as best he could, leaning over in his seat at the last second.

The jeep tore through the barbed wire, dragging a section of the fence as it made it clear. One of the tires blew out, but the jeep continued to roar forward until it crashed headlong into a tree.

Jeremy rolled out of the driver's seat. His back felt like it had been ripped to shreds, and blood leaked from large gashes the barbed wire had cut in his T-shirt. He looked over his shoulder to see the attackers giving chase. "Toni, are you all right? We have to move!"

She didn't answer and suddenly he realized she was no longer in the jeep. The barbed wire had caught her and had yanked her out. Her mangled corpse lay several yards back, tangled hopelessly in the fencing the jeep had carried with it. Jeremy knew she was dead from a single glance.

He grabbed up his pack from the rear of the vehicle and slung it onto his shoulder as the attackers opened fire again.

Suddenly the earth itself heaved under his feet and threw him into the woods as fire blossomed in a giant cloud from where Def Con had lain below it.

EPILOGUE

WHEN Jeremy came to, night had fallen in earnest. The mob had been reduced to a scattered corpse here and there. Slowly dying flames could be seen inside the remainder of the fence around the Def Con complex.

Jeremy coughed and spat blood onto the grass beside him. He looked up at the full moon, and a visible shadow stretched across it, dampening its glow. Jeremy wasn't a physicist, but he knew something wasn't right about it. His mind groped for an explanation of the strange shadow until he remembered an old episode of the *Outer Limits* he'd seen and recalled Sheena's warnings about the fragments of the wave. He knew one of them must have made contact with the sun, causing it to go nova millions, if not billions, of years early. The side of the earth facing the sun was probably an inferno of death, and even as he sat there watching the moon, a tide of fire crept its way towards him as the earth turned. He had only hours left to live, but he knew his death would be quick and he took comfort in that fact. He removed a bottle of water from his pack and twisted off its lid. The night was so beautiful, and since there was nowhere to run, he decided to make the most of it.

AMY and Joe sat on the station's roof. It was a safe place to be outside at night, a place where they didn't really have to worry about the creatures.

Joe spread out the picnic blanket as Amy got the food ready. He had cooked up some rabbit meat during the day, and Amy, though still learning, had made something close to being fresh baked bread. Joe sat on the blanket and popped open a bottle of wine. He smiled as he filled a glass for Amy and passed it to her. She took it even though she couldn't drink it, and she pretended to be thankful for Joe's sake.

He sipped at his wine as she looked him over. Amy was nervous about telling him. She had mixed feelings on the matter herself. Part of her was thrilled and overjoyed, but her rational mind questioned how wise it was to bring a child into this nightmare. She had to tell him though. It wasn't as if she could hide it much longer, and he deserved to know. Amy figured she would never get a chance to do it more perfect than tonight.

She reached for his hand. He was glancing up at the stars. The sky was odd this evening, the stars different somehow. Amy placed a palm on his cheek and gently turned his face so she could look deep into his eyes. "Joe," she said. "I have something to tell you . . . "

DEAD WEST

PROLOGUE

"**RUN**!" Mark shouted.

Brent's legs pumped as he raced to catch up to the train and Mark's outstretched hand. He could hear the growls of the dead behind him, but he didn't dare glance over his shoulder to see how close they were. Instead he poured everything he had into a final burst of speed. Mark grabbed him and pulled him onto the train.

Brent collapsed, struggling for breath as Mark, standing above him, opened up on their pursuers with his Winchester. He picked off the closest ones, his rifle spitting out spent casings.

The train gained speed and the dead fell farther and farther behind.

"Sweet Lord," Brent blurted out. "That was too close."

Mark laughed, propping his weapon against the inner railing of the car. "It's what you get for volunteering for this job."

"Maybe," Brent replied. "But that doesn't mean I have to like it."

He got to his feet and dusted himself off. "Damn. The dead aren't supposed to be this close to the border yet. No one knew they'd over-run Bloomington already. Last time we sent out a recon party, they were two towns over."

Mark nodded. "They're coming. There's no stopping them. I don't care what anyone says—it's only a matter of time until they make it to the East. Ain't nothing gonna stop them. Not even the river."

"Well, we ain't goin' down like those cavalry boys did. We'll hold the line. We've got to."

"You're lying to yourself boy. The West belongs to those things now. We can't guard the whole Mississippi River. Soon enough the dead will be across it and in the cities too."

"How can you believe that?" Brent asked.

"Simple. I believe in God. This is the End Times. It's gotta be. Hell on Earth and all that comes with it, boy. I've made my peace. Hope you've made your peace with Him too."

Suddenly, Mark and Brent were tossed about as the train's brakes began to squeal. They clutched the car's rails, trying their best not to tumble off onto the tracks.

"What the hell?" Mark screamed as the train stopped. They could hear shouting from the steam engine.

Mark grabbed his rifle, which by some miracle hadn't been lost on the tracks, then he and Brent hopped off the car and went to see what was happening. Several other soldiers from the train's small contingent were standing around, cursing. A massive tree blocked the railway. It would take too long to remove the trunk and branches from the tracks.

Mark motioned for Brent, and the two approached Captain Stephenson, who stood among the men inspecting the tree.

"Are we running or standing?" Mark asked.

Stephenson whirled on them. "Soldier, you better watch your mouth or you'll be dead before those rotting bastards ever get here."

"Yes, sir," Mark said, grinding his teeth. "But you didn't answer my question."

This was Stephenson's first command behind the quarantine line. He was sweating under the pressure, forced with only two choices that were pretty much suicide. Finally, he looked Mark in the eye. "We're standin'! I think it's time we gave the dead back some of the hell they've given us."

Stephenson addressed the thirty-five men standing around him. "Get the Gatling set up on the rear car. Make sure the damn gunner is somebody who's used one before. Everybody else, load up with as much ammo as you can in your pockets and form a defensive firing line flanking that car. Let's show those monsters the US Army won't go down easy!"

Everyone took up their positions as extra guns were loaded and placed within easy reach. Mark manned the Gatling in the center of the line, and Brent, hunched on the dirt with his rifle aimed at the horizon, found himself missing the company of the gruff and burly old-timer.

The dead came into view. Hundreds of them stampeding towards the train and its small cluster of defenders.

"Hold you fire!" Mark shouted.

Stephenson shot him a glare but knew it was an order that needed to be given. "Aim for their heads!" he added reluctantly, giving a nod in Mark's direction.

As soon as the dead entered firing range, the Gatling gun started blazing, tearing into the middle of their ranks. Everyone else tried to pick their shots more carefully, making sure the ones they aimed for wouldn't be getting back up.

Not even the spinning barrels of the Gatling could slow the dead's charge. They trampled the bodies of the fallen until they slammed into the defensive line without mercy. The line broke, half of the soldiers knocked to the ground under the gnashing teeth of the dead. A few tried to fight but died instantly as the dead overwhelmed them.

Grasping, eager hands yanked Mark off the car from behind the Gatling, and the old man disappeared in the sea of the dead.

Brent ran, tossing his empty rifle aside and jerking his Colt free from the holster on his belt. His feet crunched gravel as he darted down the length of the train. When he reached the fallen tree he knew there was no way in hell he could jump it. So he veered to the right and took off into the woods, with more than a dozen of dead giving chase.

Sweat rolled off his face and skin. In desperation, he hopped onto a tall tree and started to climb. Cold hands closed on his legs and ankles, and a set of yellow teeth cut through his uniform and into his thigh.

"God, forgive me," Brent pleaded as he pressed the Colt to the side of his head. He pulled the trigger, and his limp form fell into the waiting mob below.

ONE

GRANT looked up from the article he was composing as Edgar entered the room. He knew from the smirk on Edgar's face whatever news the man was about to share would be bad. Though they'd worked together at Harper's throughout the end of the Civil War, they'd never gotten along.

Edgar pulled out a chair and took a seat across from Grant without asking if he was intruding.

Grant met Edgar's eyes as the man stared at him. "May I help you?"

"I just wanted to tell you personally you're being reassigned. The paper needs someone out in the field to cover the new war raging in the West from the frontlines and—"

"This isn't a war," Grant interjected. "Men aren't killing men. It's a plague. They're just quarantining off half the bloody country to contain it."

Edgar cleared his throat. "Call it whatever you want, Grant, but to the paper and the government it's a war. The plague that's ravaged the frontier is working its way here, and if the army can't stop it then God help us all." Edgar reclined in his chair, tipping it off the floor. "Almost the entire army is stationed along the length of the Mississippi River, trying to hold the border between us and the dead. Good men are dying out there every day. To me, that's a war too."

"What do you want from me, Edgar? Did you just want to see how I would react when you told me I was going?"

Edgar ignored him. "The 112th regiment is about to make a push westward to see how bad things really are on the other side, and to exterminate as many of those *things* as they can. I want you to go with them. As I said, we need someone out there so that people here can know what's happening in the West. You've been in the field before. Hell, if I recall correctly, you claim you actually fought in some of the battles you covered near the end of the last war."

"Not by choice," Grant muttered.

"Go home and pack your bags. You'll be leaving first thing in the morning to meet up with the 112th and the main force of the push west. I'll have all the papers you'll need ready by then."

"Yes, sir," Grant answered coldly.

Edgar got up and vanished into the halls of Harper's, leaving Grant in peace.

He sat still for a moment, letting his new assignment sink in. If even half of the reports over the past few months were true, he was heading into Hell itself. The dead owned the West now. Allegedly, some tribes of Indians still held out against them, but those stories were unconfirmed and off the record. The paper didn't want people believing that savages could outlast civilized man, because without a doubt the western states were lost. The plague had swept through them like wildfire on a prairie, turning everyone who contracted it into a walking corpse intent only on devouring the living and spreading the plague.

Many people believed this was the End of Days as described in the Bible. New churches opened their doors here in the East every day, and revivals seemed a nonstop occurrence. Grant was not a religious man and the whole mess stunk of desperation, but even he had to admit this was like nothing the human race had ever faced in all of recorded history.

He pushed his chair back from his desk and walked over to collect his coat from the hook by the door. If there was any real hope left to be found, he would find it. If nothing else, his readers deserved the truth; he could at least give them that.

Five days later Grant arrived in Franklin. The 112th had beaten him there and were already well prepared for the East's first major counteroffensive against the plague. The plan, if it could be called that, was simply to cross the Mississippi, push as far west as possible and kill everything they came across, then fall back to reinforce the border until another offensive could be launched. The military command knew the dead didn't breed. They wanted to thin out their numbers and, step by step, expand the border westward until they reached the Pacific, making the US whole once more.

The 112th was just one of many regiments sent across the river at various points, but it was newly formed and composed of mainly green troops who'd never seen combat. Grant wondered if Edgar had assigned him to that particular regiment because they were the least likely to make it back.

He shook the dark thoughts from his head as he marched up the steps of the town's administrative building, headed to report in to the regiment's commanding officer, General Peter Alves. Alves had the reputation of being a hard ass who got things done, a competent leader despite his personality and lack of social skills. He'd climbed the ranks quickly, but always seemed to end up with the worst or most dangerous missions on his plate.

As soon as Grant walked in, a young man dressed in an aide's uniform rushed to meet him. "Mr. Grant?" he asked, outstretching his hand.

"Yes." Grant shook with him. "How did you know?"

"You were expected, sir. Besides, you sure ain't from around here. No one here wears clothes as fancy as yours. You just had to be from New York, sir."

Grant laughed. "I'm here to report in to General Alves."

"I know, sir. The general's busy though. I'm sorry. However, he did leave orders as to where you're being accommodated."

"Accommodated?"

"Sorry, sir. I mean as to which platoon you'll be traveling with."

Grant felt his stomach turn. The general was putting him off in more ways than one. "You mean I won't be traveling with the general himself?"

"No. Let's see . . . You're being placed under the care of Sergeant Robert Hank. He's a veteran, sir. The general said he'd be more than able to not only ensure your safety while you're with us, but also be able to show you what it's really like to be fighting the dead."

"Wonderful." Grant faked a smile. Things just kept getting better and better. "Where can I find this Sergeant Hank?"

"He and his men are in the barracks just across town. Do you want me to escort you there?"

"No," Grant said, and he turned and walked out of the building. He was just about done being cast aside, and he was having a tough time holding his anger in check. Surely, he figured, things couldn't get any worse.

THE dead thing raised its head to look at the surrounding soldiers, straining against the ropes that held it to the post in the middle of the training field.

"Fire!" Hank ordered.

A chorus of rifle cracks erupted as Winchesters spat empty shell casings and soldiers pumped fresh rounds into their chambers. When the cacophony ended, the dead thing still twitched and rolled its head back and forth, emitting a low, hoarse moan.

Hank spun to face the dozen new recruits who'd just riddled the thing's body with holes. "What the hell's the problem here?" he asked, screaming in the face of the closest private. "I ordered you men to kill that thing! Why isn't it dead?"

No one answered.

"You want to know why?" Hank drew his revolver and put a bullet into the dead thing's forehead. Its body slumped, limp against the post. "You didn't shoot the damn thing in the head!" Hank pointed across the river at the other shore, far off in the distance. "And when you're over there, if you don't shoot for the head you won't just be wasting ammo and my time, you'll be dead just like *it*."

Hank lowered his voice. "A headshot is the only way to take one of those things down and make sure it stays that way." He cut his normal sermon short as a man in an expensive suit approached the training area. "All of you back here in an hour. We'll try this shit again then. Dismissed!"

The privates scattered in fear of their sergeant's rage, and the man in the suit clapped. "Commendable speech," he said, not offering to shake hands. "I'm Jacob Grant from Harper's; I was told you'd be taking care of me when we go across."

"You're going to have to take care of yourself, mister. These greenhorns ain't worth a load of cow dung yet. It'll be all I can do to take care of myself."

"Nonetheless, I suppose I'm going to be a part of your platoon now, according to General Alves." Grant's eyes came to rest on the corpse tied to the post; it looked as if it had been rotting for days. "My God . . . That thing really took a dozen rounds and was still alive?"

"No, it wasn't alive. But it was still hungry. They'll keep coming at you as long as they can move."

"But it's dead now?"

"Dead as a doornail. Destroy their brain and they're restin' peaceful again like God intended."

Grant kept staring at the corpse.

"Relax," Hank assured him. "The only way you can get the plague is if one of them bites you or scratches you up pretty good." He looked Grant up and down. "You sure you're up for this, newsboy?"

"Somebody has to be. People have a right to know the truth about all this. Maybe then we can make sense of it all."

Hank laughed. "Right." He realized he was still holding his revolver and tucked it into the holster on his belt. "We ship out at first light, newsboy. I imagine you've already been on the road a while, so I suggest you try to get some rest. There may not be any for a long time once we get started. I'll show you where you can bed down."

The two men walked away from the corpse, leaving it dripping blood onto the field.

TWO

AS the sun rose above the Mississippi River, a line of heavy streamers and ferries discharged their living cargo onto the western bank. A few dozen cavalrymen hit the shore first, galloping off into the trees to make sure the surrounding area was clear of the dead; a line of infantrymen followed off the boats. Over two hundred strong, the men fanned out along the shore, taking aim at the tree line to create a safe perimeter for the rest of the regiment to come on land. The whole area was a flurry of activity. Officers ran back and forth, barking orders as Gatling gun emplacements were set up and everyone dug in. Soon the beachhead was secure, with no sign of the enemy. Over a thousand soldiers stood waiting for further orders, eager to push forward.

General Alves and his superiors were well aware this would not be a conventional war. There would be no organized resistance from the enemy. The regiment was to split its allotment of personnel into smaller search-and-destroy platoons of fifty or more men. These platoons would fan apart in a sweeping motion, moving westward ahead of the main force. Many of the platoons would be assigned a specific region or town to investigate along the way before meeting at a pre-established rally point and returning to the main force.

To form up their platoon, Grant and his men fell in with another squad led by an officer named Simon Wayne. Wayne was a distinguished graduate of West Point and would be in charge of their unit with Hank as his second. The group consisted of fifty men total, and their assigned destination was a town named Canton.

Finally the orders came and the regiment was on the move, breaking apart as it marched. As Grant's platoon broke off to head for their objective, he took one last look at the shrinking body of the main force, hoping whomever had thought up this operation had known what they were doing.

The platoon was over a day out and two days from Canton before they found their first sign of the dead. A corpse lay in the middle of the road, sprawled out beside a wagon, which looked to have been headed east before it lost a wheel. The body was badly decomposed, but one could see that more than the birds had been at it. Pieces of the man lay everywhere, as if they'd been carried off, gnawed on, and discarded. A young private named Ben fell to his knees near Grant, and his lunch splattered the dirt road. Many of the men in the platoon covered their mouths while others stood strong with disciplined faces of stone.

"Damn, boy!" a soldier named Clint said to Ben. "No sense in getting all torn up about it. He's dead and gone."

Grant turned to face Clint, clenching his fists and resisting the urge to strike him in the jaw. Instead, he pulled out his notebook and pencil and began to sketch the horrific scene.

Dalton, one of the platoon's two trackers, knelt beside the body to inspect it. "Been dead about two days. From the looks of things, I'd say there were five of the dead. Took him apart fairly easily too, as if they caught him off-guard. Poor soul didn't even have time to go for his shotgun in the wagon."

"What do we do?" someone asked.

"Bury him," Wayne ordered.

Grant approached Hank. "Why do you think he didn't get up? As one of them?"

"Look at his head."

Indeed, a patch of the man's skull was caved in. Apparently as the things had pulled him to the ground, he had smashed his head on the large rocks bordering the road.

Hank and Grant watched the men hastily dig a shallow grave in the soft dirt of the woods. No one wanted to touch the body. They had all been taught how the plague spread and they knew it couldn't be contracted by merely touching one of the infected, but not all fears are rational, Grant imagined. Finally, he offered to move the body himself. Hank helped him hoist the corpse and toss it into the sad excuse for a grave. No sooner than they were done Wayne began shouting orders.

"Okay, people, let's keep moving. Be ready. We know they're around these parts for sure now."

The platoon reassembled into a loose marching formation and continued on.

Just before dusk, they made camp in a clearing near the road. The troops were on edge whether they showed it or not. Wayne ordered them to kindle numerous fires, preferring the safety of the light over concealment. If the fires brought the dead to them, it would be a good thing, even if it would be hard to see the enemy beyond the glow.

Grant took a seat at one of the larger fires beside Ben. The private couldn't be more than nineteen years old.

"This your first time in the field?" Grant asked.

Ben nodded. "I signed up after the slave war. I want to do something for my country, to make a difference in this world somehow. I didn't think it would be killing dead men."

"It's better than killing the living," Grant assured him.

Ben looked at him, his mouth dangling open in shock. "You fought in the Civil War?"

"I did. I just wasn't a soldier. The problem with battles is that they pull everyone into them, whether you're a non-combatant or not, doesn't matter. No one takes the time to ask or care."

Grant gestured at Ben's weapon. "That's one of the new Golden Boys isn't it?"

Ben handed him the rifle. "Winchester 1866. Tube magazine, fifteen shots before reloading, sharper accuracy, and much less likely to misfire than a musket."

Grant whistled as he examined the rifle. "If we had these a few years ago, the war would've been over a whole lot sooner."

Ben smiled and reached to take the rifle as Grant gave it back. "You're not carrying a weapon?"

"No. If things get bad enough for me to need one, I expect there will be plenty lying around for me to use."

A rifle cracked on the other side of the camp. Both Ben and Grant hopped to their feet. The lingering rays of the dying sun, combined with the firelight, lit the clearing well enough to show what was happening at the edge of the camp. A pack of dead men and women, numbering in the dozens, had emerged from the woods and were darting towards the camp perimeter, howling like starved animals in a rage. The sentries and several other men were already letting them have it. Rifles blazed, their chambers spitting casings onto the grass. The dead weren't even slowing; in fact, they seemed to be gaining speed, as if spurred on by resistance.

"Aim for their heads!" Wayne was roaring from behind the hastily assembled firing line. Hank shoved the shouting officer aside and aimed his Winchester at the dead. His shot blew open the skull of a middle-aged man at the head of the pack, spraying blood and bone into the air. The man fell, trampled under the feet of the dead behind him.

Hank's action snapped the other soldiers out of their panic by showing them the dead could die. It happened too late though. Only around ten of the things took hits to the head before the pack collided with the firing line. Men screamed as cold, rotting hands dug into their flesh. A couple of them were knocked to the ground and fed upon while the rest tried to retreat.

Wayne drew his sidearm and dispatched an elderly woman chewing on the cheek of a private. "Fall back!" he urged as a man missing an eye leapt at him.

Hank stepped between Wayne and his attacker at the last second, batting the thing aside with the butt of his rifle. As he fell on top of the creature, he tore a knife from a sheath in the top of his boot and, with all his weight, drove the blade to its hilt into the thing's skull.

Grant turned to check on Ben, but the boy was gone. He'd raced forward to join the melee. Grant cursed. So much for his plan of just picking a weapon off the dead. He felt exposed and vulnerable. He knew he was too, and he had to do something—anything. He couldn't just stand here in the open. *To hell with it*, he thought, and he charged into battle.

Not far from him, a dead woman had pinned a soldier to the ground and was trying to get a clean bite at his throat. Grant tore her off the man and shoved her away. She was on her feet faster than he could believe.

Only the private's quick recovery saved Grant's life. By luck more than skill, the soldier managed to put a bullet into her left eye as she threw herself at Grant, and just like that the camp was quiet once more.

Grant took a deep breath, recollecting himself as he appraised the situation. Nine soldiers in the platoon had died in the attack. Another fifteen or more received bites or wounds and were just as dead. It was only a matter of time. Grant saw Wayne and Hank, already off by themselves, having a heated discussion. Grant headed straight for them.

Both of the officers fell silent and glared at him.

"Gentlemen, surely you were given orders on what to do with the wounded, considering the nature of the plague," Grant said. "This should not be a topic open to debate."

"You know he's right, sir," Hank said, seeming a tad less angry after hearing what the journalist had to say.

Wayne scowled. "What would you have me do? Do you think any sane, armed man is going to stand there and let me shoot him?"

"It has to be done. The sooner the better," Hank said. "If one of them turns, who knows how many more of us he'll take with him."

The rest of the platoon had already clearly divided itself: those who weren't injured wanted to be far away from those who were.

"Good Lord," Grant said, exasperated. "Did they not give you a plan on how to deal with this?"

Neither Wayne nor Hank answered him.

Grant ripped the revolver from Wayne's hand and started over to the wounded. "You men are all dead. You know it. The question is, are you going to die with honor in the service of your country, or fight what must be done at the cost of those who will carry on with this mission?"

Grant's answer came in the form of a rifle crack and a bullet whizzing by him; instinctively he dove for the ground.

A new battle erupted in the camp between the living and the dying. Men fell on both sides. Dalton, the tracker, was one of the bitten. He turned on the other wounded near him and rammed a knife into the spine of the closest soldier. As the man collapsed, Dalton took his handgun from his hip and, his hand and trigger finger moving like lightning, emptied the weapon into his companions.

It was over quickly. As the smoke cleared, Grant stood over Dalton's body with Wayne's gun and personally made sure the corpse did not rise. It was the least he could do for a man so honorable, even in the face of death. Grant tossed the gun at Wayne. "It's done now, sir," he said coldly.

He walked away without another word, leaving Wayne and the others to deal with the bodies.

THREE

AT the break of dawn, the remaining eighteen men headed west once more. No one spoke. There was nothing to be said that anyone wanted to hear out loud. They ate their midday meal without stopping, and only as the sun was beginning to set did the tired, beaten men pause to rest.

This time only one small fire was lit, and everyone did their best to stay near its light. The night watch was set up so that ten men were awake and combat-ready at all times. Grant volunteered for the first shift. He carried a rifle as well as a sidearm now, unwilling to put his life in the hands of someone else. If another full pack of the dead attacked them, there would be no survivors this time. They would be overwhelmed and there wouldn't be a damn thing any of them could do about it.

Grant found himself sitting with Clint, Ben, and another soldier he didn't know by name, listening to them talk.

"We made good time today, didn't we, Sam?" Clint asked.

Sam nodded. "I figure we should reach Canton before nightfall tomorrow."

"Sam, is it?" Grant asked, extending his hand over the fire to the leather-skinned man. "You look like you've been through this before."

"Reckon I have. I was stationed in the West when the plague broke out." Sam reached for the coffee brewing on the fire and filled his tin cup. "I'm one of the few who made it across the river before things got too bad and the quarantine line was put in place."

"You've fought these things before then?" Grant pressed, his reporter's instinct getting the better of him.

Sam stared at him with the eyes of a veteran. "We'll be better off when we reach Canton. Fightin' the dead in the open is suicide. The bastards are too hard to kill. Guess no one told that to the folks at home when they was puttin' this mess of an operation together."

"I didn't sign up for this," Ben said aloud. "I really didn't. It ain't right."

"Ain't nothing right about the dead gettin' up and tryin' to eat ya. Pull it together, boy," Sam warned. "The shit ain't even started for us yet. Last night was nothing. Wait till you see a herd of those things, over a hundred or more strong, come tearin' at ya. Then you'll have a memory that'll really haunt ya."

"We're gonna kill those bastards and send 'em back to Hell where they belong. All of them," Clint promised, gritting his teeth as he cleaned his rifle.

"This town, Canton," Grant cut in. "Do you know anything about it, Sam?"

"Not much. Think a couple hundred folk called it home. It's one of those towns that just sprang up in the rush west. The odds of us getting in and out of there alive ain't too great, but like I said: at least there we'll have somewhere to fortify and make a stand." Sam sipped at his coffee. "You boys should be getting some rest. Our watch is over and I bet we'll all be pressin' it hard again tomorrow."

The night passed with no sign of the dead, and just as Sam had predicted, the next day was filled with a rigorous march. As the squad drew nearer to Canton, their expectations of another attack rose, but none came.

Wayne himself was on point as the group entered the town. The place stank of rotting flesh and death. There was no question that the dead were lying in wait, and quite likely a large number of them.

Wayne surveyed the closest buildings and picked the one that looked the most secure. "Clint, Ben: go check out the jail. I want it secured as fast as possible. Everybody else, hold your positions and be ready to move in on their signal."

Clint and Ben darted for the building and disappeared behind its door, which swung in the breeze.

Hank tapped Grant on the shoulder as they waited. "See that?" he asked, directing the journalist's attention to the eastern side of town.

"I'll be damned," Grant muttered. "Tell me that's not what I think it is."

"Wish I could," Hank said, frowning. "It's an orphanage all right. A big one from the looks of the thing."

"You don't think . . . " Grant couldn't bring himself to finish the sentence.

"I sure do. The plague doesn't give a crap how old you are."

A gunshot echoed inside the jail. Five more rang out in its wake. Wayne was on the verge of ordering more men into the building, but Ben popped into the doorway and gave the all-clear sign. Almost en masse the squad sprinted for the cover of the building. Grant and Hank entered last, pushing the door closed behind them.

Hank spotted a heavy looking desk. "Gimme a hand!" he ordered. Grant and two other men helped shove the desk in front of the door, wedging it as tightly shut as they could. "That should at least give us some warning," Hank said, satisfied.

Ben fought through the gathered men toward Wayne. "The place is clear, sir. We only found one of the dead in here, and it was locked up in one of the cells."

"What were all the shots then?" Wayne asked.

"Ben panicked," Clint replied, emerging from the rear of the building. "And we had a hell of time hitting the thing in its head, what with it slinging itself against the bars, trying to get at us."

"What's the plan?" Hank asked Wayne as he walked up.

The dead stirred in the streets outside. Their howls seemed to come from everywhere at once. The gunfire undoubtedly had alerted them.

Wayne stood in front of his men. "We have to hold this place if we want to stay alive. I want that door and the rear entrance better secured. Use anything you can find. Get them barricaded off!" After a brief pause, he said, "In the meantime, I want men on the roof. We should have a clear view of the surrounding area from up there and should be able to pick off the dead without actually engaging them face to face."

Hank snapped into action, directing the men and making it happen.

Only Grant stayed with Wayne, not taking part in the bustle of activity.

"That's a good plan," Grant said.

"No one asked your opinion."

"I'd just like to point out the dead are going to swarm around this jail like flies. We may not have a way out of here when the time comes."

"There's always a way out," Wayne said curtly.

Hank was the first to make it to the roof. He rushed to the edge and peered down at the streets below. The dead were coming out of the woodwork. He counted over a hundred before he gave up in frustration. "Get your asses up here now!" he shouted at the other men he'd assigned to the roof. Then he dropped to one knee into a firing position and splattered the brains of a former clergyman racing towards the jail's main door. The other men joined him and soon the roof was a cloud of gun smoke, but the howls of the dead only grew louder and more numerous as shell casings showered the rooftop like rain.

Something thudded into the door of the jail so hard it shook the desk braced against it.

"They're here!" a soldier shouted in warning.

The door began to shake as the things hammered on it from outside.

"Get the ladder to the roof taken down!" Wayne yelled. "Those men up there need as much time as we can give them! Be prepared to retreat into the holding cells. We can back ourselves in where they can't reach us, but we'll still be able to blow their asses to Hell. And damn well make sure someone thinks to get the keys!" he added.

Dead fists punched through the door with the sound of splintering wood, and the heavy desk was easily pushed aside under the weight of the mob. The men opened fire as the dead started to pour in, bottlenecked by the doorway; the soldiers didn't even wait for Wayne's command.

Grant scurried up to the roof and then kicked the ladder to the floor. There was no way in Hell he was going to lock himself away, surrounded by those things straining to get at him. Hank and the others were far too busy blasting the dead in the streets to notice him. Grant choked on the acrid clouds of gun smoke, which hung in the air all over the roof. "Ammo!" he heard someone yell.

"Ain't no more, son!" Hank called back. He noticed Grant and snatched the journalist's rifle from his hands. "Here!" Hank tossed it to the soldier. "Make it count!" To Grant, he said, "Get us some more ammo up here!"

"I can't!" Grant screamed over the gunfire. "They got in! It's a bloodbath down there!"

"Shit!" Hank paused to think for a second, then shouted for the men on the roof to hold their fire. The soldiers stared at him in confusion, and he peered past Grant into the jail below. The howls of the dead around the building were too loud for him to hear what was happening downstairs. All he could see through the hole was a surge of dead people pushing over one another towards the cells at the rear of the building. His face had become a mask of stone. "We're dead," he finally admitted.

"How many are left in the streets?" Grant asked.

"Too many. They're packed half a dozen thick all around the walls of this place."

"But they've stopped coming?"

"Just about. Guess most of 'em are here by now."

Grant raced to edge to see for himself. "We just need to get off this roof and make a run for it."

"Through all of them?" Hank pointed at the sea of snarling faces looking up with hungry, hollow eyes.

"You gentlemen didn't happen to bring along a Ketchum did you?"

Hank laughed. "No. Grenades aren't safe to carry on a mission like this, but . . . I think we can make something that'll work just as well as what you're thinking. We'll need a distraction though."

From the soldiers around them, Hank hastily gathered the components he needed to fashion a homemade bomb. It was going to take most of their ammo, but he hoped it would be worth it. "Any volunteers for the distraction?" he asked without looking up from his work.

"I'll do it, sir," Ben said, stepping forward.

Grant started to protest, but Hank somehow sensed it and cut him off. "Good on you, boy. If any of us make it out of this Godforsaken town alive, I swear your sacrifice will be remembered."

When Hank was ready, Ben lowered a rope over the west edge and climbed down to hang just above the reach of the creatures, screaming and taunting them with his dangling legs. The dead swarmed beneath him in a frenzy, and more and more drifted around the building to converge beneath the young private.

Hank lit the fuse on his bomb and tossed it into the street on the eastern side. Another rope followed quickly after it, even before the explosion came. The roof shook—Ben, unable to hold on, fell into the grasping arms of the dead, and on the other side of the roof, men slid down the rope to the now mostly cleared street below them. Those who hit the ground first took potshots at the closest dead to buy time for the others. Then as a whole, the remnants of the platoon ran towards the edge of town and the cover of the trees.

INSIDE the jail, Wayne and two other men were using the last of their ammo on the dead. The things flung themselves over and over into the cells, stretching their arms between the iron bars. One of the other two soldiers had already been scratched, but Wayne was waiting till the last possible second to put him down. He wanted as many of the dead sent back to Hell as he could manage.

When the explosion hit the street outside and shook the building, it caught Wayne and the others off-guard. The soldier who wasn't wounded careened into the hands of the dead, and Wayne saw them tear open his throat. Blood sprayed into the air.

The explosion weakened the building's structure just enough for the cell door to give way under the mass of bodies ramming against it.

A rotting hand grabbed Wayne's face and shoved its fingers into his eyes. He shouted in the face of death, fighting even as he fell.

AS the men from the roof neared the edge of town, their legs pumping beneath them and their breath coming in ragged gasps, they saw movement in the trees. A flood of small figures emerged to meet them.

"Sweet Jesus!" someone cried out. "They're just children!"

More than three dozen orphans stood between the men and their hope of survival. They were all dead.

"Keep moving!" Hank ordered. "Fight through them!"

The soldiers and the children collided in a running brawl. To Grant's right, a child grabbed a man by the thigh and sent him sprawling. Before he even had a chance to scream, the children climbed all over him, tearing him apart with their tiny hands.

A young girl, who must have been no older than twelve when she died, dropped the doll she'd been cradling and reached out for Grant as maggots swam in the gray flesh of her contorted face. She growled, baring red-stained teeth, and Grant shot her in the head with his Colt. He didn't take time to watch her body fall.

"This way!" someone shouted, and Grant changed his course to follow the sound of the voice.

FOUR

GRANT collapsed on the ground of a small clearing in the woods, his muscles burning from being pushed past their limits.

"I think we've lost them for the moment," Hank said as he and the other four survivors finally came to a stop.

"About damn time," Clint spat and dropped to the ground, checking his rifle. They had been on the run for nearly two hours and were exhausted.

"We can't stay here long," Sam said.

"I know," Hank agreed. He rested his weight against the trunk of a tree. "We're never going to make it to the rally point. It's too far, especially since we just backtracked away from it to stay alive."

"This mission has gone all to Hell." Clint loaded his last rounds into his rifle. "I vote we hightail it home while we still can."

"There has to be some farmsteads in these parts," Sam thought aloud. "It's possible we could find some horses left alive while we head east. Make the trip a lot faster."

Hank nodded. "That settles it then. Let's get going before we have company."

Grant wearily pushed himself to his feet as the exhausted men got back on the move. "Anybody got anything to eat?" he asked.

Hank handed him a hard biscuit from the pouch on his belt. "Go easy on it. There may not be anything else for a while."

Grant thanked him for the food and nearly shattered his teeth on it. Stale or not, he had to admit the bread tasted wonderful. He couldn't remember the last time he'd eaten, and his body needed something if he was going to keep moving. He cursed himself for spending far too much time behind his desk at Harper's.

"Wait!" Clint said suddenly. "I think I know where we're at. We passed this area on the march in. If I'm right, there should be a farm not too far from here to the north."

"Well, what are we waiting for?" Hank asked. "Lead us to it."

The farm was a large one. Fields of corn and wheat rustled in the wind as the men approached its barn. The horse inside had long ago starved to death, and flies buzzed over their remains. The house was empty as well, but at least they'd found a place to take shelter for the night. After a quick raid of the house's pantry for a cold supper, they opted to stay in the barn despite the smell, sleeping high above the floor in the hayloft.

At the crack of dawn, they looted the last of the edible food for breakfast, then set out eastward once more. They found the road their regiment had marched in on and followed it towards the Mississippi River and the army's beachhead. It seemed like every other hour of the long trek, they could hear the howls of the dead in the distance. Sometimes the cries came from behind them; other times they came from ahead—the men had no choice but to continue on.

"We must have pissed them off," Clint said. "They weren't this far east as we came in."

"Or maybe other squads have already retreated to the beachhead along this road and the dead followed them," Grant pointed out. "Either way, it was just a matter of time until they headed east. That's why we were sent here, to stop them before they did. It's what a disease does; it spreads."

"Holy shit!" Clint exclaimed. A supply wagon sat in the middle of the road ahead of them. Two horses were harnessed to it, very much alive, though in poor shape and clearly spooked. Bodies covered the road around the wagon, and an overturned Gatling gun lay in the wagon's bed; a soldier's body was propped against it, rotting in the heat of the sun.

Clint broke into a run for the wagon.

"Clint!" Hank shouted, but the private didn't even slow down.

As he reached the wagon, the soldier on the Gatling snarled and sprung at him. It wrestled him to the ground, and with jagged fingernails it slashed his cheek.

The others advanced more cautiously with Hank in the lead, checking bodies as they went.

"God help me!" Clint wailed, managing to roll out from underneath the dead man's assault. He drew his Colt and jammed the barrel against the man's forehead.

At the sound of the shot, the woods around the road roared to life with the hungry cries of the dead.

"Get the horses loose!" Hank barked, swinging to meet the corpse of a farmer that charged at him from the trees. Hank put a shot into its chest to slow the thing down, then put a second round into its face. The farmer hit the gravel road with a thud.

With his knife, Grant cut one of the horses free of its harness. The terrified animal fought to run as the dead poured onto the road, and Grant was barely able to hold it in place. Had the horse not been a trained military animal it would have been long gone the second he managed to get it loose.

Grant and Hank exchanged a sad glance as the others fired wildly to stem the tide of the dead.

"Go!" Hank ordered.

Grant didn't hesitate. He mounted the animal and kicked its sides. The horse didn't need any encouragement; it cut a path through the dead and charged away from the battle. Grant didn't look back as the gunfire turned to screams.

Hank was the last to fall. He stood alone on the road as the dead circled him. His empty rifle smoked in his hands. "Come on, you pieces of shit! Come on and end this!"

He met the first one head-on and busted its skull with the butt of his weapon, but then, moving as one, the dead dragged him to the gravel, gnawing on his flesh even before his body hit the road. Hank screamed as they ripped his intestines from his stomach and passed them around. An ugly, deformed corpse with no nose leaned over and assaulted him with its rank breath. The thing tore into Hank's throat, and blood spurted into its face.

Except for the chewing sounds, the road had fallen silent.

NEAR dawn, Grant's horse gave out and he was forced to continue on foot toward the beachhead. Far in the distance, he could hear cannons discharging, and clouds of smoke rose from beyond the trees.

Longing for his rifle, Grant paused and drew his Colt. He counted three rounds left in the chamber and hoped they would be enough to see him the rest of the way.

As he stood, weapon in hand, a dead woman staggered out of the bushes to his right. He jerked his gun up, but held his finger on the trigger. *She's blind*, he realized.

The bulk of her face was gone, as were her eyes, and her tissue looked burnt, as if she'd been caught in an explosion. A long trail of her insides spilt from her waist and dragged on the dirt behind her as she lumbered forward, oblivious to his presence. A low moan rose from her throat as she continued past Grant, deeper into the woods. He couldn't keep his eyes from following her. He felt a mixture of hatred and pity he didn't think he'd ever be able to describe for his readers should he make it home.

When the woman had vanished, Grant turned and continued towards the sound of the battle. The gunfire was louder now, and the cries of dying men intermingled with rifle fire. He reached the edge of the trees and ducked down as two dead men raced past him into the conflict on the river's shore. The whole riverbank was a mass of blood and bodies, most of which lay unmoving. Only here and there in scattered formations were there soldiers left to hold the beachhead. Grant couldn't distinguish the wounded from the dead in the sea of human flesh that littered the shore.

The army was in full retreat. Men were paddling small boats into the river's currents as massive steamboats continued to fire at the shoreline with cannon emplacements. Grant heard the hiss of an incoming ball and ducked even lower as it exploded among the bodies.

As blood fell from the sky, Grant hopped to his feet and made a dash for the river. Hundreds of dead Indians were swarming out of the woods upstream. It looked as if all the tribes had finally united against the invading white man. Many of the dead clutched tomahawks out of instinct or some lingering phantom of their humanity, though it was clear they didn't know how to use them. Several of them noticed him and with a cold, curdling war cry changed their course, running headlong in his direction.

In that moment, Grant knew the West was truly dead. If a people so noble and so courageous had failed to survive, what hope did Easterners have against them?

Grant chose the clearest route to the water, dodging the arms of a corpse sitting on a mound of its own shredded flesh. Its legs were nowhere to be seen.

Grant hit the river and waded in without slowing down, splashing his way along until the bottom was out of reach and he was swept up by the currents. The water was freezing cold, a brown mixture of blood and mud; he swam as hard as he could.

Through the thick clouds of smoke hanging on the surface of the water, he could see the fleet of mighty steamboats more clearly, the last great defenders of the eastern shore. As the current tugged him south, he struggled to swim eastward. His left foot brushed something underwater and he felt a hand close around his ankle. His head splashed under and he came face to face with the bloated remains of a fat man trapped in the rocks below.

Water flooded Grant's lungs as he tried to scream, and moments later the murky waters of the Mississippi flowed a tiny bit redder.

EPILOGUE

PRESIDENT Johnson stood before Congress. Most of the faces stared at him with open contempt, still riled at him for allowing the Southern states into the Union after the slave war without harsher punishments for their transgressions. Even now, in the face of the darkness brewing in the West, they wanted their vengeance. Did they not understand what was happening in their own country? Were they too lost in the past to save the future? He prayed not.

"Gentleman, I have asked you all to gather for this emergency session because this morning I received some most bleak and frightening news. Our push westward has failed and our army is in a state of retreat."

Murmurs and gasps of horror rose in the crowd.

Johnson steadied himself and continued. He knew he would take the blame for the army's failure in the long run, assuming he lived long enough to see things return to normal.

"It is worse still, I'm afraid. I have been informed that the dead are now crossing the Mississippi in enough numbers to be a threat to us all. The plague has come ashore in the East, good sirs, and if we do not stop it now, we'll have no other chance."

As the room broke into chaos and panic, Johnson paused to take another deep breath and prayed he would be strong enough to lead this country to victory over such an unnatural and unholy foe.

He called for order and the congressmen settled enough for him to be heard.

"Now, gentlemen, this is what I suggest we do . . . "

As he laid out his plans for the next line of defense, outside in the streets of Washington a homeless man staggered out of an alleyway. A woman turned to him on the busy corner to ask if he was in need of help. The man's hands closed on her neck as she tried to scream.

Bystanders recoiled in horror as the man pulled her close and bit into the top of her skull. The authorities came running to see what the trouble was, and the end of the world truly began.

THE RATS

ONE

WARREN snuck a glance through the boards covering the living room window. The dead were everywhere, at least three dozen of them wandering up and down the street in search of their next meal. He doubted very much that they would find one. They didn't seem intelligent enough to search the houses on their own, and the monster wasn't here to lead them anymore.

The thing had just up and left an hour ago after it had guided the dead into the Petersons' home. Warren supposed it had thought they were the last ones hiding on this street, and he was glad the thing was gone. The dead he could deal with, but that monster had been something beyond his comprehension.

It was what they called a demon, and it looked like a rat, with four razor-sharp primary teeth and beady black eyes that reflected moonlight, only the thing stood on two legs, seven feet tall. Just like a man, though there was nothing human about it. It reminded him of some kind of fairy-tale demon. He could've sworn it had hissed in frustration when it left the neighborhood without prey.

"Daddy," Emily said, placing her tiny hand on Warren's hip.

He looked down into her sad blue eyes. "What is it, honey?"

"Mommy wants you to come back to the basement."

Warren nodded. He picked up his P-90 from where he'd propped it near the window and followed his daughter downstairs into the candlelit room. As he entered, he made sure to shut and lock the heavy door behind him.

Jessica was staring at him, her green eyes bloodshot from a seemingly endless flood of tears that she cried every time they managed to get Emily asleep.

"Don't worry, baby," Warren said. "The dead can't get in here and that thing is gone. It's not up there now. Everything's going to be okay."

Emily wandered over to Jessica, who scooped her up. Warren could tell Jessica wanted to scream at him for locking them into this tiny basement to die, but she was holding her tongue for their daughter's sake.

"The worst of it's over," Warren tried to assure her. "It's just a matter of time until the dead wander off and we can make a break for it."

Jessica nodded, trying to force a smile.

A scratching sound filled the room.

Warren frowned. "What the hell is that?"

"I don't know," Jessica said. "It started while you were upstairs. It starts up and then dies down every few minutes."

"Why didn't you come and get me before now?" Warren asked, holding in his rage.

"I . . . I think it's coming from behind the washer," Emily said. "It's not the monsters trying to get in, is it, daddy?"

"No, I don't think so. The monsters are all up on the street." Warren moved over to the washing machine and slid it away from the wall. The second he did, he knew he'd made a terrible mistake. The whole section of wall behind it had been scratched away, and a mass of rats came pouring into the basement.

"Oh God!" Jessica yelled.

Warren sprayed the rats with his P-90 on instinct, and the gun boomed in the small space. He fought helplessly to stop the rodents, realizing that he was the only thing standing between them and his family. Trying to get a better aim at their center mass, he backed away from the wall and smashed one of the rats beneath his heavy boot. Emily squealed behind him and Jessica cried out in pain as the rats raced their way up her legs, eating holes into her flesh as they went.

"No!" Warren screamed.

And then the walls gave way and the entire room flooded with rats, so many that he drowned in them as their teeth ripped and tore into his skin.

WARREN awoke in a shower of glass as a bullet blew out the window above his head. At first he could feel the rats all around him, but he managed to shake off the nightmare as he rolled from the car's backseat onto the floorboard, taking his M-16 with him. His family had died long ago, but he was still alive and wasn't going to die if he could help it.

"What the hell is going on?" he shouted, not quite ready to hazard a look outside.

Matt slammed into the side of the car near the shattered window. He was panting and nearly out of breath. Warren glared up at him, silently demanding an explanation. Outside the car, the gunfire had stopped.

"Are you okay, sir?" Matt managed to ask.

Warren stepped out of the car and, brushing chunks of glass off his clothing, took a look around. The sun was just beginning to stir in the morning clouds. Jenkins and Scott stood out in the field, well beyond the camp perimeter. Behind Warren, inside the large circle of vehicles which made up the convoy, the camp was a flurry of activity as people started their day. Clearly, they weren't under attack, which left Warren more than a bit pissed off at the rude awakening. Only a single body lay between him and his men in the field.

"Jenkins didn't mean to, sir," Matt said, sensing Warren's anger. "I was relieving them from their watch and somehow one of the dead slipped—"

Warren started marching towards the two men in the field, and Matt fell in behind him without another word.

"Mornin', boss," Jenkins said, grinning. Scott stood at his side, looking like a child who knew he was about to be dragged to the principal's office for a spanking. "You sleep well?"

Warren punched him, and Jenkins staggered backwards, spitting out a bloody tooth. He recovered quickly, but not fast enough to dodge the butt of Warren's rifle; it hammered his stomach, and he collapsed to his knees.

Warren shoved the barrel of his M-16 into Jenkins's face. "I'm only going to ask you once. What the fuck happened?"

Before Jenkins could reply, Scott said, "One of the dead was headed into camp. We didn't see it until it was long past us. Jenkins took it out, but he missed with his first shot. It took two to hit it."

Warren gritted his teeth. He had lost count of how many times he'd given this same talk to the sentries. "Didn't I teach you that if it was only one or two or a handful, you reposition yourself between them and the convoy before you start shooting? The things are too damn slow to be a threat in small numbers."

Scott and Matt nodded, but Jenkins spit another mouthful of blood onto the ground and looked up at Warren as if ready to tear out the man's throat with his bare hands. "I got the fucker, didn't I? Isn't that what counts?"

"And you nearly got me in the process. If your shot had been a bit lower, we would not be having this conservation and the convoy would be another man down. There are so few of us left already, do you really want to see somebody else die from you being stupid? I, for one, have seen enough death to last me a lifetime."

Jenkins didn't answer. He got to his feet and wiped his mouth with the back of his hand.

"You'll be more careful next time," Warren informed him, then glanced at Matt. "You sure that corpse is the only one?"

"Pretty sure. The gunfire will draw any more in the area to us, but I don't think we're in any danger. This area was mostly deserted even before the rats."

"Jenkins, stay with him. You're going to be pulling double duty today. Scott, go and get some rest. If any of you need me, I'll be trying to find some damn breakfast before the next round of shit hits the fan." Warren turned to look toward camp.

Almost fifty vehicles, ranging from a beat-up Dodge Shadow to a tank and two APCs, formed the defensive circle around what could be the last of the human race. There were less than one hundred and fifty people in the convoy, but right now that small number seemed like a whole city to him. Every one of them had their own tales of loss and grief. No one had escaped the horror that had swept over the world like wildfire, and yet they continued on. Just like him, he guessed, they were too stubborn to die. Maybe it was just the survival instinct, or maybe it was some last spark of hope that kept them going.

Warren had lost everything he'd ever cared about, and he would never find a new life for himself—he accepted that. He had been a solider before Hell rose up and spilled out over the earth, and he was still a soldier now. He had a job to do, and he was damn well determined to keep these folks alive for a shot at the future.

Inside the camp, families were eating breakfast together. People were trading goods and services. Gerald and his crew were working on one of the older trucks in an attempt to keep it viable. Not a single person appeared to have been bothered by Jenkins's shots. *And why would they be?* Warren wondered. The roaming dead were as much a part of everyday life as living on the run. It was simply safer to be on the road and moving. The convoy had the arms and manpower to handle any number of the dead or rats short of a massive wave, and that was an unlikely thing to encounter here in the middle of nowhere. The rats were the real danger, and because of them, putting down roots was like signing your own death warrant. The rodents had a tendency to show up on your doorstep, and they always found a way to get inside. They liked enclosed places where their prey had nowhere to run.

"Boss?" Scott asked.

Warren tore himself from his thoughts. "What?"

"Are we moving out today?"

Warren forced a smile, trying to make a joke of his answer. "Don't know. I would guess so. We've been here too long already. We stay much longer and the rats may try to make a go for it."

Scott laughed.

Warren shook his head, wishing he were joking, then made his way toward camp.

SITTING in the command APC, Mike took a sip of the instant coffee in his cup, essentially swill warmed by one of the campfires. People these days loved fires. He imagined they thought the flames might keep the rats away—they just didn't or couldn't understand how intelligent the pests had become.

No one knew how or why it happened. In the beginning, there were only a few scattered reports of rats attacking people, lost in the whirlwind of disasters on the nightly news. It wasn't until a massive swarm of rats consumed every tenant living in a large apartment building in New York that people started to notice. Even then, the changes in the rat species were far overshadowed by the walking dead. As the corpses swept across the nation, eating everyone in their path, the authorities told people either to stay in their homes and wait for help or travel to one of the safe houses set up by FEMA and their ilk; the general population followed the advice and unwittingly gift-wrapped themselves for the rats. Rising up from the cellars and basements, or in some cases just pouring through windows, the rats devoured everyone they found. Humanity had lost the war before it ever began.

It wasn't at all like the movies. If you were bitten by a dead person, you didn't contract some virus or disease and become one of them. The dead were merely the tools of their rodent masters, foot soldiers to a greater power. However, if a rat bit you, you did rise again when you died. The disease gestated until the death of its host, after which it rewired the host's brain to carry out the will of the rats. Scientists suspected it was some kind of evolutionary glitch, something new the rats secreted when they bit someone, something that acted like a virus but wasn't. It made the dead into cattle for the rats, both a food supply and a mindless herd. The scientists theorized endlessly on the cause—at least until the demons showed up.

Mike shuddered as he thought about it and thanked God the demons were small in number, even now, five months after the world had crumbled into Hell.

Mike set down his coffee on the APC's dashboard and started crunching the numbers in his head again. Any way he looked at it, they were pretty much screwed if they didn't reach the base soon, and they would need to raid another town if they were going to keep going at all.

Mike turned and gazed out the passenger window to see Warren staring back at him. "How long have you been standing there?" Mike asked as he climbed out of the vehicle.

Warren showed him two rows of tobacco-stained teeth. "Long enough to see from the look on your face things are worse than I thought."

"You're too good at your job, Warren."

"How's that?"

"We have too many people and not nearly the food or fuel we need to keep moving. If it hadn't been for you and your men, most of us would be dead by now."

Warren grunted. "I could go shoot some people at random if you like."

Mike chuckled, though a part of him wondered if Warren was serious. "No, really. We need fuel, Warren. Most of the vehicles are running on fumes."

"You sure this place we're headed to is worth all the trouble, Mike?"

"I'm sure. With a few modifications, the rats will never be able to get inside unless we let them in. This place is solid. I only hope the military isn't waiting on us there. They may not be too friendly, but I can tell you, the place should be stockpiled with enough supplies to keep us alive and safe for years. It'll give us time to figure out how to beat the little bastards once and for all." After a short pause, he said, "But in order to get there, we'll have to make another raid. It's the only option."

"We lost a hell of a lot of good men last time, boss."

"I know." Mike grabbed his map from the APC and rolled it out on the hood. He pointed out three hand-drawn circles. "I've been giving it a lot of thought during the four days we've been camped, and these, I think, are our safest targets."

Warren studied the map. "Jericho is out. That place is overrun, you can bet on it. And Livingston . . . I wouldn't want to take a team that far from the convoy."

"Well then, I guess Greensburg is the target," Mike conceded.

"Yep, but the convoy's been here too long. We'll have to risk moving as we hit it. Divide up what fuel is left so you guys can get on the road while my team is gone." Warren placed a finger on the map. "I say we move the whole convoy here, somewhere closer to Greensburg but not too close, maybe around the Jones Creek area. I want to be able to hightail it back to you as quick as possible if there's trouble on either end."

"Okay. That's settled. I'll make the announcement and we should be able to make Jones Creek by nightfall if we hurry . . . But you should know there's no room for failure in Greensburg. If you return without the fuel, it's over."

Warren nodded and went off to gather his team for the job.

MICHELLE sat up, pushing the sleeping bag off her. She clasped her hands and stretched them high above her head as her long blond hair spilled over her shoulders.

"Good morning, sleepy head," Benji said. He handed her a bowl of oatmeal, which he had just taken off the fire. "Looks like we're having your favorite again."

Michelle made a disgusted face and reluctantly took the bowl. "It stopped being my favorite a long time ago. Any chance you have some eggs and bacon?"

"We might if you started sleeping around for it," he joked. She was his sister, but he wasn't blind to the fact that most men in the convoy would give almost anything to wake up beside her. Michelle wasn't thin but she wasn't chubby either, one of those biological marvels that filled out perfectly in all the right places. Her blond hair and blue eyes were an added bonus.

Unfortunately for the men of the convoy and Benji's stomach, she was also a tomboy, if that term could be applied to someone slightly past twenty-five years old; she had fought more than her fair share of the dead, and had kept her brother on this side of the grave all by herself until they'd stumbled upon the convoy. But even then, she wasn't content to just sit back. She'd joined Warren's team of soldiers as fast as she could and began to train under Warren himself.

"Don't mess with me this early in the morning, little brother, or I might have to beat the shit out of you," she said.

Benji feigned shock. "You wouldn't dare."

"Just because you're gay doesn't make you a lady, Benji, and the glasses aren't going to save you either if you keep screwing around with me." Michelle laughed and plunged a spoonful of oatmeal into her mouth.

Benji fished a cigarette from his jacket pocket and lit up.

Michelle waved angrily at the cloud of secondhand smoke. "I thought you didn't have any of those left."

"So did I," Benji replied. "I had some luck last night and won nearly a full pack off that redneck you work with."

"Jenkins? How the hell did you end up playing cards with him?"

"Don't know. He just decided to join the game last night at Mike's. Had a run of bad luck and kept going like he couldn't stand to lose to the little queer guy."

"Don't fuck around with him, Benji, I mean it. The guy's on the edge."

He waved a hand dismissively. "He's harmless. It's your damn boss that gives me the creeps. That guy not only redefines the term *bad ass*, but the word *cold* too."

"Warren's okay."

"How would you know, sis?" Benji grinned. "I haven't met anyone in this convoy who knows anything about the man other than he was some kind of elite soldier or something. So is there something you'd like to share with me, or . . . ?"

Michelle shrugged. "He's okay, Benji. He's the kind of guy you trust. That's all I know."

"Better you than me, I guess." Benji set down his already empty bowl. "It's going to be a busy day, sis. They just finished making the announcement that we're moving out."

"Shit." Michelle laughed. "I was just beginning to break in the patch of dirt I've been sleeping on."

AFTER the announcement that the convoy was moving out and people began to pack, Mike saw Gerald storming across the camp towards him. He wished he could avoid the man, but the camp simply wasn't that big.

"We're not ready," Gerald told him. "I got one truck half torn apart that we're still trying to fix, at least four cars need work on their tires, and there's—"

Mike cut him off. "Look, Gerald, I'm sorry. I didn't ask for all this anymore than you did, but we have to move and we have to move now. Staying is too great a risk. We'll leave the truck if we have to. Just do the best you can."

"Just give me one more day," Gerald pleaded. "We can't keep leaving vehicles behind. Pretty soon we're not going to have room for everyone if we do."

"What do you want me to do, Gerald? I know you're working your ass off—we all are—but if we don't reach the base, and soon, we may never make it."

Gerald sighed, knowing he'd lost the argument. "All right. But please tell me we're not moving far. Some of the cars can't handle much more yet."

Mike shook his head. "We're just headed up the road to Jones Creek, far enough to buy us some time and get closer to Warren's next raid."

"Can I go with them this time?" Gerald asked. "Those guys don't know crap about what parts we need to keep going in the long run. I swear they must never read the lists I give to Warren."

"Gerald . . . "

"Yeah, yeah, I know. I'm too important and all that crap. You'd think the apocalypse would've spared more than one engineer, eh?"

"Oh, I think one's quite enough if they're all like you, Gerald."

He let Mike's remark slide and changed the subject. "Guess I better go give Warren's jeeps a once-over before his team heads out, huh?"

"I think that would be a good idea."

Mike smiled as the engineer hurried off, leaving him alone with his thoughts. The man could be a damn pain in the ass, but Mike needed him—the whole convoy did—so there was no choice but to endure his constant whining about the state of their equipment. Besides, he was right: everything was falling quickly into disrepair.

"GOOD luck," Mike said as Warren slid into the passenger seat of one of the convoy's three military jeeps.

"You too," Warren said. He glanced at the madhouse around them, people loading up the last of their things and making sure nothing was left behind for the rats to find. He didn't like leaving the main group with less than half of its trained defenders, but he had no choice if they were to survive long term.

Raising his hand over his head, Warren gave the rest of his team the signal to roll out. His driver, Matt, fired up the jeep's engine and led the others onto the road towards Greensburg.

'Let's hope they make it back," Benji said, walking up to Mike.

"Warren always comes back." Mike placed an arm around the younger man's shoulder. Though many in the convoy didn't approve of their relationship, Mike had stopped trying to hide it. Some secrets couldn't be kept in such close quarters. "Let's get to the command vehicle and get this show on the road."

TWO

WARREN flicked the lighter, taking a deep drag off what might be his last cigarette as the sun sank in the sky. He stood on the hilltop above Greensburg, looking into the remains of the town, and Michelle and Matt stood at his side. Behind them, the three combat jeeps were parked in a row; Jenkins and Daniel leaned against one, inspecting their weapons.

Scott had gone ahead on foot to recon the outskirts of the town and should have been back by now. The team hadn't seen or heard any signs of trouble from below, but Warren could feel tension in the air, the fear and dread that gripped soldiers just before the shooting started. "How long?" he asked.

"He's been gone nearly two hours," Michelle said, and Warren grunted in reply.

"We got a plan, chief?" Jenkins taunted him from behind.

"How about you drink a nice tall glass of shut the fuck up?" Matt said, quoting one of his favorite films.

Jenkins pushed away from the jeep and stood up straight, his cheeks red with anger.

"Enough," Warren said. "My guts tell me there's a demon behind Scott being late. Maybe more than one."

The others fell silent. Even Jenkins settled back against the side of a jeep, keeping his mouth shut for once.

"Scott's never late," Warren continued. "He's too damn good for the dead or the vermin to take him down without him getting off a couple shots."

"Where does that leave us?" Matt asked, looking to Warren for direction.

"We're going into Greensburg and we're going to take what we need, demons or not." Warren tossed his smoke aside and walked past Matt to the jeeps.

"Whoa, hold up!" Daniel cut in. The hulking mass of muscle that he was, he still managed to sound like a frightened child. "Didn't you just say there may be demons down there?"

Warren climbed into the driver seat of the closest jeep and turned its key, revving the engine. Only then did he speak. "We have to get those supplies or everyone in the convoy is dead, not just us."

"You heard the man," Michelle barked. "Daniel, you can ride with me and Jenkins. I don't want you stuck alone with Scott gone."

The big man scrambled over to join them as Warren peeled out down the hill, barely giving Matt time to hop in the jeep.

The road into Greensburg was filled with abandoned cars. There was no sign of the dead—even the true dead. It was odd not to see picked-over skeletons littering the street. Clearly the rats had swept through this area some time ago.

The wreckage filling the roadway forced the team to slow down so much that Warren almost wished he'd brought the tank to clear a path. As the team finally rolled into town, the dying sunlight vanished from the sky, and night fell over them.

Warren scrapped the lists of needed supplies in his head, focusing solely on fuel. Something wasn't right here, and the sooner he could get his team in and out the better. He ordered the jeeps to a halt at the first gas station and dispatched Michelle and her crew to find a tanker truck, which they would use to haul the fuel. He and Matt secured the station and went to work on getting the pumps operational; luckily most stations had a backup generator, and it was just a matter of getting it running.

By the time the tanker drove up with Michelle at the wheel and Daniel and Jenkins following her in the jeep, the lights were on at the station. Warren said a quiet prayer of thanks that his information about the town had been correct. There weren't many places left with easily accessible fuel tankers. Daniel and Matt leapt into action and began filling the massive tanker to its brim.

Michelle approached Warren, and his eyes lingered on her long legs for a moment before he realized he was staring. He cursed himself for his weakness and got to business. "Well?"

'No sign of Scott. We haven't seen a single rat or walking corpse either. It's as if this whole town is just empty."

'Shit." Warren grimaced. "It's a trap. The rats must have been watching the convoy."

Michelle retreated a step, as if afraid he might lose it. "But if it's a trap, why aren't we dead yet?"

'It's not that kind of trap," Warren explained, springing into movement. "Finish filling her up, then get the hell out of here!" he told Daniel and Matt. "I don't care where you go, but don't head to the rally point—no matter what happens. Understood?"

Both men nodded.

"Keep your radios on and stay sharp. We'll be in touch as soon as we can." Warren sprinted to his jeep, motioning for Michelle and Jenkins to follow him. "The fucking demons are making a move on the convoy. We've got to get back there—now!"

THE dead came out of nowhere and the rats followed in their wake. The convoy had been in the process of setting up a new camp, and the handful of trained fighters Warren left behind simply weren't enough to organize the would-be defenders. Hundreds upon hundreds of the dead surrounded the camp's perimeter as nearly everyone with a weapon opened fire. Most of the bullets struck rotting chests and arms without real effect; worse, some of them struck legs and kneecaps, creating crawlers who wormed their way beneath the protective line of vehicles into the already terrified mob of civilians. Only a headshot stopped the dead.

One woman, in her attempt to flee, ran in front of the M-60 mounted on the command APC, and Mike, unable to turn the heavy gun away in time, watched her body splatter into a bloody pulp.

Benji sat behind him atop the APC, spraying the dead with an AK-47 cranked up to full auto.

Waves of rats poured beneath the shambling legs of the dead, using the corpses as cover as they raced towards camp. The convoy's flamethrowers were the only defense against the vermin, but if Mike ordered them to be employed now, with the rats under cover the way they were, the whole convoy would be overwhelmed by a sea of flaming corpses. Somewhere in the battle a man howled as the rats washed over him, pulling him to the ground as their teeth tore into his skin.

Mike watched as Gerald and two of his mechanics struggled to load a group of children into an escape van. The engineer blasted a dozen rats into blood and bone with his shotgun. As he went to pump another round into the chamber, a cold gray hand latched onto his weapon and pulled him face to face with one of the dead.

At that moment, the ground itself seemed to shake, nearly blowing out Mike's eardrums. He lost his balance and fell from the top of the command car, but Benji grabbed him by the shirt at the last possible second and kept him from falling off completely. He helped Mike climb back up, and they looked around for the source of the quake.

Some idiot had tried to fire the tank's main gun, but the shell had detonated against a clog of rats that had been searching the barrel for a way in. The combat vehicle was now a flaming mass of wreckage and secondary explosions as its remaining ammo expended itself in the blaze.

Mike could see Benji shouting something at him but couldn't make out the words over the ringing in his ears. A dead hand reached up from below and took hold of his ankle, trying to pull him from the vehicle. Benji slid to Mike's side, pressed his 9mm sidearm against the creature's head and pulled the trigger. Mike jerked free as the thing toppled backwards to the ground.

More explosions rippled through the convoy, lighting up the night like flares. Many of the cars and trucks were engulfed in flames.

Mike heard the bullet before it slapped against his skull. As Benji leaned over him and the darkness swooped down over his vision, Mike realized too late that he hadn't been able to alert Warren and his team to the attack.

MICHELLE could see the fires raging where the convoy was supposed to be camped, red and orange flames leaping up into the darkness.

Warren slammed on the brakes and the jeep came to a screeching halt on the road.

"What the hell are you doing?" she screamed.

"We're too late," he said; he sounded hollow. He went to slam the gearshift into reverse, but Michelle bolted from her seat. Warren turned to Jenkins. "Why the hell didn't you stop her?"

Jenkins didn't answer. He was frozen as if in some kind of shock, his eyes transfixed on the carnage in the distance.

"Shit." Warren jerked the gearshift into park, then swung his feet onto the asphalt and ran after Michelle.

She was tall and fast, made even faster by the adrenaline pumping through her veins, but Warren managed to grab her from behind and bring her to a halt. "Michelle, it's over."

"No!" She tried to shove Warren off of her. "My brother's there—we have to help them!"

"Michelle—"

She elbowed him hard in the stomach. Any other man might have fallen from the blow, but Warren's training took over; he spun her around and smashed his fist into her cheek.

Michelle toppled to the road. She got on her knees and looked up at Warren with a burning rage in her eyes. He didn't have time to argue with her. They had to get out of the area before the rats from the convoy discovered they were there.

He kicked Michelle in the head, and she fell over, eyes rolling up to the whites. Then Warren picked her up and tossed her into the jeep's passenger seat.

Jenkins was beginning to come around. "What . . . what are we going to do?" he asked.

"Survive." Warren gunned the engine, and the wheels spun out as he doubled back the way they had come. "Mike!" he said into his radio.

"Mike, if you're out there, bring anyone you can to the second rally point. Mike!"

The radio remained silent.

"It's like you said," Jenkins reminded him. "We were too late. They're all dead."

Warren tossed the radio aside and focused on the road in front of him.

"HEY there, sis." Benji smiled as Michelle opened her eyes. At first she thought she was dreaming, until she tried to sit up and a sharp pain stabbed through her head.

"Whoa." Benji gently pushed her back down. "You had a pretty rough knock to the head." He laughed. "I told you that Warren guy was a psycho. Maybe next time you'll listen to me."

Michelle looked around at her surroundings. She was lying on a makeshift pile of bedding stretched out on the dirt. The sun was high in the sky, and she could hear people talking in the distance.

"The convoy was burning." Tears ran down her cheeks. "I . . . I thought you were dead."

"I almost was," Benji replied. "Less than twenty of us made it out of there alive."

"Mike?" she asked.

"Mike's fine. A bullet grazed his head, but he's fine."

Michelle squeezed Benji's hand and smiled. He nodded and smiled back.

"Where are we?"

"About seventy miles closer to the base Mike's been leading us to." Benji shook his head. "We're down to one overcrowded van, a pickup truck that's nearly falling apart, and the tanker and jeeps you guys brought with you from Greensburg."

"That doesn't sound too hopeful."

"Actually, in a kind of sad and sick way, Mike says we're better off. We can move faster now and we're a smaller target. Mike said the rats may even think they got us all and leave us alone if we're lucky."

"I doubt that."

Benji gave her a funny look. "Warren said the exact same thing."

"Where is that bastard?"

"He's off with Mike. I think they're discussing a faster route to the base since we don't have as many people to worry about now. Mike talks like we might be able to reach the base in just over a day if we keep pushing straight when we roll out." Benji paused, "A day, Michelle, can you believe it? A single day."

"Good." She tried to sound cheerful. "Then maybe I won't have to eat your burnt oatmeal anymore."

Benji shot her a playful injured look. "Just get some rest, okay? We'll be moving soon."

She promised she would, and he scurried off to where the others were. Michelle closed her eyes and tried to think of the future, but all she could see were the flames of the convoy burning in the night.

Hours later, the convoy ventured on toward the base. Michelle found herself riding shotgun next to Warren in one of the combat jeeps, with Benji in the seat behind them. She understood why Warren had knocked her out and she tried to forgive him for it. Benji wasn't happy about sharing a jeep with the guy who had punched out his sister, and he wasn't happy about being separated from Mike either, but he'd promised to stay with Michelle this time.

Their jeep was in the lead, followed by the pickup and the van, both crammed full of the remaining survivors. The tanker truck was next in line, with Daniel and Jenkins's jeep bringing up the rear.

The scenery left much to be desired. Barren sand sprawled out around them on all sides.

"We'll be there soon," Benji tried to assure Michelle. She wondered if he was actually trying to convince himself.

"Has Mike told you what this base is?" Warren asked, taking them both off-guard.

"It's a bomb shelter," Benji answered. "Like the kind they took the President to when all this started happening."

'No. No it's not," Warren said. "But you're right, they did take the President to a place like what you're talking about. Him, the other VIPs, and the men assigned to protect them all died horribly. The rats were waiting for them underground."

"Warren, stop it. There's no way you could know that," Michelle said.

Warren ignored her. "Where we're going isn't a bomb shelter or some kind of bunker, though they did gut one and build the base inside of it. It's a research facility, a state-of-the-art, self-contained place of nightmares. It's one of the most sterile and impenetrable places on Earth. The base was designed to keep the government's worst experiments contained should something go wrong, but I think it will keep the rats out as well . . . As long as it hasn't been breached by someone else before we get there."

"What were they working on in the base?" Benji asked, hating himself for believing Warren but realizing it was just the kind of place Mike would lead them to.

"Bio-weapons, viruses, new types of killer radiation—how the hell should I know? I doubt if Mike even knows for sure. Regardless, it will keep us alive and we'll be a hell of a lot better off than we are outside."

After that, the three of them rode on in silence. Benji leaned into his seat and stared up at the sky. He knew Mike had been some sort of high-ranking scientist before the world ended. Everything Warren had just told them made perfect sense, but what bothered Benji was how much Warren knew. Why hadn't Mike told him more about the base if he'd shared this much with Warren? And was what Warren said about the President true? Warren didn't come across as a guy who made shit up, so just who the hell was he? Benji promised himself to confront Mike about Warren when they were all safe.

He closed his eyes, tired of staring at the clouds and the sand, and dozed off to sleep.

THE small chain of vehicles came to a stop outside the massive steel fence encircling the base.

The group got out of their vehicles like expectant kids on Christmas morning and gathered at the gate, filled with new hope and relief to have finally arrived. A sign hung on the fence, proclaiming that this place was government property and off-limits to the public. It warned civilians to stay away and also boasted that intruders would be shot, but Mike explained that it was just a ruse to help keep the base secret.

"The gate's locked. That's a good sign," Warren said to Mike. "But how do we open it?"

"Just shoot the lock off. The defenses up top don't really matter. It's what's under the sand that's going to keep us alive." Mike could see Warren's military mind unwilling to sacrifice something as small in the grand scheme of things as a locked gate, so he added, "We can use one of the cars to brace it or maybe find a way to chain it back ourselves if we need to."

Warren called for Daniel to bring him his weapon and used the high-powered rifle to destroy the lock. A cheer rose from the survivors of the convoy and people rushed through the gate as it swung open.

"Wait!" Warren screamed, but no one listened.

Mike put a hand on his shoulder. "Let them have this moment. I doubt there's any need to worry until we actually get inside the complex proper. If there was still a military presence here, we'd already be dead or under fire. We'll take it slower then. I promise."

Warren reluctantly agreed, but moved the lever of the rifle to load another round into the chamber.

THREE

MIKE sipped at his cup of coffee, savoring the flavor as he flipped through the stack of paperwork on his desk. He and the others had been living in the base for a week and it still seemed like a dream. They were as safe as they could be in a world gone to hell. They had food, running water, electricity—he even had a damn office again.

There was so much to do ahead of them. They had yet to finish a full inventory of the base's massive stockpiles, and they hadn't even begun to explore the research that had been conducted there before the rats came. Maybe there was something they could use as a weapon against the creatures. Anything seemed possible.

The first things they had done after moving in were simply the basics: getting the place as operational as they could, assigning everyone living quarters, and setting up a watch shift for the base's security room; they had also assigned a team to make contact with other survivors via the base's communications array.

Everyone was happy and finding a way to contribute—everyone except Warren. The man had become withdrawn now that he had accomplished his mission. He was a soldier by blood, and damn good at his job too, but it appeared that after he'd gotten everyone to the base, his job was at an end, at least for the foreseeable future; while Mike hated to think that the man felt useless, he had to confess he was thankful they had no reason for his protection.

The base also had an armory, so he'd assigned Warren the task of inventorying the weaponry and devising the best plan to defend the base, should the rats breach the compound. He knew Warren took the task seriously, but he also understood it wasn't what Warren was really trained to do.

Someone knocked on the door to his office. Mike placed his coffee beside the paperwork on his desk as Benji let himself in. Mike instantly saw the mischievous look on Benji's face and knew that his plans of working through the morning were pretty much shot to hell. He smiled as the younger man entered and shut the door behind him.

A classic Beach Boys tune echoed in the hallway as Brent sped along on a skateboard. He let out a scream of pure joy as he reached the hall's end and jumped into the air, pulling off a Tony Hawk-style stunt. He landed and, keeping his momentum, turned to head back the way he'd come.

He nearly lost his balance and barely managed to stop when he saw Warren standing in his path. He grabbed up the board and snapped to attention. "Sir," he bellowed over the Beach Boys.

"Music's a bit loud, isn't it, Private?"

Brent rushed over to the portable stereo he'd looted from one of the base's work areas and shut off the song halfway through. "Sorry, sir, won't happen again."

Warren hid a smile. He wondered if he was ever as young as Brent was. "It's okay, Private, and please stop calling me *sir*." Warren nodded at the skateboard. "Looks like fun."

"Yes . . . " Brent caught himself before he ended with the word *sir*. "It is."

"At ease, soldier. I didn't come by to give you hell. I'm working on a list of the stuff in the armory for Mike and just thought you might want to help me finish it."

Brent visibly relaxed. "Love to, sir."

Warren shot him a look. "Call me Warren, damn it, or I will end up kicking your ass after all, got it?"

Brent nodded and started to collect his stuff from the hallway.

"Leave it," Warren ordered. "It shouldn't take us long. You'll be surfing the corridors again before you know it."

The base consisted of four levels. The top held the administrative areas, and the second floor housed a mixture of supply storage, generators, the armory, and things of that nature. Both the third and fourth story contained a mixture of quarters, labs and the like, but unique to the third were the communications room and security area.

Warren and Brent got into the elevator, and Warren hit the button for the second floor. As the doors closed, he spoke up. "I've been meaning to ask how you got out of the attack on the convoy alive. Most everyone credits you with saving their lives, but I wanted to hear from you what really went down out there."

Brent shifted uncomfortably. "I just did what I had to do."

"I know that, soldier. I'm not looking to place judgment. It's a miracle any of you got out. I just want to hear how you pulled it off."

Brent took in a deep breath and started his explanation. "We were all tired and hungry. You know how tough life on the road could be, and that was an especially bad day after you guys left. We had a hell of time getting to the rally point. Gerald was raging worse than usual, and we were forced several times to stop just so he and his crew could jury-rig some of the vehicles to keep them rolling. When we finally made it there, all anyone wanted to do was rest. There were more of the wandering dead around than usual, so Mike ordered me to round up some volunteers to help deal with them. None of us were concerned . . . well, not really. We just figured the slightly higher number of the dead came from being closer to a formerly populated area. I sent the regulars to their posts and was still trying to get some people to help us out when all hell broke loose.

"Suddenly the dead were pouring like rivers out of the hills all around us. I'd never seen anything like it. They just kept coming, wave after wave of them, staggering towards the convoy. I rushed to the perimeter to try to take command of the convoy's watchers, but the panic in the camp was too great. Almost everybody with a gun started shooting. We started having our own people caught in the crossfire . . . " Brent paused; *crossfire* wasn't the correct word, but he couldn't think of another one. "Some idiots were trying to shoot at the dead all the way on the other side of the camp from them. Then things got worse.

"The rats came in, using the dead as cover. I saw Mike on top of the command car with that little guy he spends so much time with. Mike himself was using the car's mounted weapon. I knew I couldn't reach them, so I couldn't ask him what to do. Rationally I guess I knew we couldn't use the flamethrowers against the rats with so many of the dead around, but I went for them anyway. My mind kept screaming that they were our only hope against the rats. Even an automatic rifle is nearly useless if you're facing a swarm of them.

"I made it to the supply truck, grabbed the closest flamethrower and lit it up. Something must have snapped in me because I just let go with it. I started torching everything that moved. The rats began to keep away from the area I was in, and I realized most of the camp was already on fire. Somehow the tank had exploded."

"The tank exploded?" Warren asked.

"Yeah, it was a nightmare. Anyway, a few others flocked to my position to keep the dead off me, and suddenly my little burning patch of the camp became an island of safety from the rats. We held off the dead long enough to load up anyone we could in the closest vehicles that weren't on fire, and then we rolled out. We had to leave the truck with the flamethrowers, and it blew just as we made it out. We lost a car from the blast. I will never forget seeing those poor people being burnt alive, but I think it's what saved us and let us get away. We tore a streak out of there and just kept running until Mike's little buddy heard you on the radio and we were able to meet up."

"Stop blaming yourself," Warren told him. "It sounds to me like you're the only reason anyone's alive from the convoy. I would have done the same things you did. Guess I should be glad I left you behind."

Brent tried to smile.

"Well, soldier, let's go see what we've got on hand in case the rats come calling."

"Yes, sir," Brent said, and Warren let the "S" word slide as they entered the armory.

AT 1600 hours on their seventh day at the base, the survivors assembled for the first time to discuss their plans for the future. Mike had organized the meeting and had chosen the mess hall for the location.

By the time he and Benji entered the room, everyone except for Darren, who was working on the base's systems while on watch in the command room, were already waiting on them. Benji broke away from Mike's side and took a seat at the front of the small group near Michelle, Warren, and Brent.

"Good afternoon," Mike began, looking out into the faces before him. "I know you're all as glad to be here as I am, so let's start with a bit about where we're staying. Long before the world fell apart, the government and the military were experimenting with ways of waging war that, if unleashed, could have brought about a hell similar to what we live in today. There are bases like this scattered across the U.S., but *this* base . . . this base isn't like any of the others. It's beyond them.

"The most deadly bio-weapons man ever conceived were being designed here. Only a select few in the government knew this place existed. During your stay here, you have likely noticed some of the rooms are sealed off. I don't have the codes to access those doors, and I am not certain we should open them even if we could. From top to bottom, this base was built not only to keep unauthorized personnel out, but to contain the things that were being created here if something went wrong. This base is, beyond the shadow of a doubt, the safest place in the western world—maybe the whole world. In short, I believe we are as safe here as we're ever going to be."

Mike paused, letting his words sink in. "So that brings us to the issues of actually living here. Most of you in at least some sort of fashion have helped take stock of the useful things this base contains. We have running water, an unlimited, shielded supply of it, so thank God for that. There's enough food to keep us from starving for years without rationing. And Warren was quite pleased with what we found in the armory. He believes we have the firepower to make a stand if the rats find this place. The sole real concern of the base is power.

"Though it's partially solar powered and has a wide array of batteries and generators to help recharge them, our fuel supply is limited. Eventually some of us may be forced to venture out to obtain more, but for now we're okay. I don't see the need for an expedition aboveground at least for a month or two. Thus, I suggest we enjoy what we've been blessed with. We have plenty of time to come up with viable solutions to the fuel issue. It's time for us to rest and live a little again in a world where so many others don't have the luxury."

Benji cleared his throat and got up to stand beside Mike. "We may have everything we need, but there's still a lot of work to be done. We need people to cook, clean, pull watch shifts, and people to try to make contact with other survivors. And people to plan for what the future may bring. The world may be dead, but life goes on and so does work.

"Now that we're not on the run anymore, we need a better assessment of just what everyone is capable of and what duties they would like to take on in our new home. I'll be meeting with each one of you over the next day or so to see where everyone can be the greatest help, then we'll come up with a duty roster so everyone knows where they stand and exactly what they're responsible for. Each of us will pull our own weight from now on."

Mike motioned Benji to silence. "With that said, if you have any questions, you're welcome to approach Benji or myself at anytime, and we'll do our best to address them."

As the meeting broke up, Mike judged that most people seemed not just hopeful but happy. He was sure eventually there would be complaints and disputes over everything from assignments to living quarters, but as a whole, things were going well and the group was on its way to a real future.

Mike followed Benji out of the breaking crowd and into the base's control center, where Darren was working in one of the terminals.

"How did the meeting go?" he asked.

Mike smiled. "As well as could be hoped for. How are things going here?"

Darren shrugged. "I know you picked me to help out with this because, other than you, I'm the only person in this group with any computer skills . . . " he smiled and shook his head, "but I just ran a geek squad for an electronics store. This shit here . . . " he gestured at the room around them, "this is some hardcore stuff. I'm doing the best I can, but it's way beyond me. Without the pass codes you had, I doubt I'd even be in the system yet."

Mike nodded. "I know what you mean. Computers were never my specialty either. I used to just take this stuff for granted when I was a researcher, and when I took over as an administrator . . . " Mike sighed. "Well, let's just say delegation is a wonderful thing." He slid a chair over to where Darren was working and sat down. "I think between my casual understanding of the system here and your knowledge of hardware, we should be able to get everything online, given time. We did get the lights on," he said, trying to ease the tension with a joke. "So what's still not operational at this point?"

"Most of the internal and external security measures. I haven't been able to gain access to the security camera feeds, or whatever the hell the more advanced system is that overlaps them in the programming."

"That would be the base's bio-scanners, I think."

"Bio-scanners, right. This whole damn base is like something out of *Torchwood*."

"What?"

"*Torchwood*? You didn't watch a lot of sci-fi, did you?" Darren laughed. "Forget it. Doesn't matter. Anyway, we do have power. I have control over all of the base's doors except the ones that I think lead into the high-clearance labs and a few of the more scientific supply areas. I *have* gotten the communications array working, including the intercom system. One thing scares me though. If this base's bio-scanners, or whatever you called them, were ever triggered to a threat, there's no way in hell I'd be able to override them. We'd be trapped down here."

"I don't see how that's a problem," Benji chimed in. "Have you read Warren's report on the armory? We could just blast our way out if it came to that."

Mike and Darren looked at him as if he were an idiot.

"Benji, do you really think they'd build this place to where someone down here could get out if something went wrong inside of it?"

"Darren's right," Mike agreed. "I doubt a point-blank nuke could rupture this structure. If it goes into lockdown, we're finished . . . but at least it won't be the rats that get us."

"You got that right," Warren said, making them all jump as he appeared in the doorway.

"What the hell are you doing here?" Mike asked.

"Not much to do around here, in case you hadn't noticed. Besides, I had something I wanted to ask you. But if you're busy, I can come back."

"No. No, not really. We're still just trying to figure things out in here. What was it you wanted to ask?"

"Just something I've been wondering about since we got here and found the main outer doors open. I can't believe no else has asked it yet."

"Well?" Mike prompted.

"Where the hell is everyone, Mike? You don't build something like this and leave it unmanned. I don't care if the F-ing world is falling into Hell; even if people were called out and some abandoned their duties to try to reach their families, someone would have stayed. Shit, Mike, we haven't found a single corpse."

Mike stared at Warren as the soldier's words sank in. "My God . . . You're right. How in the hell have we been so stupid? There should have been a skeleton crew at least to keep the base operational. This place is too much for the government to just write off." Mike whirled on Darren. "We need the security systems online now! We have to know if we're alone, or if there are others in the base with us."

"Be my guest," Darren said, getting up and offering his tools to Mike.

"Shit!" Mike plopped into Darren's seat and ripped open a panel on the console. Darren moved out of his way. "Where the fuck do you think you're going?" Mike snapped at him. "Get back here and help me!"

Benji glanced at Warren and caught what appeared to be a quick smile pass over the man's rough features. "I'll get us some coffee," Warren said and turned to leave the room.

As Warren left, Benji found the nerve to speak up again. "But wouldn't we have seen anyone by now if they were here?"

"This base is huge, Benji," Mike answered without looking up from his work. "And they'd know it better than we do. For all we know, they could be holed up in a safe room somewhere, biding their time."

"Biding their time for what?"

"A chance to take back the base," Mike said.

Warren returned minutes later with a steaming cup of coffee in his hand. He took a sip as he watched Darren and Mike fighting with the base's systems. They'd long since given up any fix short of manually bypassing the security protocols.

"Damn it!" Mike shouted. "This is taking too long!"

"Uhh . . . Mike," Warren said, trying to get his attention. He didn't look up. "Mike."

"What?"

"There's no army hidden in the base to try to kill us," Warren said calmly.

Mike almost ignored Warren and went to throw himself back into his work, but he caught a glint of humor on Warren's face. He stopped and glared at him. "How can you know that?" he asked carefully.

"The armory," Warren informed him. "When Brent and I were cataloging it, we noticed a few things missing from what should have been there. Two rifles, a handful of pistols, some ammo. Just a bit here and there. The other inventory reports you had for the meeting showed similar things, just a bit missing here and there. The way I see it, there were likely one or two people living in this place when got here—maybe three if someone was injured. They likely saw us coming but for some reason couldn't close the main doors in time, so they grabbed what they could, locked down the labs, and tucked themselves away when they realized there were too many of us for them to fight. Right now, I bet they're tucked away, scared shitless, waiting on us to leave."

"You knew there was someone else here this whole time and you're just now telling me a week later?"

"No, I suspected. When I overheard about the problems you were having with the security systems, that confirmed it for me. You've been able to get the ones outside working just fine, but the internal ones . . . That's because they shut them down hard to protect themselves. It's what I would've done in their place. Though if these people were anything like me, most of us would be dead, picked off one or two at a time to even the odds, which makes me think these people, whoever they are, aren't looking for a fight. They've had their chance to strike first and they let it slip by."

"So you're saying we shouldn't be worried?" Darren asked.

"No, I didn't say that. We need to find them. We need to let them know we're not a threat before they get so desperate they do something stupid."

"I've got it!" Mike shouted. The security console came to life. Not just a random screen here and there but the whole board of monitors, showing eight of the interior rooms, including the one they were in. They could now cycle through the cameras and, in theory, see most of the base, but more importantly the bio-scanners were online too.

Darren double-checked Mike's work. The last thing they needed was for the system to short out or blow.

Mike clicked on the bio-scanner screen and a two-dimensional map of the base appeared. Little green dots spotted the map, most of them moving.

"Those dots represent everyone alive in the complex. See how there are four dots here?" Mike pointed at the room they were in. "That's us. So five of you came back from the fuel run and eighteen of us escaped the attack on the convoy, so how many dots do we have?"

"Twenty-four," Warren answered. "One person too many."

"But how do we know which dot isn't one of us?" Darren asked.

"Normally, I would say we couldn't," Mike said, "but luck has made it easy for us." He pointed at the screen again. "He or she is camped out in the number-four lab. We haven't been able to get into the high-security labs yet, so there's no way that's one of us."

"I think it's time we paid them a visit," Warren said, ready to get down to business.

"Hold on," Mike urged. "We may have gotten these systems online, but we still can't open those doors. I don't think going down there and banging on them is a good idea for any of us."

"So what do we do, Mike?" Warren asked, clearly annoyed. "Station a guard by them twenty-four seven and wait for whoever it is to get desperate enough to come out on their own?"

"Actually, I was just thinking we'd use the base's intercom. We can talk to whoever it is in there without putting any of our people at risk."

Warren thought it over and nodded. "Agreed. But I'm still going down there, just in case whoever's in there gets spooked and comes out, guns blazing."

"Take Brent and Michelle with you. No sense in taking unneeded chances; besides, Michelle's a hell of a lot more diplomatic than you are."

Warren scowled. "Give me ten minutes to round them up and get in position." With that said, he stormed out of the room.

"Damn," Darren commented. "That man is ready to kick some ass."

"He's always ready," Mike said. "I'm just glad it's not ours.

FOUR

KYLE stirred on his makeshift bed. His dreams had not been pleasant, hadn't been since the darkness came. Hell, they never had been pleasant, he admitted to himself. He wasn't the kind of person who had nice dreams.

He sat up, dropping his bare feet onto the metal floor of the lab and scratching his eyebrow. His back ached from using a lab table as a mattress.

Ever since he had gone into hiding a week ago, he hadn't been able to shower or shave properly. It bothered him more than the dregs of shit food he'd been living on since he'd locked himself in the lab.

When the intruders first broke in, he had cursed himself for not repairing the outer doors. He should have done it as soon as he arrived, even before he brought the base's systems online. But he'd thought the world was dead, and to save time and energy he'd decided to turn on systems as needed. The intruders had taken him so off-guard, there was no way he could've sealed them out. So he'd taken what precautions he was able to, locking down security systems, disabling a few key systems—or at least turning them off again—and grabbing what he thought he'd need to survive until they were gone. Kyle had never imagined they would take up residence in the base. In the heat of the moment, he'd only seen them as looters, not refugees, and now he was paying the price.

He dressed and began to search through his dwindling rations for something he'd be able to stomach for breakfast.

Suddenly a voice filled the room, startling him so bad he dropped the granola bar he'd just dug out of the pile.

"Hello," the voice said. "My name is Michael Stevenson. We mean you no harm. Please use the base's intercom to respond if you can hear me."

Kyle raced to the lab's door and snatched up one of the two M-16 rifles propped against the wall.

They'd found him. Though he had hoped he wouldn't be discovered, some small rational part of his brain knew this would happen.

"Hello. Please respond if you can hear me," the voice continued. "My name is Michael Stevenson. I am a former director of this facility. Please, we mean you no harm."

Kyle stood by the lab's door, knuckles white from his tightening grip on the rifle. His eyes darted to the intercom panel on the far wall.

Had they been able to access the base's security measures despite his efforts, or were they merely guessing that someone else was here with them? Were they military or civilian? From the glimpses he'd caught of them on the exterior cameras, he was inclined to guess the latter, but if so, why would they have a former director with them? Was the voice lying about who he was? If not, then Kyle knew he was screwed. If the man was who he claimed to be, then surely they'd repaired the scanners and would know exactly where he was at all times, even if he made a run for it. Worse, they would know he was alone. Likely there were armed men already waiting on the other side of the door.

Guessing he had no other option, Kyle set aside his rifle and walked towards the intercom panel.

"STILL nothing?" Darren asked.

Mike scowled at him. "You're sitting right here. Have you heard anyone?"

"Maybe the intercom in that lab just isn't working," Benji said.

"I very much doubt it." Mike pressed the intercom button again and started to repeat his message. "Hello," was the only word he got out before another voice came over the comm.

"I heard you the first few times. What do you want?"

Mike blinked, taken aback by the eerie, calm sound of the voice. "Well, for starters we'd like you to come out and talk with us face to face."

"I'm sure you would," the voice answered. "The question is, if I open the door to this lab, are we going to talk, or are your men going to put a bullet in my head?"

"We mean you no harm." Mike tried to sound reassuring.

"You'll have to forgive me if I don't take your word on that."

"What's your name?" Mike asked.

"Kyle."

"Okay, Kyle. If you don't come out, we will eventually find a way to open the door or cut through it. Things could go badly for both of us if it comes to that. If you're afraid we're military or raiders, we're not. We're just people who need a place to stay. We're simply trying to stay alive like you are."

"Answer me one thing, Michael Stevenson: have the rats won?"

Mike looked at Benji and Darren, then turned back to the intercom. "Yes, the rats won. We haven't seen any other survivors or heard any comm. traffic in a long time. I believe the human race is nearly extinct."

Kyle's laughter echoed through the intercom's speakers. "That's not what I meant. I meant did they win the war?"

Mike glanced at Darren for help, but Darren shrugged.

"Didn't you hear me?" Mike asked Kyle. "The human race is almost wiped out. I'd call that a victory."

"Okay," Kyle said suddenly, struggling to control his amusement. "You've convinced me. Tell your people to stand down. I'm coming out."

In the corridor outside of the lab, Warren, Brent, and Michelle watched as the heavy metal door parted from the wall and slid open. Behind it stood a man who appeared to be in his early thirties. He was thin, and unwashed brown hair topped his head. His features, accentuated by glasses, were narrow and bird–like, yet attractive in a geekish sort of way. He carried himself with an air of confidence that usually came from military training, but his clothes were civilian and dirty, as if they hadn't been changed in a while.

The man held out his empty hands in front of him. "I come in peace," he said, grinning. "Take me to your leader."

Brent and Michelle couldn't help but laugh at the absurdity of his statement.

Warren, however, didn't laugh. "Turn around and put your hands on the wall."

"Or what? You'll shoot me? My name is Kyle, by the way. Nice to meet you too, though I didn't catch your name."

"It's Warren. Now I suggest you do as I say before you start to piss me off more than you already have."

"It figures people like you would survive," Kyle said, appraising Warren. "You're a hardcore soldier and trained killer, aren't you, sport? I know your type."

Warren gritted his teeth. "I'm not going to ask you again."

"No, I imagine not." Kyle turned and placed his hands on the walls, legs spread.

Warren moved in and patted him down for concealed weapons. When he saw that Kyle was clean, he stepped back.

Kyle turned around, looking over Michelle's body and drinking it in. He bowed to her. "My dear lady, perhaps after the guns are put away I might learn your name."

Michelle noticed she was still pointing her gun at him and lowered it. "Michelle," she said apologetically.

Kyle shot a parody of a salute at Warren and said, "If you would be so kind as to lead the way, I believe your boss is waiting on me."

Warren led Kyle through the complex, leaving Brent and Michelle behind in an attempt to draw attention away from what was going on. So far only a few people knew about Kyle's presence and Warren wanted to keep it that way until they knew for sure how things would play out. Luckily most people in the group kept to themselves or at least to certain cliques. Originally the convoy group had been so large and so hectically nomadic it was nearly impossible to get to know everyone. People were beginning to loosen up now inside the safety of the base, but still the odds were in Warren's favor.

He and Kyle only passed a handful of people on their way to the control room, and no one seemed to notice anything out of place. Warren had left his rifle with Michelle, and his sidearm was nothing out of the ordinary; the group was used to him storming around the base with a gun.

Mike, Darren, and Benji were waiting on them as they entered. Mike stood up from his seat at one of the security consoles and extended his hand to Kyle. "I'm Doctor Michael Stevenson, but please call me Mike."

Kyle took his hand and shook it. "Nice to meet you, Mike. And who might these gentlemen be?"

Mike introduced Benji as his aide and Darren as the group's computer specialist, though the title was a bit of an exaggeration. "And you've already met Warren," Mike concluded. "He's our head of security."

Kyle chuckled. "I gathered as much."

Mike offered Kyle a seat and sat down near him. "We've got a lot of questions for you, Kyle. How about we start with why you're here? As far as I know, this base was officially decommissioned when the plague hit, and the operating personnel relocated or were sent out into the field. A single person being left here just doesn't make sense. A skeleton crew or the sort I could believe, but not one person. Were you stationed here, or did you come here after things went to hell like we did?"

"Or we could start by asking who the hell you are?" Warren butted in. "Your accent doesn't sound like someone who's spent a long time in the U.S."

"Kyle Weathersby," Kyle said to Warren. He sighed and turned back to Mike. "I imagine you want the long answer. Okay. I am, or rather *was*, a representative, shall we say, of the British government, dispatched by the United Nations in attempt to discover the fate of the United States. The U.S. was one of the first countries to 'go silent' as all hell broke loose around the globe. I set foot upon American soil for the first time twenty-four hours after my government lost contact. I, along with my similarly well-armed associates, quickly found ourselves on the run, fighting for survival, with no way home. Most of the members of my team died in New York. Those of us who made it out lost contact with home.

"We set out for your capital and reached it to join forces with the remains of your leadership, at least those who weren't already dead or whisked away to a shelter somewhere. One of those survivors was a person of some importance in your C.I.A. He knew of this facility, and a small group of us decided to head for here since home was unreachable and your nation had crumpled. I was the only one to make it here still breathing. I've been here ever since, staying alive and using the comm. channels to listen to the fate of the world above.

"I honestly thought I would die down here alone before your group showed up. I had gotten so used to the idea, I hid rather than chance dying at your hands. I couldn't bring myself to make a stand against you, knowing how rare human life is becoming in the world." Kyle stopped. "Is that enough of an answer for you or do I need to elaborate?"

"So you're military?" Warren asked.

Kyle shook his head. "No, I was a field operative. There's a difference. I was an agent, not a soldier."

Warren glowered at him.

"Does it really matter?" Mike asked them, taking control of the situation again. "Kyle, you said you had been listening to what was going on out there. Is the rest of the world as bad off as we are here?"

"Do you even know what's happening?" Kyle asked.

"Are there people still broadcasting?" Darren interrupted.

"No." Kyle's voice became flat and cold. "I hadn't heard anything for a few days before you arrived."

"So the rats rule everything now?" Mike asked, praying he was wrong about the answer he expected to get.

"No. They're at war with the other factions of Hell."

The room fell silent. Kyle felt their eyes burning into him, and finally he continued. "The wolves are still trying to complete their hold of Canada. The squids rule the seas and most of the islands. The bats are facing pockets of human resistance in Russia. The snakes have pacified Asia and are already making strikes against the bats, which hasn't gone well for them if the human accounts are to be believed. I haven't heard anything about Australia, and South America has been silent since days after the U.S. fell apart. As to my home, it was holding out against the dead, but the last word I got were my orders to come here.

"The only constant in all of it is the dead. Each group of demons, or whatever one chooses to call them, seems to use the dead as their primary foot soldiers in their secondary war against us. So with the demons at war and humanity nearly gone, I would be forced to say that if anyone 'rules the world,' as you put it, it would be the dead."

Mike leaned close to Kyle. "Stop it. I am sorry for whatever happened to you, but there are no such things as demons. Hell doesn't exist. Everything that's happening out there is the combined result of a virus and an aberrant evolutionary spike in the rodent species."

Kyle held his ground. "Believe what you wish. I don't care. I'm just telling you what I've seen and heard. Hell has been loosed upon the earth, and because of where we are, we are going to die. Maybe not today, maybe not even for a year or two in this base, but we are going to die. Unlike most of the other factions, the rats just want us gone and they'll stop at nothing until their borders are clear of our infestation."

"Mike, we've all seen those creatures with the rats," Darren argued. "Warren and some of his crew even nicknamed them demons. He may be telling the truth."

"Or he may be completely crazy! We have no way to verify who he is or any of his claims."

Kyle reached into his pocket and slapped down his U.N. identification card in front of Mike. "And I recorded some of the transmissions I spoke of. If you haven't fired them while jury-rigging the base's systems, I suggest you listen to them yourselves."

Warren watched Mike closely. He could see that the man refused to accept anything Kyle had told them, but as much as his own instincts told him not to trust the U.N. agent, Warren had to admit his story had the ring of truth about it. "What do we do, Mike?"

"Lock him up until we figure out what's really going on."

"Mike," Benji interjected, "we can't do that. He has rights."

"I'm not suggesting we kill him! I just think we should keep an eye on him until we know he's not crazy. For his sake and our own."

Kyle said nothing, resigning himself to the group's judgment.

"I agree with Benji," Darren spoke up. "This guy knows this place better than we do. Frankly, we could use his help, and he hasn't done anything."

Mike turned to Warren. "I want you to find somewhere to lock this man up and make sure he stays there."

"Sorry, Mike, they're right. We need him. If there's a chance he can get this base fully online and the main doors locked down, he's a hell of a lot more use to us here than tucked away somewhere. Everyone else deserves to know he's here as well, and what he knows too. We're all in this together."

"Did any of you listen to the crap he claimed was happening? Demons, Hell on Earth—I mean, my God, come on." He slammed his fist into the console beside him. "He needs to be locked up."

"Benji," Warren said, "get the group together for another meeting. I want all of us there, understand?"

Benji nodded, though it pained him to go against Mike.

"And Mr. Higgins, you're going to stay right here for the moment and help Darren with his work. If you so much as think of doing anything that would put us at risk, I will personally put a bullet through your damn skull."

Mike threw up his hands. "So that's it then? I'm out just like that, and you're all listening to Warren instead of me?"

"Mike, we're grateful you got us here," Warren said, stepping closer to him. "No one's saying we don't respect you, but rats or no rats, this is still a free country where people get to decide what's best for them. None of us has the right to decide things for this group alone."

Mike rocked back in his chair. "Fine. Fine. Do what you think you need to do. I won't stand in your way."

Warren nodded. "Benji, the meeting . . . "

Benji leapt up and scurried out of the room, glancing back at Mike as if to say he was sorry.

"Do things always work so smoothly for you guys?" Kyle asked, unable to resist his tendency for dark humor.

Two hours later, the survivors of the convoy gathered into the mess hall. Mike, Warren, and Kyle sat at a table facing the rest of the group. Warren finished explaining who Kyle was, how they'd found him, and what Kyle had told them about the state of the world. "So that's what we know. Darren has spent the last few hours working on retrieving some of the transmissions Mr. Higgins spoke of. Darren?" Warren motioned for him to start.

"I have rigged the transmissions to play into the room for all of us to hear at the same time," Darren said, walking over to the room's intercom panel. "They're random, and most likely some of them will be garbled, but the base's computers have translated them into English where needed; this was the best I could do." Darren punched a button on the intercom and the transmissions began to play.

"To anyone who can hear me, this is Captain Vladimir Nabov of the Soviet Home Guard. Please send assistance. We are cut off and running out of ammunition. The push to free the capital has failed. The main force is broken and shattered. My men and myself have taken shelter inside a cathedral outside of Moscow. Conventional weapons seem to have little effect on the enemy beyond slowing them down. Three of them alone decimated my entire unit with their bare hands, without a single loss to their forces.

"For whatever reason, the creatures themselves will not attack us inside these walls; however, we are far from safe. The bats . . . the bats come in waves, hundreds at a time, pouring through the shattered windows. So far, we have beaten them each time they've tried to overrun us, but we cannot hold on much longer. Please, in the name of God, if you can hear us, we need assistance."

The intercom crackled and the broadcast changed to a voice with a heavy French accent. "So it's me again. I'm still on the air as of now. I think I have enough fuel to keep the generator running and the heat on for another day or two. I don't know why I'm doing this. I doubt actual people are listening to this anymore, but it helps me stay sane. Once a radio geek, always a radio geek," the voice joked, then turned sad.

"They took my wife yesterday. We left the station to see if we could find some food. We'd used up the stuff from the vending machines and the stuff for the lounge fridge, despite careful rationing. We snuck out the rear entrance and were heading for Baker Street because we knew there was a grocery on that block. The thing must have caught our scent or something, because we were being quiet and as careful as possible. It came tearing out of an abandoned car it must have been sleeping in. It wasn't a wolf either. We didn't see any of those.

"This thing was one of their leaders, a full-on monster in the flesh. Must've stood eight feet tall. It went straight for Margaret, tossing me aside like trash." The voice had become heartbroken and on the verge of tears. "When I got to my feet again, she was screaming and it had her skirt torn open, just . . . just taking her right there in the street.

"I lost it, I guess. I had a metal bat with me that one of my friends had kept in his office, and I started beating the hell out of the thing's head. At first, it grunted like I was a mere annoyance, and it kept rutting away. Finally, it turned and I caught a glimpse of its yellow eyes before it backhanded me. When I came to, they were gone. Margaret's blood was smeared onto the street where she had lain, but I don't think she's dead."

The voice cracked, as if trying to hold back tears, and the speaker paused before continuing. "I think I'll be seeing her again soon," the man said with heavy sadness and an edge of fear. "She'll change if she's alive, then she'll remember me. If the male of her pack allows it, she'll be coming. I spent most of last night, before I got too drunk to stand, strengthening up the barricades on the doors and windows downstairs, but I've heard tell of those things tossing around cars. When she comes, she will get in."

The transmission ended and a new one started up, but this time there was only the sound of men and women screaming in the distance, as if they weren't at their equipment and had merely left it on. When the screaming stopped, a chorus of hissing noises could be heard before the transmission ended and the next began.

"Mayday! Mayday! This is the USS McDaniel. We are under attack! I repeat: we are under attack!" The sound of small arms fire and ripping metal could be heard loudly in the background. "The squids are everywhere! The bigger ones have breached the hull in several places, and the smaller mutated ones are climbing onto the deck. We're being boarded. Help us! Help . . . " The transmission became static and cut off.

"That's all I have been able to piece together so far," Darren informed the group. "We have been getting a constant live broadcast from Mexico, but it's just a constant buzzing noise now. I swear it sounds like a swarm of insects talking."

Warren stood up behind the table he was at. "Thank you, Darren. As you've heard, the transmissions do confirm Mr. Higgins' stories about what has happened to our world. He has also presented us with proof that he was indeed working as a British operative as part of a joint U.N. taskforce sent to the U.S. days after our country fell into complete collapse. None of this information directly changes our situation, but we are left with the question of what to do with Mr. Higgins himself. He has extensive knowledge in many fields that could be of use to us, and his presence will not adversely affect our resources. I would like to ask if he might be allowed to stay."

Murmurs of shock ran through the group. Michelle spoke up first. "Are you suggesting that you and Mike have actually thought of kicking him out? I mean just sending him out there to die?"

Mike stood up beside Warren. "Transmissions and IDs can be faked. We don't really know who this man is. I believe he may be unstable and a threat to our continued security. There are no such things as demons, yet Mr. Higgins firmly states that multiple factions of Hell have somehow been loosed upon our world. He believes these factions are at war with one another for the control of our planet. Does that sound remotely sane to any of you? Our problems come from the rats and a mutated viral strand, which has somehow caused an evolutionary jump in the rodent species."

Darren looked Mike in the eye. "I think believing something different than what you do is not cause to sentence a man to death. As far as I'm concerned, he's already a part of our group by being human and alive."

"Those transmissions sounded pretty real to me," Daniel chimed in. Words of agreement spread through the small crowd.

Seeing he was defeated, Mike sat down and left Warren with the floor.

Kyle, who had been smiling the whole time, suddenly jumped out of his seat like a lunatic. He pointed at something behind the group, and heads turned to the back of the mess hall where Jenkins was leaping to his feet, trying to claw his .45 free from its holster.

A rat sat beside him, sniffing the air. With its blazing red eyes fixed on Warren, Mike and Kyle, it screeched and charged at them, baring its large primary teeth. Its screech quickly turned into a hiss of anger and superiority.

As it made a path towards them, Michelle jumped out of her chair and crushed its skull underneath the heel of her right boot. Warm blood leaked from its eyes as she picked up its corpse by the tail and tossed it towards the back of the room. The group quickly spiraled into panic.

"Hold on!" Warren ordered. "Everybody settle down—now!" The room fell silent at the fury in his voice. "If there were more of them in the room, they'd be attacking us already. Darren, get up to the control center and run a scan. Jenkins, Michelle, go with him! Everyone else, stay the fuck where you are. If they have made it in, the last thing we need to do is split up and take off running through the halls."

Darren, with Jenkins and Michelle in tow, had already sprinted out of the mess hall. Warren grabbed Kyle up by the front of his shirt. "Are there rats in this base? Have you seen any before?"

Kyle knocked Warren's hand away from him. "No. If they're here, they must have followed you. How did all of you get here?"

"The damn cars," Warren said, realizing what Kyle was suggesting. He turned back to the crowd as the intercom blared to life and Darren's voice flooded the room.

"The base is clear. That thing must've been alone. But Warren, you and Mike need to get up here as fast as you can."

"Everybody stay calm!" Warren barked. "Go to your quarters, seal the doors, and we'll let you know what's going on as soon as possible. Now go!" Warren looked over the crowd as they poured out of the room. Mike and Kyle were running side by side for the control room and Warren cursed as he took off after them.

Warren was the last one to make it. He looked at the external camera screens the others were staring at and simply breathed the words, "Oh shit."

Darren nodded gravely. "Yeah, it looks pretty bad." Rows upon rows of rotting bodies stumbled around above the base, and literally thousands of rats skittered about beneath the corpses' feet.

"My lord," Mike whispered and pointed at one of the screens showing the main doors. "Are those the things you're calling demons?" he asked Kyle.

Two massive creatures were looking down the shaft that led to the complex's inner doors. They stood seven feet tall like humanoid rat monsters from a child's nightmare. As Kyle spoke, a clawed hand fell over the camera's lens and the screen went black.

"Yep, those would be them," Kyle confirmed smugly.

"How the hell did they find us?" Mike wondered.

"They followed us." Warren drew his sidearm and checked its magazine. "Kyle said the rats want all of us dead and their borders clear before they launch into the war he's told us about. Think about what our convoy must have looked like to them. It was likely one of the last large gatherings of us anywhere in the U.S. They planned the attack on it and they've come to finish what they started."

"Yeah, but how did they know where to follow us?" Jenkins asked.

"We had to leave the vehicles up top. They must have recognized them by our scent, then all they had to do was look around. With those damn huge open doors, where the hell else could they think we've gone to?"

"The bio-scanners are still showing we're clean so far," Darren said with a shrug. "But if one got in, others probably will. It's just a matter of time."

"The rat was a scout," Warren and Kyle said almost at the same time. Warren snarled and Kyle gestured at the blank screen. "I'd be worried about the demons. Who knows how many are up there? The two we saw are enough to tear apart the inner doors alone, given time." Kyle plopped down in a chair. "This is your base now, your group. You guys make the call. Are we going to fight or run?"

"Where could we run to?" Mike fumed. "If this place isn't safe, where the hell is?"

"My home was still standing when I left. We could try for there," Kyle offered.

"You're forgetting something." Warren slid his gun into the holster on his belt. "In order to get out, we're going to have to go past them . . . And on foot. They've torn the vehicles to shreds, you can bet on it."

"So there's no other option?" Michelle asked. "We make a stand or die?"

"Looks that way," Daniel answered.

"Great," Michelle said bitterly. "Anybody got a plan as to how we do that?"

"We could lock down the upper levels. Buy ourselves some time to think," Darren suggested.

"Are you insane?" Michelle appeared on the edge of exploding in his direction.

"No, wait." Warren gave her a stern glance. "He may be onto something. Kyle, can you control the lockdown? Choose which doors to seal?"

"Yeah, sure. You want to lead them down a path, keep them from spreading out and using their numbers against us? I can do that, but remember, we don't know how the lone rat got in. There's no guarantee we won't be facing them from two or more places regardless."

"If we're going to make a stand, doing it gives us more of a chance than not trying it." Warren pointed at the layout of the base on the scanner screen. "Try to force them through here."

Kyle spun around in his chair and went to work laying his preparations.

"Daniel." Warren laid a hand on the hulking man's shoulder. "Go round up everyone you can who knows how to use a weapon in close quarters. Michelle, Jenkins, go break out the flamethrowers." Warren placed a finger on the screen. "We'll meet them here in the main corridor, two doors in from the main ones. They shouldn't have time to break in any more than that before we're in place."

"What about everyone else?" Darren asked.

"Arm them and send them back to the mess hall until we see how this goes on the upper levels. If it goes well, the rats may cut their losses and bug out."

"I doubt that," Kyle said, looking over his shoulder at Warren as he worked.

"Me too, but if they do, it'll be our window to make a run for it. If not, taking us out is going to cost them. They'll have to pay heavily for every foot they make it inside."

FIVE

BY the time Warren reached the spot on the upper level where the group had opted to make their stand, the others were waiting. Daniel and Jenkins wore the flamethrower units, which would be the group's core defense. Michelle and Brent, being better marksmen, carried assault rifles; it would be primarily up to them to hold off the burning dead. Mike and a young woman named Brook stood behind them, armed with scattershot shotguns to deal with whatever rats made it through the flames and to cover the group's retreat, if it came to that.

Warren had arrived late because he'd stopped to place several charges on the corridor walls farther down in order to slow the enemy if they were forced to bug out faster than they planned. Already, the demons were pounding away at the last inner door.

"Looks like you made it here in the nick of time, boss," Michelle said, smiling.

Warren returned her smile and readied the bulky, eight-shot grenade launcher in his hands, taking aim as the door fell inward and an angry demon met them with a half-surprised screech.

"Light 'em up!" Warren yelled and pulled the trigger of his weapon. The grenade caught the monster in the chest, knocking it backwards in a mass of blood and bone.

The defenders rose up from their makeshift cover as rats came pouring towards them. Twin jets of flame streaked into the passage-way, frying the lead rats as they ran headlong into the blazing streams. The rodents began to realize they were not gaining ground and with-drew as the dead came staggering in.

Daniel and Jenkins fell back, and Warren, tossing aside his launch-er in favor of an AK-47, joined Michelle and Jenkins as they opened up on full auto, spraying the dead in the confined space. Warren and Jenkins quickly switched to placing their rounds for more effect as Michelle kept up the onslaught, pushing the corpses back as best she could. Despite their efforts, the dead gained ground.

Mike stepped up and fired around Michelle as she paused to reload. Brook stayed in the rear, and she was the one to notice the rats using the dead for cover. "They're coming back!" she screamed, unable to fire with her friends in front of her.

Pressing themselves against the walls, Warren and Brent reloaded, then resumed firing as Jenkins and Daniel took the center, smothering the floor of the corridor in flame. More rats squealed, dying as they were cooked alive, but the dead paid no attention to the fires swirling about their waists; they continued to press forward. The base's defenders were ever so slowly being forced to retreat.

Then Daniel's flamethrower ran dry. "Incoming!" he shouted and ran behind the others as the rats made a renewed push forward. Jenkins cranked up his flame and engulfed the whole corridor in a sea of fire.

"Fall back!" Warren ordered.

Kyle, who was watching the battle from the control room, sealed a door behind them as they retreated deeper into the complex. When the door slammed shut, the defenders paused to regroup. Benji came running up to them with a new flamethrower in his hands. Daniel grabbed it and began to strap it onto his back.

"Thank you," Warren told Benji. "Now get the hell out of here!"

Benji turned and fled as the pounding on the door started.

"Grenade again?" Daniel asked.

"Can't," Warren replied. "Not enough cover this time."

"What about the demon?" someone shrieked.

"We're going to have to shoot the fucker!"

The monsters bashed through the door, and it flew inward, slamming Brent into the wall and cutting his body nearly in half. Blood and intestines spilled from the long gash across his stomach.

The demon sprang at them like a force of nature. Michelle and Warren blasted it, and spent round casings clattered to the floor around them. It howled in pain but kept moving straight into the heart of the group, clawing away most of Jenkins's face. His finger tightened on the trigger of his flamethrower, hosing Daniel and Mike. Daniel's flamethrower exploded, and Jenkins's erupted soon after.

Michelle and Brook managed to evade the blasts, ducking away around a corner. They got to their feet as the demon came around the bend, stumbling, its whole body ablaze.

Brook watched in horror as Michelle stepped up to it and stuck the barrel of her rifle against its face. She pulled the trigger, and its head splattered from a point-blank, three-round burst. "That's for Warren," she whispered as its body toppled over with a thud. Michelle stared at the burning thing with tears welling up in her eyes until Brook yanked her backwards by her shoulder, screaming for her to come on.

Kyle's voice boomed over the intercom. "Run! Get to the lower levels! I'm locking down the top completely—run!"

Brook dragged Michelle into a lift and didn't let go until its doors sealed behind them. Michelle slumped to the floor, shaking with sobs. Brook kneeled beside her and took her in her arms.

The lift didn't stop until it reached the bottom level. Darren met them and helped Michelle to her feet. "Kyle's on his way here, sealing the last of the doors manually behind him."

Michelle took a deep breath, steadying herself. "How long?" she asked.

"Kyle said he didn't know. If they work their way to a lift and come down its shaft, less than an hour, tops." Darren reached out and put a hand on her arm. "I'm sorry about Warren."

She slapped his hand off her. "We don't have time for this. I'm the only one left who has real training in fighting the rats. I've got to do something to try and stop them." She marched off towards the mess hall with Brook and Darren reluctantly following her. "These people need to know what's coming," she said without looking back.

Benji was standing inside the doorway to the mess hall as Michelle entered. She shoved him aside before he could ask where Mike was, and every pair of eyes in the room turned towards her.

"Warren's dead," she stated in a hollow voice. "So are Mike and the others."

The news hit Benji like a fist to the gut. He fell to his knees with tears flowing down his cheeks.

"The rats are inside the base and coming for us. We have less than an hour."

The other survivors remained silent, stricken with terror.

"There's no way out," Michelle informed them. "I know none of you are soldiers. Most of you never used a gun before the rats came, and some of you probably don't think you can, but we're it. What we do in the next few minutes will determine who we are and what our lives meant. We can sit and wait for the rats to gnaw us into bits, or we can go fighting like Warren and the others did. It's up to you, but I need to know this instant where we stand."

"Haven't been too keen on waiting around my whole life," a big man named Paul said.

A redheaded woman in her early thirties spoke up next. "Those things took my husband when the convoy was attacked. I say we kill as many of those little pieces of shit as we can."

Corrie, who'd been serving as the group's main cook, pushed herself to her feet; she was in her forties, overweight, and she had a horrible complexion. "You point me at 'em, honey, and I'll blow the bastards to pulp," she said, pumping a round into the chamber of the 12-gauge she carried.

"Are we all in agreement then?" Michelle challenged them, slinging her rifle onto her shoulder so that it pointed at the ceiling. A chorus of approval echoed in the mess hall as Kyle entered behind Michelle.

"Rallying the troops, I see," he said, laughing.

Michelle spun around, taking a swing at his face. He caught her by the wrist and twisted her in front of him, pinning her arm against her own back.

"That's cute. It really is." Kyle gave her a kiss on the cheek as she broke his hold and bolted from him. "Whoa, beautiful. We don't have to die today. There is another way out of the compound without going through the bulk of the rats."

"What?" Michelle asked, struggling to keep her anger in check.

"The rat," Kyle said, "the one that got in alone. It used the bak door. There's an old part of the base that doesn't show on the scanners. It isn't part of the base proper, so to speak. It was part of the original bomb shelter built on this spot before your government remodeled this place into a high-tech death factory."

Darren was stunned. "If that's true, why didn't you tell us about it before?"

"Didn't know about it myself until a few minutes ago. I know this place went on beyond the steel walls we called the base, but I didn't know they were still accessible until I saw a demon just appear on the bio-scanners as I was running for my life. Since as far as I know they can't walk through rock, I figure it came from a tunnel in the old base and ripped its way into this one."

"What does all that mean?" Paul asked, trying to keep up.

"It means if we can take out a single demon and maybe a much smaller force of the rats and the dead than the one up top, we can get the hell out of here and have a shot at staying alive."

"Where's the tunnel?" someone called out.

Kyle kept his eyes on Michelle. "It's in the emergency stairwell between this level and the one above it, only on the other side of the complex. If we're lucky, the rats will spread their numbers thin on the level above us, thinking some of us are hiding on that floor. We'll hopefully have even less of them to fight through."

"Michelle," Darren said, "could we really do what he's saying?"

"Maybe. If we had more weapons."

"We don't and we're wasting time," Kyle spat. "I can't do this on my own, or I'd be gone already. We go now with what we have, or we die here without question. It's as simple as that."

Paul motioned for Michelle to go. "Get going. I can't do what he's asking, or I'd go myself." He thumped his chest. "Heart condition. I wouldn't survive the running."

Corrie moved to stand beside him. "I'm staying too." She gestured to a group of people keeping to themselves at the rear of the mess hall. "Most of us would stay and hope the rats pass us by or overlook us. Some of us are too scared to go out there if there's the slightest chance we'll be safe where we are. Take who you can and go. If the rats do find us, we'll buy you some time."

Michelle was shocked by Corrie's offer and the bulk of the group's refusal to go. She didn't know what to do. These folk were her responsibility.

Benji stood up, sniffing and wiping at his cheeks. "You go on, sis. I'll look after them. Mike and Warren both would've wanted someone to survive."

"Benji . . . " she started in a quivering voice, but he grabbed her and shoved her at Kyle.

"Get the hell out of here, sis, before I kick your ass for once."

Kyle winked at Benji. "Thanks," he said as he darted for the door. Darren, Brook, and a redheaded woman named Anne raced after him. Michelle hesitated long enough to hug Benji and give him a peck on the nose, and then she followed Kyle's group.

The others watched them go, then closed the mess hall doors and started barricading them with tables, chairs, and whatever else they could find inside the room.

SIX

"THIS way!" Kyle led his small band of escapees around a bend in the corridor. They ran, making it across the lower level to the stairwell door without any unwelcome encounters. They stopped at the entryway. They could hear the shuffling feet of the dead above them on the other side.

"What the fuck?" Darren whispered to Kyle. "Shouldn't they be pouring in here already?"

Kyle smiled darkly, as if he knew something the others didn't. "Never question a good thing," he said, then he swung the door open before anyone could move. Two corpses turned to face them, totally taken off-guard. Kyle dispatched them both with his pistols, then dove up the stairs.

"Shit!" Michelle leapt after him, trying to cover him as best she could with her rifle.

MINUTES before Kyle entered the stairwell, the head Rat King had stood at the hole he and his three brothers had torn through the base's metal wall, communing with his children deeper in the base. His instincts had told him to head to the lowest level, but his children had found a trail of blood on the floor they were currently on. He could feel their joy as they tasted it. It led them to a series of doors that appeared to have been left open just for them. The trail ended in a great red pool at the second stairwell leading down.

The fastest of his children detected noises and smells behind the door, and they informed him that there were humans hiding down there, preparing to face them. *This is the place where we'll feast*, the rats told him.

Sympathetic to his children's eager pleas, the Rat King dispatched them and his brothers to enjoy their prize. He kept a contingent of the dead with him, however, totaling nearly three dozen in number. He was relishing the taste of flesh via his children's senses when the sound of gunshots below snapped his psychic link. He half-howled, half-screeched as the flavors faded from his mouth, then, snarling, he moved to deal with the man who'd taken such pleasure from him.

AS Kyle reached the second level, he skidded to a halt, staring straight into the face of the largest rat demon he'd ever encountered. It looked pissed off, and it threw itself at him. Kyle barely avoided its claws by hurling himself over the stairway's railing. He toppled over the side, grabbing the base of the rails so fast and so hard the impact broke one of his fingers. He screamed but didn't let go.

The Rat King moved towards him like a cat playing with its victim as Michelle reached the second level with Darren and Brook at her side. Brook blasted the creature with her shotgun, and the scattershot tore tiny holes across its skin.

Michelle's rifle clicked empty as she jerked the trigger back. She cursed, tossing it aside.

Moving in front of her, Darren fired a trio of rounds from his .45 into the monster as it spun to face them.

AFTER Michelle left, the people in the mess hall barely had time to barricade the double doors before they heard noises in the corridor outside. Something struck the doors so hard the whole barricade shook, and Benji watched in horror as monsters slowly pushed their way in. Chairs and tables clattered to the floor as the doors swung inward.

"Fire!" Paul roared.

Rats streamed through the debris of the barricade, but the two massive demons held everyone's attention.

Benji was closest to the entrance, and, unleashing a battle cry his sister would have been proud of, he ran straight at the lead demon, firing his 9mm over and over into its chest. The demon grimaced and snarled in pain, but kept walking and swatted Benji across the room with a wave of its hand; he struck the far wall and landed in a mass of broken bones, and as the darkness took him, his last thoughts were of Michelle.

People screamed all around the room, some dying at the hands of the demons, others falling under a whirlwind of hungry rodents. Soon, only Corrie and Paul were left alive.

They fought their way into a corner of the room and kept shooting. Paul was pale and sweating, barely standing as he ripped a rat off his arm where it wiggled, gnawing deeply into his biceps. Corrie was covered head to toe with small bleeding bite marks. She took aim and blew half a dozen rats to pieces with a well-placed blast from her shotgun.

Paul's eyes rolled up in his head as he cried out in pain and collapsed. The rats covered him almost instantly.

"Oh God, please," Corrie wept, flinging a rat from her hair and bringing her shotgun up to face the demon walking towards her.

"God is dead," it said in broken English. "This land is ours now."

The small rats backed off as the thing leaned in to lick the blood off Corrie's face with its long black tongue. Its breath stank of death and decay.

Corrie's shotgun fell from her trembling hands as the rat demon placed a claw between her legs. Her eyes bulged as its finger poked inside of her through her clothes. The creature mimicked a human smile as best it could and jerked upwards, gutting her from groin to neck before she even had time to scream.

THE Rat King laughed as it lifted Darren with a single hand and threw him against the stairwell wall so hard the sound of breaking bones echoed above the chaos of the battle.

Realizing the scattershot in her weapon was useless against the monster, Brook took advantage of the distraction and slipped past the beast into the hole that led to the tunnels beyond, leaving Michelle and Kyle on the stairs. A dead man dressed in a blood-covered police uniform stumbled toward her. Brook shoved the barrel of the shotgun into the corpse's mouth and blew the man to hell.

Back in the stairwell, Michelle drew her sidearm as Kyle struggled to climb over the railing back onto the platform. Anne knocked Michelle aside and let loose on full auto, her AK-47 chattering, spraying a stream of bullets into the Rat King's stomach at point-blank range. The monster retreated, leaving a pool of blood where it had stood.

Kyle swung himself onto the platform, cradling his broken hand in pain. "Don't let up!" he yelled. "Kill the damn thing!"

The Rat King lashed out at Anne with a long arm, and her head disappeared from sight as it bounced down the stairs.

"No!" Michelle screamed and launched herself at the monster. It gawked in surprise as she crashed into it and sent it careening over the side of the stairs. Even before its body had crashed into the floor below, Kyle was dragging Michelle toward the hole in the wall. "Run!"

As he darted into the tunnel and saw Brook sprinting down the passageway into the distance, he dropped a time-delayed grenade onto the ground behind him. He ran on at full speed, dragging Michelle by the hand until the force of the blast hit them and sent them rolling into the dirt. When the dust cleared, they saw that the hole into the stairwell had collapsed, but they could hear the Rat King clawing at the pile of debris that separated them. Kyle got up and yanked Michelle to her feet.

"What do we do now?" she asked.

"We keep running." Kyle smiled and sprinted after Brook.

EPILOGUE

KYLE sat at his desk. The world had ended but the paperwork went on. His superiors wanted a full report on his trip to America.

He sighed and got up, letting the work wait. He poured himself a glass of wine from the office's bar and looked out his window into the streets of London. War raged between the military and the dead, but Britain was holding. A tank made its way down the street, surrounded by a squad of heavily armed men in black, and he watched absent-mindedly, reaching up to trace the scar on his cheek that Michelle had given him. He regretted that he'd been forced to put a bullet in her skull when she'd learned of the steps he'd taken to ensure their escape from the base. He'd longed to feel her wet lips around him at least once, but Brook's lean, tan body had charms of its own, and Brook, unlike Michelle, had been able to grasp that sometimes sacrifices needed to be made for the greater good.

And she was grateful, very grateful in fact, to have a roof over her head and a warm bed to sleep in. He smirked. His job did have its perks.

He returned to his desk and picked up his pen. He'd stood face to face with the new ruler of America and had seen him badly wounded. The demons could be hurt. They weren't immortal like the legends had hinted at. They bled and could be taken out like any mortal foe.

There was hope in the world as long as Britain stood, and when it finished securing its borders and rose up from the ashes of the dead, it would be men like Kyle who would show the evil unleashed upon the earth that mankind could fight dirty too.

BIO

Eric S. Brown is the author of the upcoming releases *World War of the Dead* (Coscom Entertainment) and *Barren Earth* (with Stephen North from Library of the Living Dead Press). Some of his past works include *Cobble, Madmen's Dreams,* and *Unabridged Unabashed and Undead: The Best of Eric S. Brown.* His short fiction has been published hundreds of times and he was featured as an expert on the walking dead in the book *Zombie CSU* by Jonathan Maberry. The comic book series *Dead West,* based on the novella in this book, kicks off in late 2009 from Post Mortem Studios. He also has work slated to appear in such zombie anthologies as *Dead Science, Dead Worlds,* and *Zombology.* Eric is 34 years old and lives in NC with his wife and son.

THE RAGE PLAGUE

A NOVEL BY ANTHONY GIANGREGORIO

An unknown virus spreads across the globe, turning ordinary people into ravenous killers. Only a small population proves to be immune, but most quickly fall prey to the infected.

Isolated on the rooftop of a school near the outskirts of Chicago, Bill Thompson and a small band of survivors come to the frightening realization that, without food or water, they will perish quickly under the hot sun. Some wish to migrate to a safer, more plentiful refuge, but the school is surrounded by rampaging murderers. Without a plan, Bill and his group don't stand a chance.

Their only hope lies in their one advantage over the infected: their ability to think.

ISBN: 978-1934861196

MONSTROUS

20 TALES OF GIANT CREATURE TERROR

Move over King Kong, there are new monsters in town! Giant beetles, towering crustaceans, gargantuan felines and massive underwater beasts, to name just a few. Think you've got what it takes to survive their attacks? Then open this baby up, and join today's hottest authors as they show us the true power of Mother Nature's creatures. With enough fangs, pincers and blood to keep you up all night, we promise you won't look at creepy crawlies the same way again.

ISBN: 978-1934861127

Permuted Press

The formula has been changed...
Shifted... Altered... *Twisted.*™

www.permutedpress.com

AFTER TWILIGHT
WALKING WITH THE DEAD
by Travis Adkins

At the start of the apocalypse, a small resort town on the coast of Rhode Island fortified itself to withstand the millions of flesh-eating zombies conquering the world. With its high walls and self-contained power plant, Eastpointe was a safe haven for the lucky few who managed to arrive.

Trained specifically to outmaneuver the undead, Black Berets performed scavenging missions in outlying towns in order to stock Eastpointe with materials vital for long-term survival. But the town leaders took the Black Berets for granted, on a whim sending them out into the cannibalistic wilderness. Most did not survive.

Now the most cunning, most brutal, most efficient Black Beret will return to Eastpointe after narrowly surviving the doomed mission and unleash his anger upon the town in one bloody night of retribution.

After twilight,
when the morning comes and the sun rises,
will anyone be left alive?

ISBN: 978-1934861035

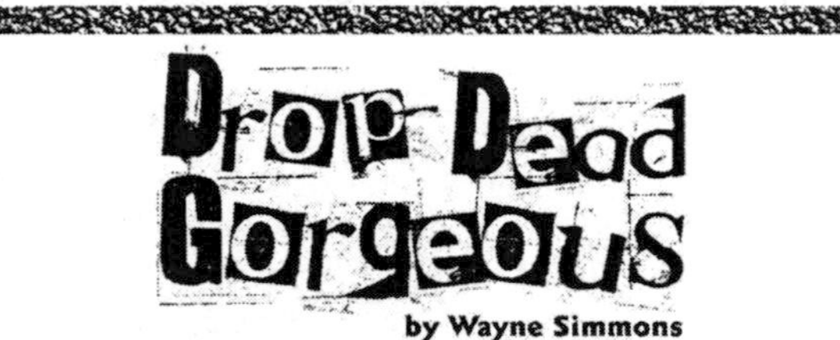

by Wayne Simmons

As tattoo artist Star begins to ink her first client on a spring Sunday morning, something goes horribly wrong with the world... Belfast's hungover lapse into a deeper sleep than normal, their sudden deaths causing an unholy mess of crashing cars, smoldering televisions and falling aircraft.

In the chaotic aftermath a group of post-apocalyptic survivors search for purpose in a devastated city. Ageing DJ Sean Magee and shifty-eyed Barry Rogan find drunken solace in a hotel bar. Ex-IRA operative Mairead Burns and RIR soldier Roy Beggs form an uneasy alliance to rebuild community life. Elsewhere, a mysterious Preacher Man lures shivering survivors out of the shadows with a promise of redemption.

Choked by the smell of death, Ireland's remaining few begin the journey toward a new life, fear and desperation giving rise to new tensions and dark old habits. But a new threat--as gorgeous as it is deadly--creeps slowly out of life's wreckage. Fueled by feral hunger and a thirst for chaos, the corpses of the beautiful are rising...

ISBN: 978-1934861059

Permuted Press
The formula has been changed...
Shifted... Altered... *Twisted.*™
www.permutedpress.com

ISBN: 978-0-9765559-4-0

"Dark, disturbing and hilarious."
—Dave Dreher, *Creature-Corner.com*

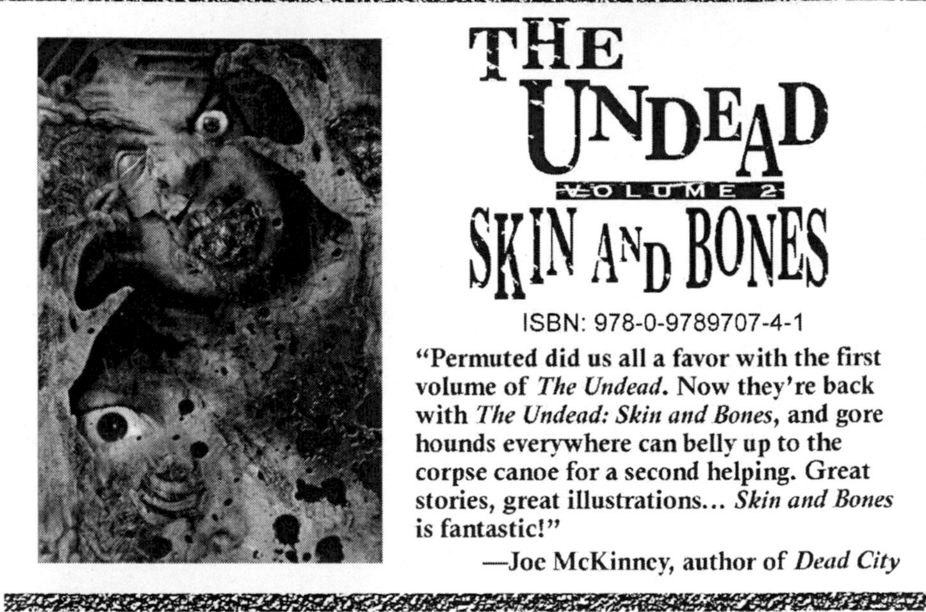

ISBN: 978-0-9789707-4-1

"Permuted did us all a favor with the first volume of *The Undead*. Now they're back with *The Undead: Skin and Bones*, and gore hounds everywhere can belly up to the corpse canoe for a second helping. Great stories, great illustrations... *Skin and Bones* is fantastic!"
—Joe McKinney, author of *Dead City*

The Undead / volume three

FLESH FEAST

ISBN: 978-0-9789707-5-8

"Fantastic stories! The zombies are fresh... well, er, they're actually moldy, festering wrecks... but these stories are great takes on the zombie genre. You're gonna like *The Undead: Flesh Feast*... just make sure you have a toothpick handy."
—Joe McKinney, author of *Dead City*

BY WILLIAM D. CARL

Beneath the dim light of a full moon, the population of Cincinnati mutates into huge, snarling monsters that devour everyone they see, acting upon their most base and bestial desires. Planes fall from the sky. Highways are clogged with abandoned cars, and buildings explode and topple. The city burns.

Only four people are immune to the metamorphosis—a smooth-talking thief who maintains the code of the Old West, an African-American bank teller who has struggled her entire life to emerge unscathed from the ghetto, a wealthy middle-aged housewife who finds everything she once believed to be a lie, and a teen-aged runaway turning tricks for food.

Somehow, these survivors must discover what caused this apocalypse and stop it from spreading. In their way is not only a city of beasts at night, but, in the daylight hours, the same monsters returned to human form, many driven insane by atrocities committed against friends and families.

Now another night is fast approaching. And once again the moon will be full.

ISBN: 978-1934861042

THE MORNINGSTAR STRAIN

THUNDER AND ASHES

A ZOMBIE NOVEL BY Z.A. RECHT

A lot can change in three months: wars can be decided, nations can be forged... or entire species can be brought to the brink of annihilation. The Morningstar Virus, an incredibly virulent disease, has swept the face of the planet, infecting billions. Its hosts rampage, attacking anything that remains uninfected. Even death can't stop the virus—its victims return as cannibalistic shamblers.

Scattered across the world, embattled groups have persevered. For some, surviving is the pinnacle of achievement. Others hoard goods and weapons. And still others leverage power over the remnants of humanity in the form of a mysterious cure for Morningstar. Francis Sherman and Anna Demilio want only a vaccine, but to find it, they must cross a countryside in ruins, dodging not only the infected, but also the lawless living.

The bulk of the storm has passed over the world, leaving echoing thunder and softly drifting ashes. But for the survivors, the peril remains, and the search for a cure is just beginning...

ISBN: 978-1934861011

Permuted Press

The formula has been changed...
Shifted... Altered... *Twisted.*™

www.permutedpress.com